Daniel Steele

Love enthroned

Essays on evangelical perfection

Daniel Steele

Love enthroned
Essays on evangelical perfection

ISBN/EAN: 9783337258009

Printed in Europe, USA, Canada, Australia, Japan

Cover: Foto ©Andreas Hilbeck / pixelio.de

More available books at **www.hansebooks.com**

LOVE ENTHRONED:

Essays on Evangelical Perfection.

By DANIEL STEELE, D.D.

Ἡ ἀγάπη ἐστὶ σύνδεσμος τῆς τελειότητος.—St. Paul.

Amor complectitur virtutum universitatem.—Bengel.

New York:

NELSON & PHILLIPS.

CINCINNATI: HITCHCOCK & WALDEN.

1875.

PREFACE.

ANOTHER book on the higher Christian life! Why should it be written? For the same reason that I should preach another Gospel sermon. Why should you read it? For the same reason that you should hear again "the old, old story of Jesus and his love." How strange it is that every one who receives full salvation gets hold of a pen as soon as he can, and blazons it abroad to all the world! It is no more wonderful than the loosened tongue of the young convert. It argues the genuineness of the blessing found. The very fact that persons who hate hobbies become, when thus anointed of the Holy Ghost, men of one idea, and henceforth push this specialty with tongue and pen as if in the grasp of an all-absorbing passion, ought to demonstrate to doubters that there is here a great Gospel truth struggling to reveal itself to the Church. Reader, do not be afraid of the multiplication of books on ad-

vanced Christian experience. The light grain
will drift off into the chaff, while the full corn
will drop into the bushel and feed the famish-
ing. It takes many men to explore a conti-
nent, many pens to portray the unsearchable
riches of Christ. Believers could have been
saved by one gospel—one photograph of the
Nazarene. But God chose four evangelists to
hold up to the Son of Man their mirrors, in
order to reflect his bright image upon our
dark world. Who shall be the limners of his
great Successor, the blessed Comforter, but
they in whom he abides, with whom he com-
munes, and on whom he has wrought his
transfiguration? The work of each of these
spiritual artists may fix some wandering eye
in a long and earnest gaze till transformed
from glory to glory by the Spirit of God.

The venerable Bishop Janes, whose zeal for
Christ, and abundant labors, are almost apostolic, in commending to the Christian public a
book on this high theme by one now associated with him in the episcopal office, uses the
following eloquent language : " Every man has
his circle of influence. Each author on this
subject will secure some readers that would

not give attention to the writings of others. Here is a power for good that ought not to be lost. Verily, if there is any subject on which we need precept upon precept, and line upon line, the theme of this book is that subject. If there is any religious truth that should be urged upon the disciples of Jesus with the sweetness of his constraining love, and the solemnity of his Divine authority, it is the truth that Christians may and ought to be holy. O that tens of thousands of individuals, filled with its bliss, and inspired by its power, were telling of its charms, and inviting to its pursuit! O that tens of thousands of spiritual limners, the Holy Ghost guiding their pencils, were actively and ceaselessly engaged in portraying the glories of this subject to the vision of the Church until every member of it, ravished by its beauties, and impelled by its attractions, would aspire to its attainment, by faith enter into its enjoyment, and then join in labors to spread it!"

These considerations, together with the urgency of many friends—one of whom, from his office of bishop of the greatest of our American Churches, is enabled to give an accurate description of the wants of the Christian public—have induced me to attempt a more permanent contribution to the literature of this high theme than can be attained through the medium of religious periodicals.

It is not the purpose of the author to bewilder his readers with pages of speculation, however strong the temptation may be, but to keep as near as possible to the teachings of the Scriptures, to his own experience, and to the testimony of others on whom the Holy Spirit has poured his illumination. It is the design of the writer, in true Pauline style, " To *testify* unto you the Gospel of the grace of God." He may not often use the pronoun in the first person singular. But he wishes it to be understood that his arguments have been forged on the anvil of his own experience. St. Paul's argumentative epistles are his experience expressed in logical form.

It is with much sorrow of heart that the writer confesses one unenviable similarity to the apostle to the Gentiles, in the fact that he now preaches that part of the Gospel which he once destroyed. Before his eyes were anointed he saw not, in the provisions of the atonement, the blessing of the fullness of Christ as a sharply defined transition in Christian experience—an instantaneous work of the Spirit by faith only, as taught by Wesley. Embracing the plausible theory of a gradual unfolding of the spiritual life without any sudden uplift by the power of the Spirit, he criticised, without the charity that is kind, the professors of this grace, magnifying their imperfections, stigmatizing them as fanatics and "pluperfects," and judging them all by an occasional glaring hypocrisy or by the extravagances of some unbalanced mind. Thus he ran into the shallow fallacy of those sinners who feast on the failings of the saints—*ex uno disce omnes*—who from one learn the character of all.

In unfolding his thoughts on this subject, the author has deemed it best to simply sketch the scheme of soteriology, or doctrine of salvation by Jesus Christ, and to elaborate only that which relates to the privileges of advanced believers. This will account for the apparent lack of symmetry in the treatment of the whole question of human salvation. Although the author has addressed special classes of his readers in the concluding chapters, he has not restrained himself from occasional exhortation in the process of his argument. Whenever the temperature rose to a white heat, he has thought it wise "to strike while the iron was hot." It may not forestall criticism by confessing, in advance, to this violation of the strict rules of logical development. The purpose of the writer has not been so much to create for himself a high reputation as a dialectitian, as to lead willing souls unto "the blessing of the fullness of Christ" by the shortest path. It is our devout prayer that these utterances of a soul filled with "joy unspeakable," and sometimes almost "intolerable,"* may contribute to the fulfilling of the Pauline petition, "That ye may be filled with all the fullness of God."

Dr. Payson thus beautifully illustrates the relation of various classes of Christians to Christ. He conceives them as ranged in concentric circles around the radiant form of our Immanuel: "Some value the presence of their Saviour so highly that they cannot bear to be at any remove from him. Even their work they will bring up, and do it in the light of

---

* " The Still Hour."—*Prof. Phelps.*

his countenance, and while engaged in it will be seen constantly raising their eyes to him, as if fearful of losing one beam of his light. Others, who, to be sure, would not be content to live out of his presence, are yet less wholly absorbed by it than these, and may be seen a little further off, engaged here and there in their various callings, their eyes generally upon their work, but often looking up to the light which they love. A third class, beyond these, but yet within the life-giving rays, includes a doubtful multitude, many of whom are so much engaged in their worldly schemes that they may be seen standing sidewise to Christ, looking mostly the other way, and only now and then turning their faces toward the light."

To induce those who are in the second and third circles to yield to the drawings of the Son of God, and gladly enter into the inner circle, and ever abide in the joyful presence of the crucified Lamb of God, is the motive of the writer, who, amid his pastoral and pulpit labors, and the more exhausting studies in preparing a commentary on a portion of the Pentateuch, has found refreshment in setting up along the path of his own experience a few guide-boards for the benefit of those who may wish to walk in the same path. The writer cannot dismiss his book without invoking upon his readers the Pauline blessing, as translated by Bishop Ellicott, "Abstain from every form of evil. But may the God of peace himself sanctify you wholly; and may your spirit, and soul, and body, be preserved entire, without blame, in the coming of our Lord Jesus Christ. Faithful is he that calleth you, who also will do it."

DEFINITIONS.

Much controversy on the subject of Christian Perfection has arisen from the use of terms having various meanings. It is our purpose to notify the reader whenever we pass from one signification of a term to another.

I. HOLY. 1) Set apart to the service of God. Applied to persons and things.

2) Morally pure, free from all stain of sin. Persons.

3) In the New Testament the original Greek word is used technically to designate all justified believers, and is translated by the word "saints" or holy ones.

2. HOLINESS.   The state of, 1) Consecration to God.
2) Moral purity.

3. SANCTIFY.   1) To hallow, to consecrate to religious
uses.   "I sanctify myself."—*Jesus.*

2) To make pure, to cleanse from moral defilement.
"The very God of peace sanctify you wholly."—
St. Paul.

3) Sanctified—In the New Testament used technically to designate the justified.

4. SANCTIFICATION.   Holiness.

5. THE MORAL LAW.   1) Unwritten; the sense of moral
obligation felt within.

2) Written; the Decalogue, with its (1) Prohibitions;
(2) Precepts.   Also the two tables, prescribing
(1) Duties to God; (2) Duties to man.

6. SIN.   1) *Actual.* A willful transgression of the known
law of God.   Sin of commission, disobedience to
a prohibition.   Sin of omission, neglect of a precept. "Sin is the transgression of the law."—*St.
John.*

Sin, (2) *Original* or *inbred*—often without any adjective, and always in the singular number—a
state, not an act.   Native corruption of the
moral nature derived from Adam's apostasy.   A
lack of conformity to the moral law.   Under the
remedial dispensation it involves no guilt till approved by the free agent and its remedy is rejected.   It is intensified by acts of sin of which it
is the source. "All unrighteousness is sin."—*St.
John.*

7. PERFECTION. As applied to man. 1) *Legal* or *Adam-ic*. Entire conformity to the moral law. "I have seen an end of all perfection, (for) thy law is ex-ing broad."—*David*.

2) *Celestial*. The complete restoration of both soul and body in the glorified state after the resurrec-tion. "Not as though I had already attained, either were already perfect."—*St. Paul*.

3) *Ideal* or *Absolute*. The combination of all con-ceivable excellences in the highest degree. As-cribed only to God, and not to beings capable of endless progress. "I am perfect."—*God*. "If I say I am perfect, it shall also prove me perverse." —*Job*.

4) *Evangelical* or *Christian*. The loving God with all our heart, mind, soul, and strength, and our neighbor as ourselves, with the complete ex-clusion of every feeling contrary to pure love. "Love is the fulfilling of the law."—*St. Paul*. "The bond of perfectness;" the sum total of the virtues.—*St. Paul* translated by *Bengel*. "There is a twofold perfection, the perfection of the work, and that of the workman."—*Bishop Hop-kins*. The former is legal, the latter is evangeli-cal perfection, which is nothing but inward sin-cerity, and uprightness of heart toward God, although there may be many imperfections and defects intermingled.

CONTENTS.

14 *Contents.*

LOVE ENTHRONED.

CHAPTER I.

LOVE REVEALED.

WHAT a mystery is love! We cannot define it; we can only indicate it by describing the occasion on which it arises in the soul. If human love is inexplicable, Divine love is an ocean too deep for the plummet of man or archangel; too broad to be bounded by the thought of the loftiest intelligence in the universe. He who knows not in his inmost consciousness the love of God, will find this book sealed to his understanding. It can only be unlocked by the key of experience. Love is not a product of the reason. It is the free play of the spiritual sensibilities in the possession of its object. God is not only love, but he is love revealed. The perfect love of God toward man is designed to call forth perfect love toward God in man's bosom. Though the mirror on which that love is reflected is broken into uneven planes and reflects a distorted image,—though the human soul at its best earthly estate under grace is shattered by infirmities and incurable imperfections,—yet the love which man cherishes toward God may flow with all the united force of his being. The history of God's intercourse with men is the chronicle of his love. This is the only history which will outlive time itself, and escape the conflagration which will burn up the world and all the works therein. This will be our text-book forever. We can contemplate no more sublime and ennobling theme. The brightness of the material universe pales before the splendors of the Divine character—that central fire which kindles the souls of seraphs in heaven and melts the hearts of sinners on earth. Thus is the science of the divine Heart infinitely above the science of the almighty Hand.

In love revealed there are ceaseless wonders. Our surprise is ever new when we discover that God so loves our entire race that he gave his well-beloved Son to the humiliation of the manger, the mockery of Gabbatha, the agonies of Gethsemane, and the ignominy of Calvary. But this was but the beginning of his beneficence. Since the Son of God has gone up to be glorified and worshiped by all the celestial orders, the loving Father has bestowed an abiding gift, the Holy Spirit, to whisper in the ear of spiritual death the words of life, to pardon penitence, and fully restore the lost image of God. The greatest marvels of the gospel scheme are not in the facts of Christ's earthly life, death, and resurrection, but in the wondrous transformation wrought by the Holy Spirit in the soul of the believer who apprehends the exceeding greatness of his power to us-ward who believe. A less surprise is the fact that the eternal *Logos* should inseparably unite himself with a spotless human body and soul than that the Holy Spirit, co-equal with the Father and the Son, should first completely cleanse a polluted man, and then change his heart from a " cage of unclean birds " into " a holy temple " and make it the habitation of God. This is a mystery of mysteries with all who have experienced the love of God perfectly shed abroad in their hearts. The age of miracles is not past. Jesus changed

2

unresisting water into wine, but the Holy
Ghost transfigures the sinful soul bristling with
antagonisms, transforming depravity to purity
by the mighty alchemy of love. The power
to effect such revolutions in character constitutes the standing miracle of Christianity.
"Instead of the thorn shall come up the fir-
tree"—tenderness instead of cruelty—"instead
of the brier shall come up the myrtle-tree"—
the gentle graces instead of stinging hatreds—
"and it shall be to the Lord for a name," indicating his nature, and "for an everlasting
sign, that shall not be cut off." The Holy
Ghost, holding up to the gaze of the world
specimens of his sanctifying power in the form
of purified characters and inspired activities
for Christ, is the ceaseless miracle-worker attesting Christian truth in an age of intense
materialism, selfishness, and unbelief.

God has begun to save every human soul.
He has already saved the entire race from the
extinction threatened in the instantaneous ex-
ecution of the death penalty upon Adam and
Eve in the garden of Eden in the moment of
their first transgression. The remedial dispensation began with the promise that the Seed

of the woman should bruise the serpent's head.
The children of the pair banished from Eden,
and fallen from their high estate, are born in
the likeness of their sinful parents, with tre-
mendous proclivities toward sin in the strength
of their passions and the bent of their wills.
Yet they come into being under the dispensation of mercy. They have a gracious ability
to repent. They are saved from that complete moral inability which paralyses the will
of the fallen angels in the direction of obedience to the moral law. This inability to resist
the downward tendency of their nature, and
to turn from sin, is, through the influences
of the Holy Spirit, procured by Jesus Christ
for all the race. "He will reprove the world
of sin, and of righteousness, and of judgment."
Through the atonement every soul is in a salv-
able state. By assenting to the facts and truths
of the Gospel, and by relying solely on its Author, every penitent sinner may be saved from
the guilt of sin. If any one fails to submit to
the Divine plan of salvation, the merciful purpose of God is defeated, and the initial salvation never becomes actual and final. Through
an abuse of the godlike attribute of freedom

man may withstand all the suasives of the Father, Son, and Holy Spirit, and create for himself a destiny of endless sorrow. The human will is an independent fountain of causation, itself uncaused in all its moral volitions. "Whatever the good man is, he is through God and his own will; the evil man, however, is so only through his own will, for evil is falling away from God." Hence the following theological axiom of Fletcher: "All damnation flows from man, all salvation flows from God." He saves all that he can without a violation of the sacred prerogative of freedom. "Turn ye, turn ye— why will ye die?" Thus love is revealed as dominant over this world; not a fondling sentimentalism, but a holy principle, ever acting in accordance with wisdom and justice; saving the penitent, persevering believer, and consuming with flaming fire all who, by incorrigible disobedience, thrust from themselves the cover of the atoning blood.

The extent of this conquest of love over the believing soul in the present world, is a theme which has elicited intense interest through all the Christian ages. At times the grace of God has been magnified, and many

have proved that he can do " exceeding abundantly above all that we ask or think ;" while
at other times this great Christian privilege of
evangelical perfection, or perfect love, has
gone into an eclipse, partial or total, and the
Church has groped in the darkness, benumbed
by the chilling cold.

CHAPTER II.

LOVE MILITANT.

SO long as sin is in the world love must make war against it. Jesus came forth from the bosom of the Father's love to send a sword upon the earth. The cross is a center of forces hostile to sin. The sinful soul is a fortress filled with armed enemies to Immanuel. The successive approaches of love to its conquest and complete possession are—

1. The offer of pardon through the atoning blood of Jesus Christ.

Justification, or the pardon of sin through faith in Jesus Christ, is an act which takes place in the mind of the Moral Governor of the universe, whereby he removes guilt, or severs the link between sin and punishment, and accounts the penitent believer in Christ as if he had never sinned. It does not change the nature from wicked to just, as its Latin etymology—*justus* and *facio*—would signify. It is a work wrought *for* the soul, and wholly external to it, and is by faith only. No member of the human family, Jesus excepted, can successfully plead that he has perfectly kept the law of God, and is in consequence of his good works worthy of His approval. " By the deeds of the law shall no flesh be justified." From making this plea "every mouth is stopped." We are in no sense of the term acquitted. We are, after conviction and condemnation, pardoned through executive clemency, induced by the mediation of the Son of God.

But a pardoned criminal is not necessarily a good citizen. Pardon has changed his relation to the law, but not his hostility toward the governor. A change must take place within him. He must be reconstructed. We now come to the second step in the conquest of the soul by love divine.

2. Regeneration, or the New Birth, is a change wrought within the soul by the power of the Holy Ghost, creating within the soul a new spiritual life, a life of loyalty and love.

By nature men are the children of wrath. They are spiritually dead. The faith faculty exists, but is in a paralysis so far as spiritual objects are concerned. The divine life be-

gins with the seed of God implanted in the
soul. This is the new principle of love. "For
the love of God is shed abroad in the heart by
the Holy Ghost." The phrase "love of God"
may signify either God's love to me or my love
to God. In this quotation it has the former
meaning. The Scriptures teach us that God
is love. But this is not enough to give me assurance of his favor so long as I read that he
is angry with the wicked every day. Therefore, so long as I have a tormenting sense of
guilt, I must be filled with painful forebodings till I have a positive and personal assurance that I am taken out of the class of the
condemned, and am reconciled to God, who
loves me, even me. This is the witness of the
Spirit, the third advance toward the complete
conquest. He is styled the Spirit of Adoption, because as such his chief message is to
attest to the believer his pardon and sonship.
When this glad evangel resounds within, love
to God springs up responsive to his great love
to me. This is a new motive power. It reinforces the ethical feeling, the sense of obligation
to right action. The bare perception of right,
with no strong impulse toward it, while the

appetites and passions are drawing in the opposite direction, constitutes the painful warfare between the flesh and the spirit, entailing upon the latter the sense of degrading bondage.

> "I see the right, and I approve it too;
> I see the wrong, and yet the wrong pursue."

But this new motive makes it easy to obey the law, because we love the Lawgiver. Hence love is the fulfilling of the law; not as a substitute for keeping the precepts and abstaining from the prohibitions of the moral law, but as an inspiration of the very spirit of obedience. But this new principle is spoken of by St. John as only a seed when first implanted. It implies future germination, growth, and fruitage. It is to spread its branches till it fills the heart, and by absorbing all the fertility of the soil, and by completely overshadowing all other plants, destroys their life. Till this maturity of the seed, the moral condition of the heart will be mixed; good and evil will struggle for the ascendency. Nevertheless, if faith in Christ—the weapon of victory—continues, the actions will be right, though the result of painful effort to keep the moribund

evil within from breaking out into manifestation. For manifestation is the tendency of
every principle. After the maturity of love,
the Divine seed, all its antagonists will be
excluded. Evil will still be presented to the
choice, but from no foothold within. Perfect
love will cast out, not only fear, but all the
hateful progeny of depravity. This is entire
sanctification. It began with the seed-grain
of holiness sown in regeneration.

There is no new principle involved. The
oak is only the acorn unfolded. Yet regeneration, completed in sanctification, is not the
highest up-reaching of the Divine life in the
soul. It is only the beginning of its whole-
ness. All the forces of the soul, for the first
time, move Godward. "Unite my heart," says
the Psalmist, "to fear thy name." He prayed
for perfection in Divine love, when every warring foe shall be removed and all the powers be
subsidized for the service of God. Up to this
point the old nature, though dying, has lin-
gered and mingled with the new. Dying unto
sin and living unto God have co-existed. The
destructive and the reconstructive processes
have gone on side by side. There is an absolute

end to the former when there is nothing more
to be destroyed : there is no end to the latter. The negative work must of necessity end
when sin is dead ; the positive work of spiritual
adornment, strength, and growth, must go on
so long as the soul is capable of advancement.

It becomes necessary at this point to indicate the salient points of difference between the
new birth and that maturity of Christian character which St. Paul denominates the "measure of the stature of the fullness of Christ."

The relation of regeneration to entire sanctification is that of a part to a whole. There
are other specific differences.

1.) In the state of mind preceding each. In
the one case the eye is fixed on the past sins,
and a sense of guilt and repentance fills the bitter cup ; in the other, the soul looks inward
upon itself, and self-abhorrence for the unlovely qualities disclosed to the anointed eye
is the dominant feeling, without, however, a
sense of Divine wrath.

2.) In the object for which the soul strives—
pardon in the first case, and purity in the second.

3.) In the manner of attaining these blessings. Both are by faith ; but the penitent

sinner lays hold of Jesus dying on the cross,
while the regenerated aspirant after a clean
heart more distinctly apprehends Jesus living
on the throne. The one thinks of his mercy,
the other of his almightiness. There is a difference in the submission of the will. The
sinner, thinking chiefly of his own salvation,
surrenders, grounding his weapons like a conquered rebel. The regenerate soul, like a
patriot seeking the salvation of his country,
gladly pours all his possessions into the treasury, a free-will offering, and counts it a privilege to enlist, soul and body, in the army.
The one cries, "God be merciful to me a sinner;" the other prays, "Father, glorify thyself in me." The consecration of the latter
is far more intelligent, deliberate, and in detail, because of his superior self-knowledge
under the illumination of the Holy Spirit.
His eager cry is,

> "Welcome, welcome, dear Redeemer,
>   Welcome to this heart of mine.
> Lord, I make a full surrender,
>   Every thought and power be thine,
>   Thine entirely, through eternal ages thine."

4.) But the greatest difference is in the blessings received. Regeneration is a great and

glorious change. It is the beginning of the
new life. The regenerate man is a new creature in Christ Jesus. To him all things have
become new. New heavens are above, and a
new earth is beneath. He has been translated
out of darkness into a marvelous light. The
angel of mercy has descended and rolled away
the stone from the sepulcher, and the dead
soul has come forth. The great Emancipator
has descended to the prison-door with the
trump of jubilee at his lips and the key of
deliverance in his right hand. Regeneration
is a wonderful change—a new creation, an
emergence out of darkness —a manumission
from the most abject slavery, a resurrection
from the dead. Yea, more than all this. By
adoption he becomes a son of God, an heir,
a joint heir with Christ. Like Joseph, he
goes from the prison to the throne. Yet like
Joseph, he is still in Egypt. A wilderness
intervenes between him and the Land of
Promise. Toward that Canaan he turns a
wistful eye, for to him it is

> " A land of corn, and wine, and oil,
> Favored with God's peculiar smile,
> With every blessing blessed."

He longs for that rest, and looks for the Joshua who shall lead him in, conquer his foes, and allot him his portion on the mountain of God. The justified state, glorious though it be, is eclipsed by the outbeaming splendors of a more excellent glory yet unattained. There is a sense of vacuity still in the soul, and a feeling that there is an attainable fullness in Christ correlated to this felt want. As the hart panteth after the water brooks, so pants this unfilled soul after God. Unrest, hungerings and thirstings after righteousness, gratitude for the stream, and a longing to follow it up to the fountain, characterize the justified state. The marvelous light sometimes fades away into twilight; clouds often overcast the sky; and there are times when neither sun nor stars appear. O for an abode on some mountain summit, which lifts its head above the clouds into the eternal sunshine! a dwelling-place in the land of Beulah, where the sun shines day and night all the year round!

5.) The witness of the Spirit is intermittent in the justified state, and abiding in entire sanctification, excluding every doubt. Here is a marked distinction. Constant assurance is

requisite to perpetual rest in Christ. This
comes only from the Comforter abiding in the
fullness of his grace. Before regeneration the
soul trusts in Jesus Christ; but before entire
sanctification we must believe in the Holy ·
Ghost, the Sanctifier, inasmuch as he has a
distinct office.

6.) A still more important difference lies in
the sense of defilement which humbles and
distresses the justified soul, and the delightful
sense of inward purity which is felt when the
Sanctifier makes his conscious abode within.
The promise seems to be fulfilled on the
earth. " They shall walk with me in white,
for they are worthy." This assurance of heart-
cleansing is something more than an inference
drawn from the soul's easy victory over temptation; it is intuitively perceived under the illumination of the Spirit. The Sanctifier is not
satisfied with doing his work only in the mysterious depths of our nature; he reveals the purification to our consciousness, filling us with joy
unspeakable. Whether this revelation is *the*
witness of the Spirit in the technical language
of theology or not, it is the voice of the Comforter speaking very comforting words : "I have

washed thee with water from all thy filthiness, and from all thy idols I have cleansed thee."

7.) The justified or regenerate person often finds it difficult to say sincerely and heartily, " Thy will be done." Self still asserts its existence as a force opposing the will of God. There is, at times, a painful duality in the soul, " the flesh (self-will) warring against the Spirit." At such times there is little peace and less joy. Entire sanctification completely harmonizes the conflict by enabling the human to acquiesce delightfully in the Divine will. "Christian perfection," says Fletcher, " extends chiefly to the will, which is the capital moral power of the soul, leaving the understanding ignorant of ten thousand things, and the body ' dead because of sin.' "*

8.) The joy that attends perfect love, in its depth, solidity, richness, and permanency, far transcends the joy of the regenerate state. It is the testimony of many witnesses, that in point of ecstatic emotion the transition into entire holiness is far more wonderful than the translation of the penitent believer from the darkness of spiritual death into the kingdom

* Checks, vol. ii, p. 489.

of light. But this is not always the case. As some are converted without a sudden and sharply-defined joy, like a tropical sunrise, ever memorable in their history, so some mount up into the heights of perfect love as gradually as the dawn climbs the eastern sky. But even in these cases, there is a moment when the rising sun pours his light upon their waiting eyes.

9.) An important distinction between these two states of Christian experience—the new birth and the fullness of love—lies in the distinction between the *gift* and the *Giver*. We may selfishly clamor for the gift, but with a perfect identity of interest with Christ do we welcome to our hearts the Giver of every good and every perfect gift. Hence the superior permanency of the Giver over the gift. The latter may be evanescent, while the former abides. The former is a lighted lamp, but the latter superadds the vessel filled with oil, which typifies the Holy Spirit.*

3. Adoption is the incorporation of a person into the family of God, with the investiture of all the prerogatives of sonship and rights

* See Dean Alford on the Parable of the Ten Virgins.

3

of heirship. It is an exalted honor. "But as many as received him, to them gave he power to become the sons of God, even to as many as believe on his name." "For as many as are led by the Spirit of God, they are the sons of God." Earth's highest dignities sink into meanness in contrast with "the row of glorified brothers, with the Son of God at the head." This adoption is simultaneous with justification and regeneration, and is attested by a special message from God to the believer's consciousness.

4. The witness of the Spirit, which has already been alluded to in this chapter, is the testimony of the Holy Ghost immediately to my soul, assuring me that I am born of God, and that the blood of Christ has washed away my sins. The messenger is called the Spirit of Adoption, because it is one of his peculiar offices to inspire the joyful cry, "Abba, Father." It differs from the testimony of the fruit of the Spirit in this, that in the latter there is an inference that we are sons of God, because we see the correspondence between their characteristics as noted in the Bible, and those observed in ourselves. This inference

will never be indubitable and satisfactory,
much less joyful, unless it be preceded by the
direct witness as above defined. Both must
go together. The inferential or corroboratory
must always accompany the immediate testimony of the Spirit, as a safeguard against
deception and fanaticism. While the direct
voice must be added to the indirect testimony
of the Spirit, which is the attestation of our
own consciousness, in order to keep us from
sinking into despair or falling into a flatter-
ing and fatal mistake, the direct testimony of
the spirit of adoption must be preached and
held up as the privilege of the child of God,
in order to that faith requisite for its reception.
In the great revival under the preaching of
Whitefield and the Wesleys, ninety-nine out
of every hundred of the converts attested their
reception of the spirit of adoption speaking
directly to their hearts. This privilege was
specially presented to penitents by those
great evangelists, and emphatically by the
Wesleys.

The direct witness of the Spirit is, in usual
cases, especially in young converts, intermittent, either through fluctuations of faith, or

through some mysterious, but doubtless beneficent, law of the mind.   In Christians of eminent devotion to God and strong faith, these
intervals are infrequent and brief, and the
tendency is toward an uninterrupted testimony of the abiding Comforter, or the higher
Christian life.   This office of the Spirit is
most plainly taught in St. Paul's epistles.
See Rom. viii, 15, 16; Gal. iv, 6.   The same
is taught in 1 John iii, 24; iv, 13; v, 10.   In
figurative language Jesus taught the same
doctrine on various occasions.   See John vii,
37–39.   He explicitly unfolded this great privilege in the promise of the Comforter, John
xiv, although this comprises much more than
the witness of adoption.   The greater includes
the less.

The Old Testament hints at this blessing in
such expressions as this : " The secret of the
Lord is with them that fear him."   It is the
source of the blessedness of him " whose in-
iquity is forgiven, whose sin is covered."

CHAPTER III.

LOVE TRIUMPHANT OVER ORIGINAL SIN.

THE spirit of sin, or inbred sin, technically called original sin, because it is inherited from Adam, is the state of heart out of which acts of sin either actually flow or tend to flow. Until this state is changed, the conquest of love over the soul is incomplete. Regeneration introduces a power which checks the outbreaking of original into actual sin, except occasional and almost involuntary sallies in moments of weakness or unwatchfulness. These are a source of grief and condemnation to the justified soul. They are a humiliating, yet only temporary defeat. For there is with all well-instructed believers a resort to the blood of sprinkling, and a pleading of the promise, " If any man sin, we have an advocate with the Father, Jesus Christ the righteous." We do not say that all justified persons experience these defeats. All may, and some doubtless do, live without condemnation from the glad moment of pardon; yet the testimony of the Church shows that these are rare exceptions. The majority, in the struggle with inbred sin, are not always victorious. What is the difference, then, between sin in a sinner, and sin in a believer? The same difference that there is between poison in a rattlesnake and the virus of that serpent injected into a healthy man. The venom is natural to the reptile. He delights in it, secretes and cherishes it with pleasure. But all the vital forces of the man resist the injected poison, and rally to thrust it out of the system. We have shown elsewhere that the seventh chapter of the Epistle to the Romans was not designed by St. Paul as an ideal of the regenerate life, even in its lowest stages. But so true is the doctrine of sin in believers—inbred sin—sometimes breaking out against the enfeebled will, that a whole section of the Christian world have mistaken the struggles of an awakened legalist seeking justification by good works, and failing through the ascendency of depraved inclination, for the portrait of the Christian in his best estate in this life. This photograph of a Christless,

convicted Jew, has, alas! been set before myriads of Christians as the masterpiece of that
Jesus who came to save his people from their
sins, the best specimen of his art as a Divine
limner even when aided by the great transformer, the Holy Spirit.

This class of Christians do not need arguments to convince them of the possible existence of sin in believers. It is difficult for
them to believe that they may live on the
earth after sin is all destroyed. Since nature
abhors a vacuum in the spiritual as in the physical world, the complete and permanent annihilation of sin as a state of heart must be
attended by the infusion of perfect love, by
which we mean love in a degree commensurate with the utmost capacity of the soul.
Hence the *coup de grace*, the death-blow which
ends the war of love against sin, is a negative
and limited work, to be followed by a work
positive and unlimited. The first is the removal of all impurity, whether inherent or
acquired; the second is being "filled with all
the fullness of God." It is the adorning of the
soul with all the fruits of the Spirit—love, joy,
peace, long-suffering, gentleness, meekness,

fidelity, patience, and temperance. Since there
are some who believe that the negative work,
the destruction of the very spirit of sin, or proclivity toward sin, takes place when the soul
is born again, we will briefly present our objections to this doctrine.

1. It is contrary to universal Christian experience. In all ages and in all Christian
lands, always and every-where, resounds the
wail of truly regenerate souls over the antagonisms of Divine love discovered in them
under the illumination of the Holy Spirit. In
passing from death unto life they have passed
into a conflict not only with the world and
Satan, but also with the flesh—the perverse
tendencies of their own natures. Now one of
three things must be true. Either these have
all made a mistake in calling themselves regenerate, or they have all backslidden from
a regenerate state, or they are truly regenerate while struggling with the remains of the
carnal mind. To insist that the first is true
is to assert the delusion of the whole body of
believers in respect to the most vital point—
sonship to God. To assume the second sup-
position is to declare the apostasy of the

Church in each of its members very soon after conversion—an appalling hypothesis. The third alternative saves the Church from the theories of delusion and of apostasy, and is in perfect harmony with universal testimony.

2. It contradicts the creed of all the ortho-dox branches of the Church universal from primitive Christianity to the present day. The Greek and the Roman, the Anglican, and every reformed Church of Europe and America, agree that there is an infection of nature remaining in them that are regenerated. Augustine and Calvin are not stronger in their assertion of this fact than are Arminius and Wesley.* It is no small presumption in favor of the truth of a doctrine, that it has remained unques-tioned through all the fierce battles of polem-ical theologians, and all the reforms of the Church, and all the restatements of Christian truth. Fragmentary sects may for a time dis-sent from the orthodox opinion, and either pass away or return again to the common faith, as did Count Zinzendorf and his Moravian fol-

---

* "The moment a sinner is justified, his heart is cleansed in a low degree; but yet he has not a clean heart in the full, proper sense, till he is made perfect in love."—*John Wesley.*

lowers in London, in the last century. For a
time, these excellent people taught the entire
sanctification of the soul in the moment of the
new birth. But so contradictory was this view
to their own experience, and so destructive of
confidence in Christ on the part of weak believers, that it was at length abandoned.

So strongly have believers since the Apostolic age been impressed with the imperfect-
cure of the soul in regeneration, that many
have believed that the entire healing must be
deferred either till death or purgatorial fires
shall complete the purification.

3. It is unphilosophical. The deeper the
stain the greater must be the power of the
chemicals applied to remove it. The blood of
Christ is the cleansing power. The degree of
efficacy is proportional to the faith of the individual. No faith, no purification; perfect
trust, complete cleansing. Is it reasonable
that this perfect trust should be exercised by
an awakened sinner in his first apprehension
of Jesus Christ. Is it philosophical to assert
that one filled with doubts, and weakened
and appalled by the terrors of the Lord thun-
dering from Mount Sinai, will then put forth

his highest act of faith? We aver that it is far more reasonable to suppose that the highest capacity of faith is attained after much exercise. If the confidence of man in man is a plant of slow growth, it is natural that the highest confidence of man in God should require time for its maturity. It is certainly not unreasonable that there should be two distinct operations of the Holy Spirit to neutralize the sin in our nature, which has a twofold source—the soul's own sinful acts, and the sin of Adam injecting a stream of corruption into humanity.

The most modern statement and defense of this erroneous doctrine is found in the "Moral Philosophy" of Dr. Fairchild, President of Oberlin College. In his chapter on the "Unity or Simplicity of Moral Action," he elaborates an argument to prove that virtue, wherever it exists, is entire and complete, with no mixture of impurity; and that there is room only for its more firm establishment, persistency, and fortification by habit. He answers the testimony of multitudes of immature Christians to the consciousness of a mixed state of sin and holiness, by asserting

that these do not co-exist, but they succeed
each other very rapidly. "The general impression of deficient goodness is admitted;
and the fact of deficiency is also admitted;
but it is a deficiency which arises from the
alternation of good and evil in the heart."
He explains away the consciousness of good
and evil by asserting that "it is not so definite
as to discriminate between these two forms
of mixture," namely, concomitancy and alternation.   Just here we are impelled to ask
whether Christ Jesus has any immediate salvation from the mixture of alternation?   Whatever the kind of mixture, it needs purifying.
Are the lapse of time and the slow formation
of virtuous habits the only saviour?   We apprehend that the answer will be, that habit is
our only redeemer from this wretched state;
that the same embarrassment surrounds the
new creation of the soul as, according to Bishop Butler, attended the creation of Adam—
the impossibility of creating a being with good
habits.   According to the Oberlin theory of
the perfect purity of the soul after regeneration, the distinctive work of the Sanctifier is
no more needed.   Henceforth He should be

called the Confirmer. But this would be a misnomer, for the soul must, by the very significance of habit, establish itself by repeated virtuous acts.

Dr. Fairchild's theory contradicts the consciousness of multitudes of such minds as are able to discriminate between concomitancy and alternation; even when they testify to the presence of a felt antagonism within themselves disturbing their peace and filling them with grief. The theory involves the false assumption of Dugald Stewart, that mind is capable of only a single action at one instant of time—that we hear only one note of the piano, and see only one point in the landscape, at one and the same instant—and that the apparent variety of sounds and vastness of landscape is due to the rapidity with which the mind passes from sound to sound only apparently co-existent, and the eye unconsciously passes from point to point in the landscape. This is shown by Sir William Hamilton to be erroneous. He demonstrates that the mind may, with abated force, follow two or three trains of thought at the same time.

4. But our chief objection to this doctrine is its unscriptural character. St. Paul is addressing believers, and portraying their character, when he writes, Gal. v, 17, "The flesh lusteth against the Spirit, and the Spirit against the flesh. These are contrary the one to the other." If the Apostle had been writing to counteract this modern error which confounds two distinct operations of the Spirit, regeneration and sanctification, he could not have more expressly antagonized it than he has in this passage. For he asserts that even in the regenerate there is a warfare between two opposing principles; and the aim of the epistle is to end the contest by the complete ascendancy of the Spirit, and the extinction of the flesh or evil nature.

But one passage of Scripture effectually demolishes this theory of the complete sanctification of the soul in the new birth. "And I, brethren, could not speak unto you as unto spiritual, but as unto carnal, even as unto babes in Christ." 1 Cor. iii, 1. These brethren, babes in Christ, could not be styled wholly, or predominantly, spiritual in their state, for St. Paul is speaking of their state, and not of their acts, which are described in the third verse. They had been born into the kingdom by the Holy Spirit, because they are styled babes in Christ, and addressed as brethren ; and in the salutation (chap. i, 2) they are styled "saints," or holy ones. Nevertheless St. Paul, with his utmost stretch of charity, cannot truthfully call them spiritual, that is, perfectly holy, for their old fleshly nature was too strongly manifesting itself. Here acts of sin cannot be said to alternate with acts of holiness, for St. Paul is not yet speaking of what they *do* but of what they *are*, and they are co-existently *carnal* and *babes in Christ*. Dr. Edward Robinson, in the earlier editions of his "New Testament Greek Lexicon," endeavored to tone down this apparent contradiction in terms by inventing a softened meaning to σαρκικοῖς, *carnal*, in this verse and in the third, as being merely "weak, frail, imperfect," and not "implying sinfulness." But it was so evident that this definition originated in the author's dogmatical opinions, and not in the principles of sound lexicography, that in his last revision he abandoned this definition of the term as applied to persons.

We have dwelt at length on this mischievous identity of entire sanctification with justification in point of time,

1. Because it tends to make young Christians abandon their trust in Christ when they discover sin still lurking within.

2. Those who do hold fast to Christ are by this doctrine excluded from seeing the great and glorious privilege of full salvation attainable on earth, and are left to a low and mixed spiritual state.

3. The census of the Christian Church in all the world would be reduced from millions to units. For, if this doctrine be true, we must count as regenerate only such as experienced entire sanctification in the new birth. John Wesley, who, from his extensive travels, and practice of personal inspection of his societies by searching questions, had a wider acquaintance with experimental Christians than any other man since the days of St. Paul, is a competent witness on this point. "But we do not know a *single instance* in any place," says Wesley,* "of a person's receiving in one and the same moment remission of sins, the abiding

* "Plain Account of Christian Perfection," page 34.

witness of the Spirit, and a new, a clean heart." If Wesley, in his more than fourscore years, never met with such a person, it is safe to say that their number at any one time in the Church universal could be counted on one's fingers.

Admitting that the dominion of sin is broken while its being still remains after the love of God, the new seed of divine life, is implanted in the heart, we proceed to show that there is a salvation from original sin in this life. All admit that sin must all be destroyed before we can enter the abodes of the saints in light. This purification cannot take place after death without involving the papal purgatory. If it is done in the moment of death, it makes the king of terrors the complete Saviour. To avoid both of these absurdities we must believe that we are to be entirely sanctified in this life.

Before the Son of God came in the flesh, a name indicative of his great work was prepared for him, and prophetically announced by the angel. That name was a heroic name in the Hebrew annals, and resonant of victory— Joshua, Saviour. He was not to save politically, but individually, not from Roman power, but from servility to sin. "He shall save his
4

people from their sins." In the promise, *His* in the Greek lacks the emphasis which would have confined it to the Jews. The word *sins* here signifies not punishment merely, " but is the sin itself—the practice of sin in its most pregnant sense." Dean Alford, by the use of this strong term *pregnant*, evidently means sin in embryo, the state of heart out of which acts of sin are born: "Lust, when it hath conceived, bringeth forth the sin." Jesus will save not only from the birth, but from the conception of sin, by lust entering in with its defilement. That this is the correct exegesis of this Scripture will be evident by attending to Peter's discourse in Solomon's Porch, in which he interprets the mission of Christ, " Unto you first, God having raised up his Son Jesus, sent him to bless you, in turning away every one of you from his iniquities." Acts iii, 26. Bengel's comment sets this great blessing in its true light: " He turns away both us from wickedness, and ungodliness (ungodlikeness) from us." He turns us away from committing sin, and removes from us the aptitude for wickedness. The sense in which we have used the term *aptitude* will soon be explained. But as if to put forever beyond dispute the purpose of the incarnation, and to point out the summits of Christian privilege so far as relates to sin, St. John says, "For this purpose the Son of God was manifested, that he might destroy the works of the devil." 1 John iii, 8. Pre-eminently the work of the devil is to produce a state of alienation from God. The first work of Satan on earth was to induce in Eve a state of distrust toward her Creator. Plucking the forbidden fruit was her act. The aptitude for this act was formed actively by Satan's artful insinuations, and passively by Eve in listening to them. To destroy the chief and crowning work of the devil, is to redeem man from this very aptitude. "Depravity of all consists in this, that in all alike is the capacity for the extremest wickedness. And it is redemption even from that capacity that man needs."* The term *capacity* is not to be confounded with *possibility.* It was possible for Adam to sin, but he must first acquire a capacity or aptitude for it by listening to those suggestions which weakened faith and chilled the ardor of love. George

* Dr. Whedon on Rom. i, 18.

Whitefield and Jonathan Edwards did not
have in their Christian maturity the capacity
to rob a bank, though it was possible for them,
under the subtle power of temptation, to have
admitted by imperceptible degrees the spirit
of avarice, and to have so far fallen from faith
in God, the great sheet-anchor of all true rectitude, so as to have taken on that capacity
for burglary. This explains the declaration
of St. John, that he that is born of God sinneth not; "For his seed remaineth in him;
and he *cannot* sin, because he is born of God."
John, having in mind one in whom the work
of regeneration has been fully accomplished
by the perfection of the regenerating principle
of love, asserts the incapacity or inaptitude of
such a soul, *while abiding in Christ*, to commit
a known and willful sin.

We conclude our argument on this point by
an examination of the assertion that in regeneration the soul is entirely sanctified because
the new birth is a Divine work, and God's
works are always perfect. Often we hear the
declaration that when God regenerates the
penitent believer he does it thoroughly; there
is no half-finished work proceeding from the

hand of the perfect and omnipotent Artist.
Now it does not follow that because God is
perfect, every thing that comes from him must
be perfect also. Look abroad through nature
and you will find many imperfections—deformed animals, trees gnarled and twisted, in
high latitudes pines dwarfed to mere ferns, in
all climes abortive blossoms and windfall fruits,
and children born with poisonous humors in
their blood, or incipient tubercles in their
lungs. God's works are always perfect where
the conditions are perfect. He does not produce perfect oranges in Alaska, nor perfect
apples in Florida, nor models in human stature in Lapland, nor Caucasian fairness of
complexion in Africa. It is thus in his spiritual kingdom. Perfect saints are developed
only under appropriate conditions—perfect
faith in Jesus Christ, evinced by an entire surrender to his will. But as the wonderful crea-
tive tendency of God waits not for perfect
conditions, but breaks forth into forms of weakness and deformity in the natural world, so
the amazing love of God does not wait for perfect spiritual conditions, but puts forth its
beneficent activities, resulting in a prodigal

wastefulness in its wayside sowings, in its stony ground crop, which makes no show in the bushel, and in its thorny ground harvest which sends no sheaf to the garner. Where faith in Christ Jesus is weak, a feeble spiritual life is the inevitable result. But when faith grasps him as an omnipotent Saviour, the uttermost salvation from sin is the consequence, and Christian manhood walks forth upon the earth in the stature of the fullness of Christ. All spiritual transformations result from the combination of two forces, the Divine and the human. Where the human is defective the resultant will be imperfect, for the Divine agency will not compensate the defects of the human co-operation. Hence the weakness of man is reflected upon the almightiness of God. Sons are born into his family having still the taint of depravity lurking in their blood, to be purged away by the cathartic of a mighty faith in the all-cleansing blood of "the Lamb of God, that taketh away the sin of the world."

CHAPTER IV.

FULL SALVATION IMMEDIATELY ATTAINABLE.

THERE is no denial that entire sanctification is necessary to admission to heaven. There is in many minds a doubt respecting the attainment of perfect purity before death. It is thought, so long as the soul and body are united, the flesh must in some degree taint the spirit. The inherent evil of matter is an old error of the Gnostics, borrowed from pagan philosophy, and early introduced into Christianity as a corrupting element. The Oriental philosophers taught that matter is uncreated and eternal, containing in it ineradicable evil; that the Creator, or Fashioner, did the best that he could with it when he shaped it into the human form; that he was not able, by any process of sublimation or refinement, to expel evil entirely from its nature, and that this inherent evil must continue to defile the soul immersed in it till death shall dissolve the loathed union. Then will the soul be in a condition to be purified, if it is curable, by drifting on rivers of fire till the stains are purged away. This is Platonism. This is the origin of the Roman Catholic doctrine of purgatory. Protestantism has shaken off the fire-purgation, but has too extensively retained the death-purgatory. After seventeen hundred years Christianity has not wholly emancipated herself from this mischievous tenet of a heathen philosophy. It is our purpose to show that there is no evil in matter or in spirit which the blood of Christ cannot cleanse, and that neither death nor penal fire, but the omnipotent Jesus, is the complete purifier of sin-stained souls, and that the only instrument he employs is the truth, and the only agent is the Holy Ghost, the Sanctifier. Our proofs will be wholly scriptural and experimental. The point to be demonstrated is this: Can Jesus save from all sin, actual and indwelling, long before death? The declaration of the angel to Joseph, " Thou shalt call his name JESUS ; for he shall save his people from their sins," does not explicitly declare when this salvation will be accomplished. But the implication is that he is to be a present Saviour, just as a physician advertising himself as a healer of cancers is understood to heal patients now, not in future years, nor a few hours before death. It is fortunate, yea, providential, that we have an inspired comment on this name by Zacharias when "filled with the Holy Ghost." With prophetic vision he saw the immediate advent of Jesus, of whom his son John, then eight days old, was to be the forerunner.

" Blessed be the Lord God of Israel ; for he hath visited and redeemed his people, and hath raised up a horn of salvation for us in the house of David. . . . That he would grant unto us, that we, being delivered out of the hand of our (spiritual) enemies, might serve him without fear, (and hence with perfect love,) *in holiness* and *righteousness* before him, (not fulfilling any mere human standard,) ALL THE DAYS OF OUR LIFE." The deliverance was to be spiritual, and not an emancipation from the Roman power ; and the result, a glad and holy service, was to ensue in this life. No language could be used to express such an idea more clearly than this. A still more explicit statement of the same great privilege of believers is found in St. Paul's brief prayer in

1 Thess. v, 23. He had just been enjoining
duties which none but those who are fully
saved could possibly perform : " Rejoice evermore. Pray without ceasing. In every thing
give thanks." John Wesley says, " I know no
higher Christian perfection than this." To enable them to obey these injunctions, and another just as difficult—"abstain from all appearance (every kind) of evil"—he offers this
prayer: "But may the God of peace himself
sanctify you wholly; and may your spirit,
soul, and body, be preserved entire without
blame, in the coming of the Lord Jesus." *

So intent is the great Apostle on giving an
adequate and explicit expression of his meaning, *entire sanctification*, that he uses a strong
word found nowhere else in the New Testament — ὁλοτελεῖς, *wholly*, rendered in the
Vulgate *per omnia*—" in your collective powers and parts," marking more emphatically
than any ordinary New Testament word the
thoroughness and pervasive nature of the holiness prayed for. Luther has very happily
translated it " *durch und durch*,"—*through and
through.* Then St. Paul has used another

* Ellicott's Translation.

peculiar term, which is found in only one other place in the New Testament, in James i, 4, and gives it the position of an emphatic predicate: "May your spirit be preserved *entire*, your soul *entire*, and your body *entire.*" He ordinarily employs the word τέλειος, "*perfect*," when he marks what has reached its proper end and maturity. But wishing to express a *quantitative*, and not a *qualitative*, meaning, he employs a term signifying "entire in all its parts," "complete," lacking nothing. Having in these strong and remarkable words indicated the thoroughness of the sanctification, Paul leaves us in no doubt as to the time, when he adds, "and *preserve* you without blame in the coming of the Lord Jesus." Through what period of time is the preservation to extend? Till the second advent of Christ. This period covers the life-time of these Thessalonians, and the space between their death and resurrection. To say that the prayer refers to the latter period is to involve St. Paul in the papal heresy of praying for the dead. Therefore the preservation which is to follow the entire sanctification can refer *only to the present life* up to the hour of death. So

plainly is this true, that no polemical writer
has ventured to twist this passage into any
other meaning. The entire sanctification here
supplicated is not only in this life, but the peculiar phraseology of the prayer implies that
it is an instantaneous work. To the objection
that the verb ἀγιάσαι, *sanctify*, can here only be
understood of the gradual spread of the principle of holiness implanted in regeneration; even
Olshausen insists that the emphasis laid on
the "very God," or "the God of peace himself," "shows that something new is to follow," some vigorous interposition of the omnipotent arm of the Sanctifier. Besides this,
the verb is in the aorist tense, denoting a single momentary act.

Before taking our leave of this wonderful
Scripture we call attention to the fact, that it
effectually refutes the Gnostic error respecting
the inherent evil of matter. In the enumera-
tion of the constituent elements of man which
are to be sanctified wholly, and preserved each
entire, we find "body," σῶμα, which is wholly
material. St. Paul knew of nothing in man
which was incapable of receiving the efficacy
of the cleansing blood of Christ. And lest

there should be any room for cavil, he speci-
fies the ψυχή, the lower or animal "soul," in
which inhere those passions and desires possessed by man in common with the brutes.
This border land between pure spirit on one
side and gross matter on the other, lies open
to the great Purifier as well as the higher element of spirit, πνεῦμα, the designed receptacle
or temple for the abode of God in man.   In
the Epistle to the Hebrews the Apostle's closet
door gets ajar again, and we hear these words
breathed into the ear of God—so much like
those just quoted as to indicate the same
pleader: "Now the God of peace, that brought
again from the dead our Lord Jesus, through
the blood of the everlasting covenant,* that
great Shepherd of the sheep, make you *perfect*
in every *good work* to do his will."   This must
be before death, for good works must be in
time.   To be perfect in them is to exclude
every evil work, that is, all sin.

2. Every Scripture in which we are exhorted
to bring forth those virtues and graces called
the fruit of the Spirit, must refer to this life.

---

* The order of clauses in the Greek teaches that Jesus was
raised through the blood of the everlasting covenant.

If these are required in perfection, as they certainly are, they must exclude their opposites. Perfect love supposes the extirpation of every antagonistic affection; perfect meekness, all unholy anger; and thus with all the other graces.

3. We argue again, that entire holiness is attainable in this life, because all the commands to be holy must refer to the present. Grammarians tell us that all imperatives are in the present tense. If they cover the future they include the indivisible now. "Be ye holy," plainly requires present holiness. "Be ye perfect," enjoins perfection to-day. "Thou shalt love the Lord with all thy heart," is a command enforcing perfect love to-day, if it means any thing.

4. The promises of sanctifying grace are available to believers now, or they are worthless. For true faith can be exercised for spiritual grace for ourselves only as it rests on the promise which includes the present moment. "Knowing this, that the body of sin might be destroyed, that *henceforth* we should not serve sin." This promise of the destruction of sin begins now, and is followed by a glorious

henceforth of emancipation this side of death. Let the reader study the following promises, and observe how manifestly they imply present fulfillment: Isa. i, 18, 25; Titus ii, 14; 1 John i, 9; iv, 16–18. Let him also remember that every command to be holy covers the present, and contains an implied promise of the aid of the Sanctifier.

5. It remains to examine one Scripture in which it is asserted that our evangelical perfection is in express terms deferred to some future time, namely, 1 Peter v, 10: "But the God of all grace, who hath called us unto his eternal glory by Christ Jesus, after that ye have suffered a while, make you perfect, stablish, strengthen, settle you." Some tell us that the adverbial clause, "after ye have suffered a while," modifies the following verb, "perfect." Let us read it in this way, and we will find that the poor souls for whom Peter prays cannot claim to be "stablished" now, nor strengthened now, nor settled now; but they must be tossed about in weakness and instability till after they have "suffered awhile." This is certainly contrary to the uniform promise of God to help in time of

need. We need the most help when we suffer.
Then again, the soul deserted of God for a while
is anxious to know the length of this indefinite "a while." How long a time must elapse
before I can claim by faith the strengthening
grace here supplicated? It is evident that
the four verbs "perfect," "stablish," "strength-
en," and "settle," are all in the same grammati-
cal construction. If we must wait a while to
be perfected, we must also wait in suffering to
be strengthened. But now suppose that, with
the best biblical scholar of the century, Dean
Alford, we attach the adverbial clause to the
verb "hath called," what will be the rendering then? "But the God of all grace, who
called you unto his eternal glory (heaven, not
now, but) when ye have suffered a little while,
himself perfect you (now,) stablish," etc. This
rendering is simple and clear. It obviates all
the difficulties of the other rendering, and
makes God a present help in our extremity.
The sufferings must be passed before the glory
can be entered. They are the condition of the
reward. This is all that St. Peter intended
by the clause in dispute. As God is ready to
pardon *now* every sinner on the earth who

comes in penitence and faith in Jesus, so is this Almighty Saviour able and willing, at the present moment, to cleanse and endow with the fullness of the Holy Spirit every believer who honors Christ by a trust in his promise of the abiding Comforter. So intense is his abhorrence of sin that he longs to wipe out the last spot that defiles humanity.

6. The experimental evidence that the blood of Christ avails to the complete cleansing of the believer before death would fill many volumes. We give the first that comes to hand.

" A few years ago the wife of a distinguished minister was lying hopelessly ill. All was mist and uncertainty before her. She longed for the purity and peace promised in the holy word, but her husband had always preached a gradual growth in grace, and completeness in Christ only at the last moment of life, and she waited for that hour in dread uncertainty.

" ' O, that I could have complete deliverance from sin now, before that fearful hour!' she exclaimed.

" ' Why not now?' the Spirit suggested.

" She sent for her husband, and as he en-
5

tered her sick-chamber, she anxiously inquired,
'Can Christ save me from all sin?'

"'Yes; he's an almighty Saviour, your Saviour, able to save to the uttermost.'

"'When can he save me? You have often
said that he saves from all sin at the dying
moment. If he is *almighty*, don't you think
he could save me a few minutes before death?
It would take the sting of death away to know
that I am saved.'

"'Yes, I think he could.'

"'Well, if he could save me a few minutes
before death, don't you believe it possible for
him to save a few hours or a day before
death?' The husband bowed his assent.
'But,' she said with deep earnestness, 'I may
live a week, or a month; do you think it possible for God to save a soul from all sin so
long before death?'

"'Yes; all things are possible with God,'
he answered with deep emotion.

"'Then kneel right down here and pray for
me. I want this full salvation now, and if I
live a month, I will live to praise God.'

"He knelt beside her bed, and poured out
his soul to God in prayer as he had never

done before. And while he prayed, the cleansing blood that makes whiter than snow was applied to her soul, and she was enabled to rejoice with a joy unspeakable and full of glory. She lived a month afterward to magnify the grace of God, and testify of the perfect love that casteth out all fear. And since that hour her husband has preached Christ as a present Saviour, able to save from all sin." *

The following experience of a Presbyterian preacher's wife who still lives, and testifies on both continents to the cleansing blood of Jesus Christ purifying her from all sin years after conversion, meets the objection urged by some that those experiencing entire sanctification are only just then converted or reclaimed from a backslidden state :—

"When I was converted my conversion was so marked, so clear, so decided, that I never could have a doubt of it. I went on for three years in the ordinary Christian way, (sometimes gaining a little, perhaps, but at other times defeated,) battling against my besetting sins—against pride and ambition, against impatience and irritability, against worrying

* "The Jeweled Ministry."

about the future, and about the petty things
of life.

"But at the end of three years I was taught
a very different way from that of making resolutions, and struggling into the Divine life,
and battling down my ambition, and pride,
and levity, and all those things which tor-
mented me. I found that Jesus Christ would
do all that work for me. After I learned this,
my life was changed. O, how changed it was!
How calm and serene it became! There was
such a resting on Jesus! He seemed to be
with me every day, and all the time; and I
looked to him to keep me from pride and ambition, and from the worriments of life, and
from anxiety about the future, and I found
that he did that work for me. He did it all
the time. He is the Conqueror of sin. If we
leave ourselves in his hands he does for us
what we cannot do for ourselves."

A widely-known deaconess, in evangelical
labors most abundant, testifies to a steady
growth up to the time when the love of Christ
was made perfect in her heart by the fullness
of the Holy Ghost :—

"For years I worked and worked to get the

Christian graces, and fit myself for salvation by Christ. And O, how hard that was! But then it was a great deal easier than to submit to Jesus. My heart chafed and found no rest until I was willing to accept the words of Christ when he said to me, "Your heart is deceitful and desperately wicked," and at the same time to accept his words when he said, "I will save you," and to trust in him. After that, doubts went from me, and there seemed to be a full resting in the righteousness of Christ, in his merits, in his atonement. There was no rest in myself, in my experiences, or aught else besides simply resting upon Christ to save me eternally, and accepting his promises to be with me every-where and every day, and to guide me in all things. In this there was peace and joy to my soul.

"All that I can think of by which to illustrate my Christian life is this, that it was like sitting in a row-boat and rowing up stream, and making progress by severe effort; until, by and by, there comes a steamer along, and the weary toiler is asked if he will not have a ride, and he steps on board, and makes the remainder of the voyage easily and pleasantly.

It seemed at first that the Christian work was hard and wearying, but after that it was God doing the work in me, God pushing me on, God leading me, God guiding. And now it is easy—easy in the family, with the little ones, every-where. For it is love—the love of God —that is working. The soul is filled with love. And O, how love will go anywheré, and count no cost, and keep no record of what it does! There is no burden at all about living for a loved object. It is perfect freedom."

We have not space for the clear testimonies of Madam Guyon, Catharine Adorna, Monsieur De Renty, John and Mary Fletcher, Hester Ann Rogers, Bramwell, Carvosso, Adam Clarke, J. B. Taylor, Wilbur Fisk, Olin, Hamline, Alfred Cookman, and a host of others, whose biographies are a precious legacy to the Christian world, and a directory to all who are seeking to find the highway of holiness.

CHAPTER V.

BIBLE TEXTS FOR SIN EXAMINED.

M UCH of the controversy about sin results from the want of accuracy in the
definition of this term.   We do not in this
chapter include in sin the involuntary devia-
tions from the law of absolute right, but willful
transgressions of the known law of God, written in his word or on the tables of the heart,
and also original or inbred sin.

Living without sin are words which shock
many persons.   It seems to them to be plucking the crown from the head of Christ, the
only sinless man who ever walked the earth,
and putting that crown upon the heads of
men.   But let us see whether sin in the human
soul really honors or dishonors Christ.   What
was the great errand of Jesus into the world?
To save his people from their sins.   So far,
then, as he does not save from sin, his mission
is a dishonorable failure.   He came to create
the believer anew, making him a new creature.

So much of the old man of sin as appears to stain and corrupt this new creature reflects discredit upon " Him that begetteth." " Ye are his workmanship." The work testifies of the skill or of the incompetency of the artist. Will any one insist that sin is a beauty and not a blemish in the work of the Divine Sculptor? In his prayer, which has been appropriately styled his high-priestly address to his Father, Jesus says respecting his disciples, "I am glorified in them." Does Christ's glory consist in sin, reflected from his followers? St. John said of the Logos, who became flesh and dwelt among us, that we beheld his glory—not a material resplendence, not worldly wealth, nor rank, nor fame, nor genius, but moral excellence, fullness of " grace and truth." These qualities in believing hearts glorify Christ. Sin is not only a shame to any people, but a shame to the God of any people. Jesus, therefore, is not jealous of the believer who, through the power of his grace, has complete victory over inward sin, and perfect cleansing from outward defilement, but he rejoices in the honor which his perfect work reflects upon his workmanship. He is not afraid that he who wears the robe of his righteousness will outshine himself, and appropriate his honors. Sin might do this, but holiness never.

But is not sin in the heart necessary to keep the soul humble? Will not spiritual pride lift itself up as soon as sin is destroyed? As well might you ask whether a man would not lift up his head haughtily when his neck has been broken. The Holy Spirit, taking complete possession of the heart, not only breaks the neck of sin, but casts out this strong man, leaving no seed of pride behind. Perfect love to Christ is perfect lowliness. When it is demonstrated that men must drink a little whisky daily in order to temperance,—steal a trifling amount every day in order to be honest,—tell a few fibs every twenty-four hours in order to be truthful,—and occasionally violate the seventh commandment that they may maintain their purity,—then we will sit down and soberly answer the objection that a little nest-egg of sin in the heart is a necessary nucleus about which all the Christian virtues are to be gathered. But does not the Bible flatly contradict this doctrine, that the freedom which Jesus, the great Emancipator, bestows, includes grace to live without sinning? Did not Solomon, in prayer at the dedication of the temple, (2 Chron. vi, 36,) tell Jehovah that "there is no man which sinneth not?" And does he not repeat this declaration in Eccles. vii, 20, "For there is not a just man on earth that doeth good and sinneth not?" We answer that Solomon, when correctly interpreted, as he is in the Vulgate, the Septuagint, and most of the ancient versions, gives no countenance to sin. These all read, "*May not sin.*" The Hebrew language, having no potential mode, uses the indicative future instead. The context must determine the real meaning. The context is nonsense in King James' version, using an *if* where there is no room for a condition—"if any man sin, for every man sins." Let me illustrate the absurdity of this translation.

At the laying of a corner-stone of a State lunatic asylum the Governor, in his address, is made by the reporter to say, "If any person in the commonwealth is insane—for every person is insane—let him come here and be cared for." We should all correct the blundering reporter, and say, *may become* in-

sane, instead of *is* insane, in order to make the
Governor talk sense. Correct the reporter, or
translator, rather, of Solomon, and let him
talk sense also, and you will hear him say,
If any man sin, for there is no one who is im-
peccable, who *may not* sin. This criticism
applies to the quotation from the Eccle-
siastes, also. But does not St. James say,
(iii, 2,) "For in many things we offend all?"
Who are the *we?* Is it St. James and the
rest of the apostles? Then these excellent
men, after blessing God, fall to cursing men.
See ninth verse. But if the *we* is used for
men generally, the difficulty vanishes. That
it is so used read the entire verse, and note
the exception to the general offending, "If
any man offend not in word, the same is a
perfect man." But the plea for continuing
in sin has one more proof-text, (1 John i, 8,)
"If we say that we have no sin, we deceive
ourselves, and the truth is not in us." This
means if we have never sinned, and so have
no need of the blood of Jesus Christ, spoken
of in the previous verse. The tenth verse
reiterates and explains the eighth : "If we
say that we *have not* sinned, we make him a

liar, and his word is not in us." This explanation harmonizes perfectly with John's strong assertion, that " whosoever is born of God doth not commit sin," that is, known and willful sin. The incorrect interpretation of the eighth verse, which makes every believer in Christ a constant sinner, is in direct collision with the asserted victory over sin, enjoyed by every one born of God.

After this removal of misconceptions arising from misinterpreted Scriptures, we proceed to demonstrate the same doctrine of a complete deliverance from sin, by referring the reader to those passages which enjoin on the believer the possession of the fullness of the Divine love, and the fullness of the Spirit. We would call especial attention to the wonderful prayer of St. Paul in Ephesians iii, 14. An analysis of this prayer will find no negative petition in it. No allusion to sin, actual or indwelling, occurs; but the eye of the Apostle sees only the positive blessing—the fullness of God. This is utterly inconsistent with the existence of sin in the soul. Paul's logical mind would have seen the impropriety of such a prayer for sinners. For such he would have entreated God for pardon, and for cleansing by the washing of regeneration, and by the renewing of the Holy Ghost. But finding them thus cleansed, as empty vessels before the Lord, he prays that they may be filled with all the fullness of God.

This subject would not be complete without an examination of that fancied *magna charta* for the necessary existence of sin in the Christian heart prompting to sinful acts, namely, the seventh chapter of the Epistle to the Romans. Does St. Paul here portray the Christian at his best earthly estate? Does he hold up his own moral photograph? To both of these queries we answer, No. St. Paul formed his style in the synagogue debates. "This explains the eminently dialogic character of the style. The ever-recurring second person, often the second person singular, shows us his co-disputant ever in his presence. By this the train of thought is varied and controlled into often unexpected and abrupt transitions. Objections, sometimes in the opponent's own words, sometimes put for him in St. Paul's words, are rapidly presented and rapidly over-ridden."

This being true, it requires great care to ascertain the character speaking—whether the author is speaking for himself, or personating another. It is a very significant fact that for the first three centuries the entire Christian Church, with one accord, applied the picture of the vanquished and despairing slave described in Rom. vii, 13–25, solely to the unregenerate man. "It seemed too low a picture for the possessor of a new Christian life, as the Apostle in the main current of thought is describing. Its application to the regenerate man was first invented by Augustine, who was followed by many eminent doctors of the Middle Ages. After the Reformation the interpretation of Augustine was largely adopted, especially by the followers of Calvin. At the present day the Church generally, Greek, Roman, Protestant, including some of the latest commentators, have returned to the just interpretation as held by the primitive Church." —*Dr. Whedon.* An examination of the preceding and succeeding passages will amply justify our conclusion that a regenerate soul never sat for this dark, sad portrait. This was never designed to depict the ideal Christian life, but is rather the portrayal of the struggles of a convicted sinner seeking justification by the works of the law. The ideal Christian life is found in the sixth chapter: "But now being made free from sin, and become servants to God, ye have your fruit unto holiness, and the end everlasting life;" also in the eighth chapter: "There is therefore now no condemnation to them which are in Christ Jesus, who walk not after the flesh, but after the Spirit." As the skillful painter puts a dark background when he wishes to make the central figure in the front more radiant, so St. Paul sets off the believer delivered from sin by holding up beside him the dark contrast of a convicted legalist vainly seeking justification by his good works. How sad the blunder of mistaking the profile of the sinner for the saint, and hanging it up for imitation by the body of believers.

We are confident in our conclusion that the Holy Scriptures nowhere apologize for sin, or in the least license it or extenuate its existence in the universe. To assert that the holy God has made sin necessary under the reign of grace is to slander the Father, and pronounce the redemptive plan a stupendous failure.

CHAPTER VI.

DELIVERANCE DEFERRED.

HAVING shown that Christ proposes to free the believer in this world not only from acts of sin, but from the sinful disposition inherent in fallen humanity, we proceed to enumerate certain ills which are the effects of sin, and wear its appearance, but have not its moral character, and are not in the catalogue of things from which Jesus promises us deliverance in the present life. These are,—

First. *Spiritual warfare.* This implies temptations. Jesus warred with temptations. "As he is, so are ye in this world." "The disciple is not above his Lord." The Christian life is a long battle, for which we are to draw arms from the arsenal of Christ's promised presence, and from the power of his word, and from the endowment of his Holy Spirit. But we do assert that we may be delivered from the most distressing and perilous form of war—a civil war; a confederacy against Christ raging in every believer's bosom. This civil war is disquieting the souls of many who have accepted Christ with a feeble faith. They are living in the seventh chapter of the Epistle to the Romans. This, as we proved in the last chapter, was never designed to be the ideal Christian life, but is rather the portrayal of the struggles of a convicted sinner seeking justification by the works of the law. The ideal Christian life is found in the sixth chapter— "But being now made free from sin, and become servants of God, ye have your fruit unto holiness, and the end everlasting life;" also in the eighth chapter: "There is therefore now no condemnation to them which are in Christ Jesus, who walk not after the flesh, but after the Spirit." An objector here queries whether the flesh, one of the triad of foes to the soul trusting in Jesus Christ, is not an inward foe, a traitor within the citadel. Certainly it is such a foe in the first part of the spiritual campaign. But the promise is, "Ye shall be cleansed from all filthiness of the flesh and spirit." The commandment is, "Crucify the flesh with its affections and lusts." The ideal Christian life in the eighth of Romans is

6

of this kind. It is a death unto sin, so that he who fully apprehends Christ, the life, is as free from the movements of sin within him as the corpses in yonder grave-yard are free from the cares which bustle at midday through the market-place. "If ye do mortify the deeds of the body, ye shall live." To mortify is to slay. The Gospel contemplates the extirpation of all antagonisms to Christ within the believing soul. But does not St. Paul say, "I keep my body under, and bring it into subjection, lest, after having preached the Gospel to others I should become a castaway!" Christ would not bless, but curse us, if he should free us from the innocent appetites which our Creator has implanted in us for the preservation of the individual and of the race. These blind and instinctive impulses must be controlled by reason and conscience. Neither St. Paul nor any other saint was so holy that his hands would instinctively drop his knife and fork the instant he had eaten exactly enough, without the intervention of the will directed by the judgment. Christ does not propose to emancipate any person from the necessity of exercising his judgment in regard to his innocent appetites.

Second. Christ has not promised to deliver us, in the present life, from infirmities. So long as we abide in houses of clay we shall be humbled by their presence. I do not say that we shall be under a sense of condemnation in consequence of them. So long as we are in this tabernacle we shall groan for deliverance from these involuntary failures and weaknesses. They need the blood of sprinkling. Hence the holiest person on earth is not beyond saying daily, " Forgive us our debts, as we forgive our debtors." But you inquire, What is the nature of those infirmities from which we are to expect no release in the present life? They are the scars of sin: the wounds have been healed. As in the kingdom of nature, so in the kingdom of grace, there is no medicine to remove the scars of wounds, none efficacious in the present life. You may mend a pitcher by the application of cement, so that it will hold water; but when you strike it there is no ring. To regain the ring of a perfect vessel, you must hand it over to the potter to be ground to powder and to be reconstructed. So it is with us in the present life. Jesus, if we will submit our shattered vessels to him, can mend us up so that we may be filled with the Spirit, but we shall not on earth regain the true Adamic ring of absolute perfection. We must be handed over to death to be reduced to dust and be built up again by the Divine Potter, when we shall be presented *faultless*, not in the obscure twilight of some distant region, but *faultless* in the meridian splendors " of the presence of his glory."

As instances of invincible infirmities we would mention *lack of knowledge* in respect to subjects upon which we must act ; hence errors of judgment, paving the way for errors in practice.

Defective memory is another infirmity which even the fullness of sanctifying grace does not remove. It was not designed to restore the intellectual powers in the present life to undecaying vigor. It quickens the dead spiritual nature, and reinforces conscience. *A fallible judgment* will be ours even when love to Christ has been perfected.

Hours of apathy and spiritual dullness by reason of our bodily organism or the state of the nerves. We cannot always prevent these states. Christ does not promise to work a miracle to keep us awake and aflame with zeal, in an atmosphere deprived of its oxygen by the carelessness of the sexton.

Third. We should be happy to inform millions of groaning saints that there is attainable in the present life a state of love to Christ so strong as to exclude *every wandering thought in prayer*. John Wesley, in his younger days, declared that such a state could be reached by saints in the flesh. He lived to see his error, and to confess it in his sermon on Wandering Thoughts. This was written to correct a practical error into which some were running, of seeking the sanctification of the *mind* as distinct from the heart. These persons believed, that by the power of the Holy Spirit the succession of the thoughts could be so controlled as to shut out every improper or wandering thought, and that the mind could be stayed upon God in such a way that no distracting thought could intrude. Wesley saw that this was putting the work of entire sanctification so high as to render it unattainable, and that the advocacy of this extreme view was doing great damage to the precious doctrine of perfect *love*, which is far different from perfect *thinking*.

To all who are in distress on this account we commend the entire sermon. The philosophy of this whole subject lies in a few words. The work of the Divine Spirit is chiefly, if not wholly, comprised in a rectification of the will. Says Mr. Fletcher, "Christian perfection extends chiefly to the will, which is the capital moral power of the soul; leaving the understanding ignorant of ten thousand things. Adamic perfection extended to the whole man." The succession of ideas is independent of the will, and hence it is not the province of grace to prevent wandering thoughts. It may partially cure the evil by drawing the soul toward Christ as toward a great magnet, so that the tendency of even our random thoughts may be toward him.

Fourth. I nowhere find an assurance that the soul believing in Christ will be delivered from all *unpleasant and improper dreams.* We desire this state of religious experience, and we express our aspiration in song :—

> "Yet in my dreams I'd be
> Nearer, my God, to thee."

We must here disagree with President Edwards, who tells Christians to scrutinize their dreams in order to ascertain their real character and standing before God. So far as my observation goes, there is no law in our dreams but the law of contraries. The most peaceable, quarrel; the most gentle and tender, commit murder; the most contented with life, plot suicide; the temperate, become drunken; and the pure, become impure. These conceptions, resulting from the day's employment, the state of the digestion, the quantity of bedding, and a thousand other causes, give no more indication of the moral and spiritual condition than they do of the person's ancestral pedigree.

Fifth. Nor do we look for salvation from sudden trepidation when any thing startling occurs, like the crash of a thunderbolt or the presentation of a telegraphic dispatch from the absent family. All this is instinctive. As there is no sin in instinctive actions, so there is in them no ground of condemnation. An eminent Christian woman received a dispatch from her husband a thousand miles away, and then apologized to me, and asked forgiveness of God, for the dishonor she had done to the cause of Christ by the emotion which her trembling hand indicated when the dispatch was

suddenly thrust before her eye. The apology
and prayer were both needless, for there was
no sin in this sudden agitation. The Saviour,
for wise reasons, defers our deliverance from
these till our feet touch the other shore; and
yet, we are commanded with Abraham "to
walk before God and be perfect."

Sixth. Nor does Jesus, the great Emancipator, deliver us from the unpleasant feeling
of our insufficiency in our labors in his vineyard. We do not accomplish a thousandth
part of what we desire to do. Fields lie waste
all around us. The good seed we scatter is
largely wasted; it brings little fruit to perfection. When we contemplate these facts, the
thought suggests itself that if we were just
right, perfectly guided by the Spirit of truth,
we should engage in no abortive labors;
every stroke would tell for the kingdom of
Christ; every word of exhortation or of instruction would accomplish its exact purpose,
like the word of the Lord "which returneth
not unto him void." We have recently heard
persons testify to such a fullness and guidance
of the Spirit that every effort to do good to
others is successful, the Spirit directing, infalli-

bly, to the susceptible persons, and suggesting the exact words needed for their deliverance. But there must be some mistake in this matter. We find no instance of this in the Holy Scriptures. The holiest men are afflicted with a sense of failure in their labors. Sinners were hardened under the preaching of St. Paul. His failure to save his brethren of the Hebrew nation produced the profoundest sorrow, so that he could wish himself "accursed from Christ;" that is, that he could make an atonement in addition to Christ's, to secure their salvation. Jesus himself, when he gazed from Olivet upon the rebellious city soon to be desolated by the judgments of God, and cried "O Jerusalem, Jerusalem!" keenly felt the failure of his ministry. If we correctly interpret the language of God the Father, we must understand that even his absolute perfections do not exclude a painful sense of failure in his unsuccessful attempts to save free agents who pervert their godlike attribute of freedom by rejecting his mercy: "I have nourished and brought up children, and they have rebelled against me." He "willeth not the death of the wicked, but rather that they would turn

and live : Turn ye, turn ye." Therefore we
do not teach the possibility of freedom from
this sense of inefficiency in the present life.
It is an element of our probation, one of the
highest tests of faith, to toil for God when we
see no fruit, to sow for others to reap, or for
the birds to snatch away, or the thorns to choke.
Was not this the bitter ingredient in that cup
which made the Son of God a man of sorrows?

Seventh. Christ will not free us from death,
nor from ills and diseases, the sappers and
miners of the king of terrors. All these shall
be put beneath the Conqueror's feet, but not
now. "The last enemy that shall be destroyed
is death." Nevertheless, when the *gift* of faith
is bestowed as a *charism*, not a grace, the sick
even in our day may be healed, and death
itself may be postponed, in answer to prayer,
as in the case of Hezekiah. I Cor. xii, 9;
James v, 15.

CHAPTER VII.

METAPHORICAL REPRESENTATIONS OF PERFECT LOVE.

§ 1. *The Dove Descending and Abiding.*

MRS. HARRIET BEECHER STOWE, in her admirable essay on " Primitive Christian Experience," uses the following language :—

" The advantages to the Christian Church, in setting before it *distinct points of attainment*, are very nearly the same in result as the advantages of preaching immediate regeneration in preference to indefinite exhortation to men to lead sober, righteous, and godly lives. It has been found, in the course of New England preaching, that pressing men to an immediate and definite point of conversion, produced immediate and definite results ; and so it has been found among Christians, that pressing them to an immediate and definite point of attainment will, in like manner, result in marked and decided progress. For this reason it is, that, among the Moravian Christians, where the experience by them denominated full assurance of faith was much insisted on, there were more instances of high religious faith than in almost any other denomination."

Here is sound philosophy, founded on facts corroborated by Mr. Wesley in his wide range of observation :—"Wherever the work of sanctification increased, the whole work of God increased in all its branches." In 1765 he found in Bristol fifty less members than he left before. He thus accounts for this decline :—"One reason is, that Christian perfection has been little insisted on ; and wherever this is not done, be the preacher ever so eloquent, there is little increase either in the numbers or grace of the hearers." When a definite point is presented to the believer as attainable immediately, all the energies of the soul are aroused and concentrated. Prayer is no more at random. There is a target set up to fire at. Faith as an act—a voluntary venture upon the promise —puts forth its highest energies and achieves its greatest victories.

But just here some people find a difficulty. They do not dispute the philosophy, but they question the fact that to believers there is in the New Testament such a distinct point, such a definite line to be crossed. They say that they fail to find in the apostolic Church any instance of such a sudden transition in the spiritual life of the justified soul. It is said that after regeneration there is a gradual development of the new life, with no instantaneous uplifts such as are insisted on by the modern apostles of the higher life. It is the purpose of this chapter to show not only numerous instances of an instantaneous uprising to a higher plane of Christian experience, but that this was the normal development of the spiritual life of primitive Christians. We proceed to show that the baptism of the Holy Ghost is identical with the blessing of perfect love.

St. Paul, in one of his missionary tours, encountered Judaizing teachers who affirmed that those who would be good Christians must be good Jews, obeying all the Levitical law. This question was carried up to Jerusalem to be decided by a council of the apostles and elders. After much discussion, Peter arose and gave an account of his preaching :—" A good while ago God made choice among us that the Gentiles by my mouth should hear the word of the Gospel and believe; and God, which knoweth the hearts, bare them witness, giving them the Holy Ghost even as he did unto us; and put no difference between us and them, *purifying their hearts by faith.*" Peter refers to his preaching to Cornelius and his staff at his headquarters in Cesarea. On another occasion he declares: "And as I began to speak, the Holy Ghost fell on them *as on us at the beginning;*" that is, on the day of Pentecost, at the beginning of "the kingdom of the Holy Ghost," as John Fletcher styles it. The apostles were then *filled*, which is the same as being *baptized*, with the Holy Ghost, for it was the fulfillment of the promise, "But ye shall be baptized with the Holy Ghost not many days hence." The conclusion is inevitable, that the baptism of the Holy Ghost includes the extinction of sin in the believer's soul as its negative and minor part, and the fullness of love shed abroad in the heart as its positive and greater part; in other words, it includes entire sanctification and Christian perfection.

Let us more clearly trace the successive steps by which we come to this conclusion. Christ promised that when he should be glorified the disciples should receive a blessing which they could not receive while his bodily presence remained with them. John vii, 38, 39. That blessing was not the forgiveness of sins, for Jesus was daily dispensing pardon. It was a blessing of an abiding and aggressive nature, making believers to be as fountains whence should flow forth "rivers of living water." Thus much is determined by this passage, that there is a blessing distinct from pardoning grace, and there is an indefinite interval between them. It remains now to show that this second bless- ing involves entire sanctification. The proofs are: 1. The account of the fullness of the Holy Spirit on the day of Pentecost, ten days after the Lord Jesus ascended to his glorified state. Acts i and ii. 2. Peter's declaration (Acts xi, 15, 16) that the effusion of the Holy Spirit upon Cornelius and his company was the same in character and effect as the outpouring at the Pentecost. 3. Peter's incidental remark in Acts xv, 9, that the Holy Ghost came to Cornelius and his house in his office of the Sanc-

tifier, "Purifying their hearts by faith." The
last text is an incontrovertible demonstration
that the fullness of the Spirit is a synonym for
entire sanctification. Since there are but two
forces which can sway the soul, the flesh and
the Spirit, to be completely filled with either is
to exclude the other. To be filled with the
Spirit is to be completely emancipated from
the flesh, or inherent depravity. To be but
partially swayed by the Spirit is to afford a
foothold in the soul for a contest between
these antagonistic powers. Gal. v, 17.

It remains to be proved that Cornelius and
his staff, or house, whose hearts "were purified
by faith " in the Spirit baptism, were previous-
ly in a justified state. We have the testimony
of the Spirit of inspiration that he was " a *devout* man, and one that *feared God* with *all his
house*, (military household,) which gave much
alms to the people, and *prayed* always." Peter,
under the inspiration of the Spirit, and standing in the presence of Cornelius and his house,
asserts, " Of a truth I perceive that God is no
respecter of persons ; but in every nation he
that feareth God and worketh righteousness
is accepted with him " — " through Christ,

though he knew him not," says Wesley most truly. To be *accepted* with God is to be *justified* by God. There was no conviction of sin produced under Peter's discourse in Cesarea, no account that these pious Gentiles "were pricked in their heart," nor was there any outcry, "Men and brethren, what shall we do." They were ready to receive the Holy Ghost, hence the correctness of the inference made by the Council at Jerusalem: "Then hath God also to the Gentiles granted repentance unto life." Acts xi, 18. The reception of the Holy Spirit in his fullness presupposes their previous repentance unto life. On the day of Pentecost so great was the manifestation of spiritual power that the believers in Christ were instantly and completely filled without the instrumentality of preaching, and unbelievers during the sermon of Peter were rapidly transformed into penitent believers, ready to submit to any test of the genuineness of their faith; even to be publicly baptized in the hated name of that Jesus whom they had personally insulted and crucified. The finishing stroke of this rapid transformation was "the gift of the Holy Ghost," with its fruits—un-

7

selfishness, oneness of spirit, "gladness and singleness of heart." But generally there was a brief interval between conversion and the baptism of the Spirit.

The people of Samaria were first converted under the preaching of Deacon Philip; "and when they believed, they were baptized, both men and women." Having never been brought into personal contact with Jesus, and having never offered personal insult to him, water baptism is not made the test of the sincerity of their repentance, so that they were regenerated before that ordinance was used. The successive steps through which they passed were, attention to the word, faith, great joy—implying a change of heart—and baptism with water.* Afterward Peter and John were sent down from Jerusalem for the special work of leading the converts on to Christian perfection. They held a special meeting. They prayed· with them that they might receive the Holy Ghost, and they laid their hands upon them, and they received the Holy Ghost, not only as the giver of special gifts, but also as a distinct and permanent spiritual endowment. Says

* See Ellicott on Eph. i, 13, and Alford on Gal. i, 16.

Dr. Whedon, " They received the Holy Ghost in his miraculous and extraordinary manifestation, not merely sanctifying but charismatic. They had doubtless been regenerated by that Spirit before their baptism, in his secret and ordinary power and operation."

The Apostle Paul found at Ephesus "certain disciples." He asked them a question which seems greatly out of place if there is no distinct work of the Holy Spirit after justification : " Have ye received the Holy Ghost since ye believed?" Acts xix, 2. We admit that there is no word "since" in the Greek text, and that there may be no allusion to time in this passage, which may be rendered: " Have ye believing received the Holy Ghost?" Reading the question even in this form, making the πιστεύσαντες a participle of means— " by believing "—and not of time—" since believing," or "having believed," (*Ellicott*)—there is nothing gained on the part of those who deny a second and distinct work of the Holy Spirit; for there lies plainly on the surface of this question the implication that Christian discipleship is not a proof, *prima facie*, of " receiving the Holy Ghost." If discipleship im-

plies this blessing, St. Paul asked an absurd
question when he thus catechised the twelve
justified and baptized Ephesian disciples. The
question propounded by St. Paul at the very
first salutation was probably the interrogatory
put to every convert to Christ who had been
converted by the instrumentality of some other
person. Ignorant of his spiritual state, and
fearing that he might not have received " the
greatest gift that man can wish or Heaven can
send," he asks this all-important question :
" Have you received the Holy Ghost since
you believed?" Should the great Apostle
arise from the dead and come into our Churches
to-day, we doubt not that this would be his
first question. We are not so sure that he
would not be more surprised by the answer of
multitudes, " We have not so much as heard
whether there be any Holy Ghost," as a permanent indweller in the hearts of believers,
although they have all their lives heard the
apostolic blessing, in which the " communion
of the Holy Ghost" is the crowning grace of
that benediction. This would be because of
its not being set forth as a distinct attainment
—a prize set before each, to be grasped by faith.

We understand that the baptism, the anointing, the fullness, the abiding, the indwelling, the constant communion, the sealing, the earnest, of the Holy Spirit, are equivalent terms, expressive of the state of Christian perfection. Wherever these terms occur, the Spirit of inspiration is pointing to that state of serene rest, that unbroken peace, that repose in the blood of Christ, that unwavering trust in God, that deliverance from fleshly desire, and that eradication of inbred sin, which come from being "filled with all the fullness of God." This great blessing is the constant theme of the Apostle Paul, especially in his later epistles. He exhorts all to be filled with the Spirit; he prays for believers that they "may know the love of Christ which passeth knowledge; that Christ may dwell in their hearts." St. Paul was a practical man, and never wasted his time in urging the impracticable, in inciting to the unattainable. According to Meyer the ordinary sequence of blessings is, (*a*) Hearing; (*b*) Faith, implying preventing and saving grace; (*c*) Baptism; (*d*) Communication of the Holy Spirit. Compare together Acts ii, 37, 38, (*a, c, d;*) viii, 6, 12, 17, (*a, b, c, d;*) xix,

5, 6, (*c, d.*) Acts x, 44, (*d, c,*) and *perhaps* ix, 17, are exceptional cases. The reason for the seeming blending of the baptism of the Holy Ghost with regeneration in exceptional instances in the Acts of the Apostles, is to be attributed to the fact that the regenerate were urged to the immediate attainment of this great blessing, so that they did attain it with the interval of only a brief period. A similar experience was that of Rev. John Fletcher, who seems to have been born into the kingdom with such a grasp of faith that he apprehended Jesus Christ as his complete Saviour a very few days afterward. In the days of John Wesley, where this privilege was held up to the young convert by the preachers, and exemplified by many believers, there are instances of the attainment of perfect love within a day or two after justification. " The next morning I spoke severally with those who believed they were sanctified. There were fifty-one in all—twenty-one men, twenty-one widows or married women, and nine young women or children. In one of these the change was wrought three weeks after she was justified; in three, seven days after it; in one, five days; and in S. L., aged fourteen, two days only."—*Wesley's Journal*, August 4, 1762.

Please observe how minute and searching Wesley was in his investigations into this subject. No naturalist in pursuit of a scientific truth could be more patient and painstaking in the collection of facts from which to make his induction. Wesley may well be called the ⟩ spiritual Bacon.

Again, two days afterward, he says of another Society, " Many believed that the blood of Jesus Christ had cleansed them from all sin. I spoke to these, forty in all, one by one. Some of them said they received the blessing ten days, some seven, some four, some three days after they found peace with God, and two of them the next day. What marvel, since one day is with God as a thousand years ! "

To our position that the baptism of the Spirit is identical with entire sanctification, it may be objected that there was no need of the purification of Jesus Christ, and yet he, the sinless man, was baptized with the Holy Ghost. Our reply to this is, that entire sanctification is a negative work—the destruction of sin ; the positive work, the constructive part, is much the greater—it is the subsidizing of all the faculties, filling all the capacities with Divine life and power. A sinless soul may need the positive when it has no need of the negative part of the work wrought by the Holy Spirit. We believe that Jesus was baptized of the Holy Ghost because that baptism, at a certain stage of spiritual development, is the normal method of advancement necessary to the perfect unfolding of the spiritual life of every soul. As many people are greatly puzzled by Christ's baptism by the Holy Spirit, as if it were a strange and abnormal thing, we will endeavor to divest the subject of some of its difficulties.

All orthodox believers admit that two distinct natures are so blended in Jesus Christ as to constitute one personality. The human nature was not changed by its union with the Divine. By Christ's human nature we mean his perfect human soul and body. This nature was subject to the limitations and laws of universal humanity. The body grew in stature, the intellect in strength, the moral and spiritual susceptibilities in capacity and beauty. "He grew in favor with God and man." To this end he made diligent use of all the means of grace, read the law, the psalms, and the prophets, prayed much in secret, fasted on important occasions, and gathered with the worshipers in the synagogues and in the temple. As a man, these means of grace were as necessary as to any other Jew who would retain the favor of God. He did not, as the Son of God, need such means for retaining his love to the Father. As equal with the Holy Spirit he did not need any endowment of the Spirit; for the Christian Church, both Papal and Protestant, believe the *filioque* rejected by the Greek Church, which declares that the Holy Spirit proceeds from the Father *and the Son.* But although the Son of God is the channel through which the Holy Spirit flows down to the world from the Father—the *fons Trinitatis,* the fountain of the Trinity—yet nevertheless Jesus, the Son of man, receives him in the way appointed for all believers—an instantaneous effusion, received by faith in the promise of the Father. In this Jesus Christ is our pattern as much as in prayer and praise. The form of the dove, and the voice from heaven, and the coincidence of the Spirit-baptism with water-baptism, were peculiarities of this blessing in the case of our Lord which are not essential to it.

What a revolution would be wrought in the Church—what a resurrection to spiritual life—what a girding with power, if preachers insisted on the duty of all believers imitating their Master in the Spirit-baptism as in the water-baptism, in the reality as in the shadow, in the thing signified as in the symbol!

O blessed Jesus, hasten that day—the day of power in thy Church, as it was when it was the first inquiry of the preacher, " Have ye received the Holy Ghost since ye believed?" Then would he who writes these words for thy glory, O adorable Saviour, joyfully drop his pen, and exclaim with good old Simeon, "*nunc dimittis*," "now lettest thou thy servant depart in peace!"

§ 2. *The Anointing.*

The anointing abideth and teacheth. 1 John ii, 27. The Anointing is a person, because he teacheth. The allusion is to the consecration of kings and priests when they are set apart from common life to sacred offices. But when God sets apart his kings and priests he pours upon them the unction of the Holy Ghost, the baptism of the Spirit, the blessed Comforter, who abides forever. The Paraclete, Monitor, or Comforter, is a gift not promised to penitent sinners, but to those who already love and obey Christ. John xiv, 15, 16. In the days of the apostles, the promise of the Father, the Comforter, was sought for by believers as a definite blessing, and was ordinarily received very soon after regeneration, (Acts viii, 15, 17,) because young converts were instructed and urged to seek it with all their hearts. St. Paul's first question to the Christian neophyte was, " Have ye received the Holy Ghost since ye believed?" And, if they had heard only of water-baptism, they were instructed in the advanced doctrine of the Holy Ghost. Acts xix, 2–5. The distinct nature of this blessing is seen in the rite of confirmation, still practiced in the Anglican, Lutheran, Roman, and Greek Churches, derived from the apostolical act of laying on hands for imparting the gift of the Holy Ghost. All these Churches are right in teaching that there is a change subsequent to regeneration, (baptism in their theology,) a sharply defined transition and enlargement of the spiritual life. Their error consists in shutting up the anointing Spirit to the narrow channels of ritualism, making an unbroken chain of successional ordinations necessary to the down-flowing of the Sanctifier, as an electric current of Divine power. He is received only by faith on the part of the recipient, whether with or without the imposition of hands. In modern times, if testimonies are to be believed, the Lord pours his anointing Spirit upon the hearts of believers without priestly intervention more frequently than with it, because those who employ the rite are apt to rest in the symbol, and to imagine that they have the thing signified.

The spiritual unction, like its symbol, anointing with oil, is instantaneous. The preparation may have extended through years; the act is momentary. The result in both cases is permanent. The man is set apart from a private to a public life—from a subject to a monarch. He is henceforth to be a king as long as he lives, though he may vacate his royalty. The holy consecratory ointment was not a simple oil, but was compounded (Exod. xxx, 23, 24) of four principal spices: pure myrrh, sweet cinna-

mon, sweet calamus, and cassia, with olive oil.
These beautifully typify the gifts and graces
of the Holy Spirit. The presence of sweet
spices only prefigures that the anointing im-
parts no acerbity of disposition, no acid tem-
pers, but only gentle and amiable qualities and
benevolent affections. The anointing ointment
was holy, and God forbade for all time, on pain
of death, any imitation of it. Exodus xxx, 33.
What does this symbolize, but that a hypocritical profession of the spiritual unction, or
fullness of the Holy Ghost, is a capital offense?
The soul, Spirit-anointed, is set apart from self,
and solemnly and perpetually consecrated unto
God, with the possibility of plucking the crown
from his brow and casting it away for ever.
Rev. iii, 11. But few sovereigns ever abdi-
cate; and few souls once crowned priests and
kings unto God ever divest themselves of the
kingly dignity conferred by the fragrant chrism
of the Holy Ghost. It is a great honor to be
born into a royal family: it is a greater to be
anointed king. Hence the anointing, says
Wesley, "is immensely greater than the new
birth;" greater in the joy unspeakable which
fills and floods the soul "anointed with the oil

of gladness;" greater in conscious dignity and power, being invited to sit with the glorified God-man on his throne, as he has gone up to share the throne of his Father. The unction of the Holy One is a greater blessing than the bodily presence of the Lord Jesus raised from the dead and daily conversing with us. "It is expedient (better) for you that I go away; for if I go not away the Comforter will not come unto you." Although the miracle-worker, who authenticates the Gospel, should withdraw, you will be the gainers, even in point of assurance, by the indwelling of his Successor in your consciousness, dispelling doubt, and giving intuitive certainty. Reader, with this Divine Indweller, you will have a thousand-fold more joy than the human presence of Jesus, magnetic as he was to those who loved him, ever gave. Your efficiency in Christian work, and boldness for Jesus, will be wonderfully increased. Hast thou, my Christian friend, received the Holy Ghost, the Sanctifier, in his abiding fullness? Do you have the constant experience of the crowning blessing invoked in the apostolic benediction—the *communion of the Holy Ghost?*

"O ye tender babes in Jesus !
  Hear your heavenly Father's will ;
Claim your portion, plead his promise,
  And he quickly will fulfill.

" Pray, and the refining fire
  Will come quickly from above :
Now believe, and claim the blessing ;
  Nothing less than perfect love."

We have assumed that this anointing is the privilege of every believer, because all such are kings and· priests unto God.   St. Paul implies that the Corinthians are generally enjoying this blessing.   He says, (2 Cor. i, 21,) " He that hath anointed us is God."   We understand the plural pronoun to include the writer and the believers addressed.*   St. John, writing to the Church universal, in his General Epistle asserts that as a body they had the anointing. " Ye have an unction from the Holy One "— Christ—" and ye know all things."   It was a grace commonly enjoyed by primitive Christians, but did not exhaust itself upon them. " The residue of the Spirit " is with Him whom giving cannot impoverish nor withholding enrich.   Christ received the Holy Ghost without measure, (John iii, 34,) not to retain, but to

* See Alford.

impart. He is the almoner of the Father's bounty, the channel through whom he pours the river of his mercy. The Father is the fountain, the Son is the aqueduct, and the Holy Ghost is the Niagara, outpouring the water of life ceaselessly and abundantly for the refreshing all thirsty, believing souls. This explains the two statements, that the Holy Ghost is the unmeasured gift of the Father, and again that Christ baptizes with the Holy Ghost. Seeing that the Son hath all which the Father hath, the Father is said to send forth the Spirit of his Son into the hearts of his children, (Gal. iv, 6,) in the name, through the mediation, at the prayer of the Son. John xiv, 16. The Father anoints believers by giving them his Spirit as he has anointed the Son.

§ 3. *The Abiding Comforter.*

Many persons, in reading the New Testament, find no such sharply-defined, instantaneous transition in the Christian life after regeneration as is taught by the modern advocates of Christian perfection. This results from their failure to identify with this blessing the baptism of the Holy Ghost, the fullness of the

Spirit, the unction that abideth and teacheth, and the gift of the abiding Comforter. It is the purpose of this chapter to show the identity of perfect love with the Comforter promised by Jesus in his last address to his disciples.

1. The Comforter here promised is not limited to the office of imparting consolation. The Greek term "paraclete" might have been rendered assistant, monitor, teacher, or guide. He illumines, and hence sanctifies, for purification is through a perception of the truth. He sheds abroad a knowledge of Christ's love to the soul. Love is the regenerating principle, the seed of God. When love becomes perfect by the full and constant abiding of the Comforter, all antagonisms are excluded, and the plane is reached which is called the higher Life.

2. Consider that the abiding Comforter is not promised by Jesus in St. John's Gospel (chapters xiv–xvi) to penitent sinners, but to believers who already love Christ. He opens his address by asserting, "Ye believe in God," and by assuring them that they are heirs to the "many mansions" in his Father's house. "I go to prepare a place for you." For

8

impenitent sinners a place is already prepared
—the place originally "prepared for the devil
and his angels." "I will receive you unto
myself," is a promise never made to an unregenerate soul.

3. The distinctive condition of receiving the
Comforter is love toward Christ evinced by
obedience: "If ye love me, keep my commandments; and I will pray the Father, and
he will give you another Comforter, that he
may abide with you for ever." Several very
important truths are here implied. First, that
love to Christ, genuine love, having the fruitage of obedience, is possible, before the Comforter *consciously* abides in the believer. He
unconsciously suggests the truth and prompts
to repentance and faith, and leads and guides
the repenting sinner. There can be no initial
Divine life without the Spirit. But he does
not manifest his presence in the consciousness
as in the advanced, or technically called higher,
life. This consciousness of the presence of the
Holy Spirit as distinguished from his hidden
operations below the gaze of consciousness, is
distinctly announced as one peculiarity of the
gift of the Comforter. "But ye *know* him, for

he dwelleth with you and shall be in you."
Up to this point the work of the Spirit may
have been observed; but the Worker has been
vailed from the view of the soul, so that there
was room for doubt whether the operation
was natural or supernatural; whether the good
thoughts, righteous purposes, and holy aspirations came from self, or from a concealed
Divine suggester. Hence, nearly all orthodox
theologians, "including Fletcher and Wesley,
agree that assurance is not essential to saving
faith, and so not necessarily connected with it.
They agree—especially the Assembly of Di-
vines, Baxter, and Fletcher—that to *doubt*, or
directly question, the presence and exercise of
saving faith by the subject, is consistent with
its presence and exercise in the same subject,"* so long as he has a sincere desire to
obey the Gospel and to receive Christ in all
his offices, bringing forth inward and outward
fruits meet for repentance, fearing God and
working righteousness. This state may be
occasionally alleviated by the witness of the
Spirit, intermittently enjoyed through weakness of faith. In this state of twilight, with

* "Saving Faith." By Rev. I. Chamberlayne, D.D.

occasional gleams of sunshine, the majority of
the modern Church are dwelling, because they
do not apprehend and claim the privilege of
the abiding Comforter,—a sun standing ever
on the meridian and pouring the full splendors
of assurance upon them. Christ gives substan-
tially the same promise, resting on the same
condition of love to him, when he says, "He
that hath my commandments, and keepeth
them, he it is that loveth me; and he that
loveth me shall be loved of my Father, and I
will love him, and will *manifest myself* unto
him." Here is the same promise of the Comforter: "He shall take of mine and show them
unto you." "He shall glorify me." "He shall
testify of me." All manifestations of Christ
are through the Comforter, except the miraculous appearing of Jesus in human form to
Saul, near Damascus, to qualify him for the
apostleship. It is no manifestation, if the Divine is not brought into direct contact with
the human. Moreover, the manifestation of a
person to a person must have a point of instantaneous recognition, however gradual may
have been their approaches to, and however
progressive may be their intimacy after, such

recognition. He had manifested himself to Mary Magdalene as a pardoning Saviour, forgiving her sins, and as almighty conqueror of the infernal powers, casting out of her seven devils or demons. But the manifestation of Christ to Mary through the Comforter will exalt him in her esteem infinitely higher than her poor conceptions of him in the flesh, and her communion with him will be a thousand times more precious than when she gazed upon his countenance and hung upon his lips. She will henceforth look for him and find him within her own soul, and not in his pathways and abiding-places in Palestine. She loved him before, but now her soul is a furnace all aglow with an affection deeper, stronger, and more spiritual than before. Her will has melted into his by the "Spirit of burning." Self has been absorbed by a union with Him who once took away her sins.

It is remarkable that Jesus should have made four distinct promises of the Comforter in one short passage in his farewell address. John xiv, 15–26. This repetition emphasizes this declaration. Let us examine the third promise: "If any man love me, he will keep my words; and my Father will love him, and we will come unto him, and make our abode with him." . To say nothing about the *we* implying, as the pronoun does, equality with the Father and the utmost intimacy with him, we call attention to the same condition, namely, love, the same test of love, obedience, the perpetuity of the promised blessing, found in the word *abode* as in the words "abide" and "dwelleth," in the previous promises. The blessing itself is more strongly expressed—"we," the Son and the Father, will come unto him. Says Dr. Whedon, "The Father, Son, and Spirit will in spirit come into union with the believer's spirit. And can any one imagine that the believer will be for ever unconscious of his spiritual guests, and incapable of realizing the actuality of their communion? The believer may enjoy a conscious communion with Christ and God."[*] We apprehend that an objection will be raised here, that Jesus had distinct reference to the one coming of the Comforter on the day of Pentecost to the collective body of believers, and that he had no reference to

---

[*] For a discussion on the Recognition of the Persons of the Trinity, see foot-note in chapter xiii.

individuals scattered along through the dispensation of the Spirit during thousands of years, and therefore the promise applies to them only in this sense—that they will be born in the dispensation of the Spirit. We answer that impenitent sinners are born under this dispensation, and yet the promise is not to them. Says the commentator just quoted, " In the coming dispensation of the Spirit the manifestations of Christ will be made to the spirits of those *who love him, and to those alone.*" This confirms the position taken by us, that the promised Comforter was not designed for the collective lovers of Jesus, and for them alone, as the inauguration of what Fletcher styles "the kingdom of the Holy" Ghost, but for individuals in all ages who fulfill the conditions—love and obedience.* We come to the same conclusion when we examine the conditions. Love is an affection for a personal object. It belongs to the individual.

---

* Says Alford on John vii, 39 : " John does not say that the words were a prophecy of *what happened* on the day of Pentecost ; but of *the Spirit,* which believers were about to receive. Their *first reception* of him must not be illogically put in the place of *all his indwelling and working,* which are here intended."

If it were something to be possessed and exhibited only by the organic body of believers—
the Church in its corporate capacity—individuals could not fulfill the conditions. We educe
the same truth from the fact of the perpetuity
of the Comforter. "He shall abide with you for
ever." The pentecostal recipients of the Comforter are all dead. Did the Comforter withdraw
from the Church when the last of the pentecostal assembly went into his grave? Is *for ever*
limited to a single generation? Jesus does not
thus trifle with human hopes. Through all the
ages, therefore, the Comforter will abide, not in
Œcumenical Councils, as the representatives of
the Church, nor in the Pope, as the representative of the Council, but in those hearts which
invite his entrance by loving Jesus and obeying his law. We have elsewhere proved that
Peter's military hearers were in a justified state,
having " the spirit of faith and the purpose of
righteousness."

We have endeavored to prove in this chapter that the spiritual development of the disciples of Christ was perfectly normal, and hence
an example for us to follow. Up to the Pentecost they loved Jesus, and were tenderly

beloved by their Master; but they had not reached that crisis which should divest them of their prejudices, spiritualize their views of Christ's kingdom, purify their hearts, and gird them with irresistible spiritual energy.

An objection may be made, that the endowment of the Spirit in the case of the disciples was necessary in order to qualify them to write infallible religious truth and narrate facts which had faded almost entirely away in their memories, and that such an endowment is not needed by us. But only a few of them were called to write the Gospels, and the Acts, and the Epistles. There were at least a hundred and fourteen gathered in that upper chamber who were not called to be sacred writers. These, nevertheless, received the Spirit of truth as did those who became theopneustic writers. Those who did not need the Spirit of truth to restore to freshness the faded tablet of the memory, did nevertheless need him to make real to their spiritual perception the truths of the Gospel. Hence to all disciples of every age he is the Spirit of reality, because he gives substance to supersensual truth, and reality to that which, to mere intellectual apprehension, is shadowy

and unreal, and destitute of power to control
the conduct and beautify the character.   If
we contemplate the weakness and inefficiency
of average Christians, paralyzed by doubt and
swayed by "things seen and temporal," we
shall not deny the need of the coming of the
abiding Comforter to gird with strength, and
to put the telescope of a perfect faith to the
eye to bring the things "not seen and eternal"
near, and make them more influential than this
corrupt world.   He embodies the sum total
of all spiritual blessings.   More willing is the
Holy Father to give him to each believer than
the mother to give the healing medicine to
her dying child, or the father to give food and
raiment to his soldier son who falls upon his
threshold naked and emaciated, just escaped
from Andersonville prison.   A singular confirmation of the statement that the Holy
Spirit, in the fullness of his grace, comprises
the sum total of spiritual good, is found in
reading Matthew vii, 11, and Luke xi, 13; the
"good things" of the former are explained in
the latter by "the Holy Spirit."

CHAPTER VIII.

THE HIGHER LIFE PRAYER.

IN the third chapter of the Epistle to the Ephesians (verses 14–21, which see) Paul's closet door gets ajar, and all the Christian ages are thrilled with his sublime whisperings in the ear of God. Come, stand by me and listen. It is an honorable kind of eavesdropping. Like his Master, Paul's most earnest entreaties are not for impenitent sinners —" the world "—but for believers in Christ, for " the perfecting of the saints." But before following the lowly wrestler through the successive petitions of this wonderful prayer, let us glance at the persons for whom blessings so great are supplicated. The Ephesian Church was composed of believers of far less culture, stability, and moral stamina than are the members of our modern Churches. They were mostly of the poor, the laboring class. These are always the first to receive Christ when he is preached in any community. They

were slaves, servants, mechanics, and day-
laborers, coming into rough contact with society, and exposed to temptations of the lowest
class—theft, fornication, brawling, and drunkenness. The Gentile converts were struggling
with their old pagan habits, making a desperate fight against the heathenish vices which
lured them on every hand. The Jewish believers in Christ in foreign cities were probably
gathered from the poor—a class whose representatives are to be found crowded into the
Jews' quarter of our modern cities, small ped-
dlers and old-clothes men, aspiring to be money
brokers and usurers—for men change their sky
and not their character by crossing seas.

Such had been the antecedents of this portion of the Ephesian Church. It would be natural to say that it is preposterous to expect
any high degree of spirituality to be attained
by the first, or even by the second, generation
of such Christians, just gathered from the bottom of pagan and Jewish society. But St.
Paul is lifted above the natural, and grasps by
faith a supernatural power, which may suddenly lift these once low-lived men and wom-
en up to the summit of moral and spiritual

excellence. These remarks have been made for the especial benefit of those who imagine that the higher life was never designed for people whose condition compels them to take what is called "the rough and tumble of life;" and that only contemplative clergymen, wealthy and leisurely women unblessed with little children, and retired business men with ample fortunes and few temptations, can walk steadily in the King's highway of holiness. But in the Ephesian Church we have slaves, subject to the abuse of haughty masters, and from infancy addicted to servile vices; artisans, poverty-pinched, because for Christ's sake they have quit shrine-making; pickpockets and burglars, (Eph. iv, 28,) still eyed with suspicion by the lovers of good order; converted harlots and whoremongers, (Eph. v, 3, 8,) wrestling with gigantic, pampered lusts; and mothers in homes of poverty, with troops of fretful children at their heels. St. Paul expects that a Church made up of such unpromising material will, through the cleansing power of the Sanctifier, be "holy and without blemish," a glorious Church, not having "spot or wrinkle."

The degree of spiritual power with which

these believers may be endowed is "according to the riches of his glory;" that pre-eminent glory which St. John beheld, not in the magnificence of the material universe, but in God's moral attributes, "shining in the face of Jesus Christ," "full of grace and truth." Here we find the illimitable measure of the Spirit's power to strengthen the believer. The power of the Comforter is equal to the glory of the Redeemer. St. Paul prays that these feeble, tempted souls may be strengthened with might by the Spirit in the inner man, to a degree commensurate with the inconceivable glory surrounding, as with a halo, the character of God. In other words, he prays for an excellence which Christ preaches in his sermon on the mount—"Be ye therefore perfect, even as your Father which is in heaven is perfect."

The next petition is, "that Christ may dwell in your hearts by faith:" thus agreeing with that most precious promise of Jesus in his farewell address to his disciples, "I will abide in you." The full significance of this brief petition is, that the Son of God should representatively, by the Holy Spirit, make his permanent abode in the believer's consciousness, rectifying his will, purifying his affections, illuminating his understanding, subsidizing and directing all his energies, and pervading every atom of his body, and filling every capacity of his spirit, making him a particle of Christ's body, " of his flesh and bones," through which the currents of his life ever flow. If Christian perfection is not sought in this petition for the abiding Christ in the heart of each disciple in Ephesus, we fail to comprehend the meaning of that term. " That ye may be rooted," like a tree, "and grounded," like a building, "in love." This is but a metaphorical expression for that perfect love that casteth out all fear that hath torment. The education of the intellect, and the discipline of the moral nature, tend toward stability of character. But this is an inferior excellence in the Apostle's estimation compared with that stability produced by love binding the soul to God as with a golden chain; the stability of a planet freely moving in its orbit around its all-glorious center of attraction. "That ye may be able to comprehend with all (perfected) saints, what is the breadth, and length, and depth, and height." The breadth and length of what? Paul has

failed to say, except by implication in the next
verse, from which we infer that it is "the love
of Christ." In what sense St. Paul has applied
these geometrical dimensions to love—a spiritual quality and without extension—it is difficult
to determine. But we believe that their meaning is to be sought in the logic of Aristotle, in
which St. Paul must have been drilled in the
university of Tarsus, the most celebrated seat of
Grecian learning east of Athens. The Greek
logicians employ the term *breadth* to denote
the *extension* of a notion, the number of individuals to whom it will apply, as, for instance,
man includes every being possessed of human
attributes. The term *depth* denotes the *intension* of a notion, the aggregate of qualities
which lie piled up one upon another, in one individual distinguishing him from all others. Sir
William Hamilton adds to these logical terms
a philosophical term, namely, *protension*, ap-
plicable only to time or extended duration.
With these terms—extension, intension, and
protension, throwing a flood of light upon the
breadth, depth, and length of divine love, we
are able to get an enlarged view of the com-
prehensiveness of this petition. "That ye may

know the breadth," is to know the vast number 'of individuals of our race embraced in the scheme of redemption. It is a remarkable fact, that as soon as love is fully shed abroad in the believer's heart he immediately over-leaps the limitations of his theology, if he has been so unfortunate as to have been educated in the belief of a limited atonement, and feels irresistibly drawn toward every lost sinner as the object of Jesus' mighty love. Hence it is that the missionary spirit is so intense in fully consecrated souls. They have been brought into the most intimate sympathy with the breadth of Christ's love. Hence they plunge into the moral cesspools in our great cities, to pluck lost men and fallen women from the fires of perdition. The secret motive power which impels them to go down into these pits, and cheerfully breathe the fetid miasmas which settle there, is, that they know by experience the amazing breadth of Jesus' love.

> " He left his Father's throne above ;
>   (So free, so infinite, his grace !)
> Emptied himself of all but love,
>   And bled for Adam's helpless race ;
> 'Tis mercy all, immense and free,
> For, O my God, *it found out me !* "

9

When Paul prays that the Ephesians may know the *length* of Christ's love, he prays for their eternal blessedness, for his love knows no limit in duration. In ordinary experience the sense of Christ's love is faint—he visits but does not abide. Hence there is a lurking fear that Jesus may cease to cherish him on whom he has once smiled, even though there should be no apostasy on the part of the believer. Such a state of experience cannot be called rest in Jesus. There is unrest and fear where there should be repose and confidence. There is no cure for this but the fullness of the Spirit, revealing the fullness and perpetuity of Christ's love to the believer. In that glad hour the believer knows that Christ can be fully trusted for the future, as well as for the present. He hears the Saviour say,

> " Mine is an unchanging love,
> Higher than the heights above,
> Deeper than the depths beneath,
> Free and faithful, strong as death. "

In the first stages of Christian life the spiritual perception is not usually strong enough to hear this voice, but more frequently the ear is not intently turned in the right direction. But in that maturity of grace in which love is made

perfect, the feeling of the permanency of the
Divine regard takes full possession of the soul,
and it becomes a certainty that he will not desert us unless we desert him. This possibility
only induces us to grasp with a firmer grip the
promise that we shall be "kept by the power
of God, through faith, unto salvation." Then
we exultingly ask, with the Apostle, "Who
shall separate us from the love of Christ?"
that is, who will turn away Christ from loving
us? "I am persuaded that neither death, nor
life, nor angels, nor principalities, nor powers,
nor things present, nor things to come, nor
height, nor depth, nor any other creature, shall
be able to separate us from the love of God,
which is in Christ Jesus our Lord." Mr. Wesley had been preaching thirty-four years before
he was "thoroughly convinced" that perfect
love "is amissible,"—"capable of being lost."
It is evident that he was not a believer in that
kind of perfect love which may be experienced
to-day and lost to-morrow; a species which
many mistaken professors avow, to the great
detriment of the genuine experience, and to
the representation of the unchangeable Jesus
as an exceedingly capricious being.

In the petition, "that ye may know the depth
and height," we have really but one dimension,
depth, which denotes the multiplied qualities
of Christ's love, or, more exactly, the various
spiritual perfections which it bestows on the
believer. As God out of sunshine and dust
makes all the varieties of color which clothe
the landscape—as out of water and sunbeams
he creates the seven colors of the solar spec-
trum—so out of human faith and the Sun of
righteousness he produces the whole rainbow
of Christian graces. To know the depth of
Christ's love is to possess all "the fruits of the
Spirit, love, joy, peace, long-suffering, gentleness, meekness, fidelity, patience, and temperance," a spiritual constellation made up of
"these gracious stars, perfect repentance, perfect faith, perfect humility, perfect meekness,
perfect self-denial, perfect resignation, perfect
hope, perfect charity."

The next petition is, that ye may "know
the love of Christ which passeth knowledge."
Divine solecism! Blessed paradox! To know
the unknowable fullness of Christ's love; to
drop the short sounding-line of human experience into the unfathomable ocean of the

Divine mercy. We understand St. Paul to assert that the love of Christ surpasses all merely intellectual comprehension and logical statement, while it is apprehended by the spiritual intuitions. All who pass into this deep experience are impressed with the vastness, the boundlessness, of Christ's love, a sea without bottom or shore. "How little of the sea," says Rutherford, " can a child carry in his hand ; as little am I able to take away of my great Sea, my boundless and running-over Christ Jesus ! " This is not a peculiarity of the experience of justification. The Ephesians had not yet been

> " Plunged into the Godhead's deepest sea,
> And lost in its immensity."

They were still only ankle deep, standing in some little land-locked bay, without any conception of the immense, the limitless, expanse of waters beyond their view, hidden by the intervening promontories of ignorance and doubt. This petition is distinctively for the "higher life," as is the next, "that ye may be filled with all the fullness of God," or more exactly, "even to all the fullness of God," even as he is full—each in your degree, but all to your utmost capacity, with wisdom, might, and love. The rhetorical redundance of this petition strikingly exhibits the richness and fullness of the Apostle's experience struggling to find utterance in words. The thought, nakedly expressed, is, "that ye may be filled with God." In logical exactness there can be no increase to "filled." But St. Paul's soul, all aglow with the ardors of Christian love, must intensify the expression by adding *fullness* to *filled*, and then crowning the thought with the tautological *all* as a finishing of the climax. We do not understand that this is a petition for the omnipresent and almighty God to compress his infinitude to the limitations of the human body and soul, as in the mystery of the incarnation, in which there "dwells all the fullness of the Godhead bodily:" it is rather a prayer for that complement of blessing, each perfect in kind, which fills the cornucopia of God's grace under the remedial dispensation, and which is ready to be poured upon all who have the spiritual capacity, the faith, to receive them. To deny that this petition is for Christian perfection would be as absurd as to deny that the sun rolls daily through the

skies. St. Paul, aided by the Holy Spirit—
we would speak reverently—could not have
penned words more clearly and unequivocally
describing the blessing of perfect love as
taught in the Wesleyan standards.

In our analysis of this prayer we have shown
that every petition is an outbreathing of Paul's
soul that the Ephesians might be made perfect
in love. There is nothing negative in it ; there
is no allusion to indwelling sin ; the aim of the
whole is for the fullness of the divine life. It
is certain that he himself enjoyed the high state
of experience into which he would lead others.
The struggling expression, the strain and cumu-
lation of words, all indicate a soul running, with
abounding joy, up this higher path, and not a
mere guide-board with its foot planted in the
ground, and outstretched, painted hand pointing out the way which " the vulture's eye hath
not seen." This heaping up terms, amplifying,
heightening, and intensifying his expression, as
if his soul was agonizing for utterance, is seen in
the doxology at the end of the prayer. " Now
unto Him that is able to do exceeding abundantly above all that we ask or think, according to the power that worketh in us." What

a conception of the "exceeding greatness of Christ's power to us-ward who believe" does St. Paul here take! Can any one believe that this was revealed to his intellect by the Spirit of inspiration, and not to his consciousness in personal experience? Who can say that the great Head of the Church stationed St. Paul as a porter to open the gate for others to enter this paradise regained—this Eden of love made perfect—while himself was tantalizingly forbidden to enter so long as he dwelt in a fleshly tabernacle? No, the Master is not so severe with his chosen servant.

This doxology is a molten stream from the glowing heart of a Vesuvius. The inward fires cannot be restrained. "A power" is working in him. This power is the measure of the marvelous work which will be wrought in every one that grasps the promises. One would think that it was enough to know that Christ Jesus "is able to do all we ask;" but St. Paul adds, " or think." Thought always outstrips language. In religious experience words are but a pitiful mockery of the reality, and "language is lame" indeed. But not satisfied with this expansion of the thought, Paul adds the word *above*, which lifts the expression to an indefinite height. He then multiplies the force of the *above* by the word *abundantly*, a term which of itself is full and overflowing. The effect of *abundantly*, put before *above*, is, in mathematical phrase, to raise it to the second power. But this does not adequately set forth the amazing wealth of blessing stored up in the power of Christ as in an infinite treasury to be unlocked by the key of faith. He immediately broadens and deepens the *abundantly* by the illimitable term *exceeding*, which so enlarges the entire conception that our minds, struggling to keep up with the widening idea, fall back upon themselves in despair, when they attempt to compass in thought *abundantly* multiplied by *exceeding*, a thing as unthinkable as infinity multiplied by infinity. Bear in mind that there is no limitation of the exercise of this power of Christ to the hour of death. On the face of every petition, in the use of verbs in the present tense, there lies *prima-facia* proof that St. Paul is praying for blessings to be enjoyed by the Ephesians immediately in this life. Recur now to the circumstances and antecedents of these Christians as portrayed in the beginning of this chapter, and add to this the declaration that Jesus is yesterday, to-day, and for ever the same, and you, my dear reader, have ample ground for your faith in Jesus Christ for this great salvation.

Reader, this very prayer has been preserved for eighteen centuries for your instruction in righteousness. The prayer is for you as much as for the dwellers in Ephesus. It was put on record as a permanent publication of the complete salvation to every generation—an inventory of the unsearchable riches of Christ—the rich gifts and blessings of which he is the almoner through the Holy Spirit. It has been answered in the spiritual enlargement of thousands of souls all along the Christian centuries.

We quote but one instance, the Spirit-baptism of a young Swiss preacher, who afterward became the bright evangelical light of Switzerland, and whose " History of the Reformation" is read throughout the Protestant world. Says Merle D'Aubigné : " We were studying the Epistle to the Ephesians, and had got to the end of the third chapter. When we read the last two verses, ' Now unto Him who is

able to do exceeding abundantly above all
that we ask or think, according to the power
that worketh in us, unto Him be glory throughout all ages;' this expression fell upon my
soul like a revelation from God. He can do
by his power, I said to myself, above all we
ask, above all even that we can think—nay,
exceeding abundantly above all! A full trust
in Christ for the work to be done within my
poor heart now filled my soul. We all three
knelt down: and although I had never fully
confided my inward struggle to my friends, the
prayer of Rieu was filled with such admirable
faith as he would have uttered had he known
all my wants. When I arose in that inn room
at Kiel, I felt as if my wings were renewed as
the wings of eagles. From that time forward
I comprehended that my own efforts were of
no avail; that Christ is able to do all by his
power that worketh in us; and the habitual
attitude of my soul was to lie at the foot of the
cross, crying to Him, 'Here I am, bound hand
and foot, unable to move, unable to do the
least thing to get away from the enemy, who
oppresses me. Do all thyself. I *know* thou
wilt do it. Thou wilt even do exceeding abun-

dantly above all I ask.' I was not disappointed ; all my doubts were removed, my anguish quelled, and the Lord extended to me peace as a river. Then I could comprehend with all saints what is the breadth, and length, and depth, and height, and know the love of Christ which passeth knowledge. Then was I able to say, 'Return unto thy rest, O my soul, for the Lord hath dealt bountifully with thee.'"

CHAPTER IX.

THE THREE DISPENSATIONS.

IN John Fletcher's portrait of St. Paul as a model evangelical preacher, he very emphatically insists upon a thorough knowledge of the three great eras of spiritual life. These he denominates the dispensation of the Father, of the Son, and of the Holy Ghost. He who is unacquainted with the peculiarities of experience under these different dispensations cannot successfully apply Gospel truth, and give full proof of his ministry. For these dispensations, though in the order of development they were successive, are now co-existent. Of those accepted of God, now dwelling on the earth, some are in the dispensation of the Father, some in that of the Son, and others in the dispensation of the Holy Spirit. The first are characterized by the fear of God, servile fear, with little love. This fear influences conduct and shapes character. They fear God and work righteousness. They are

kept from sinning, and are incited to purity
and well-doing. They have no joy of the
Holy Ghost, but only that which flows in the
channels of nature, the approval of conscience
for their right actions. Not having God's love
shed abroad in their hearts by the Holy Spirit,
they are in doubt of their acceptance with God,
and are often distressed when the written or
unwritten law thunders its threatenings in
their ears, "though visited at times with a few
scattered rays of hope." They exist in all
lands, but chiefly in non-evangelical countries,
papal, pagan, and Mohammedan. Now and
then an honest Deist, a devout Unitarian, with
the head warped by early implanted error, but
a sincere heart, may be found amid the full
blaze of Gospel truth, still serving God in the
same dispensation with uncircumcised Abram
in Mesopotamia. In this view we find ground
for charity toward the less enlightened subjects of God's kingdom, and strong motives
for the abatement of bigotry. We learn to
deal tenderly with those Cornelian souls
whose prayers and alms go up for a memorial
before God. We approach them, not with de-
nunciations, but with invitations, while we

magnify Christ, and from our own experience assure them of the exceeding greatness of his power to us-ward who believe. By indiscriminately lumping them together with avowed Atheists and willful sinners, the incautious preacher gives them needless offense, and hedges up the path of advanced truth into their minds. In Christian lands these worshipers of the Father must be distinguished from those who reject the Son because of the strictness of his requirements, the inflexible terms of discipleship, and the spiritual interpretation of the moral law planting a thorn-hedge across the path of even the sinful thought, and kindling a fire in the house of their idols. Such are wickedly rejecting Jesus Christ, and are to be addressed as sinners, whether they assume the name of Evangelicals, Universalists, Socinians, or Free Religionists. "These go on without any symptom of fear toward the gulf of perdition; whether it be by the high road of vice, with the notoriously abandoned, or through the by-path of hypocrisy, with pharisaical professors."

"Under the dispensation of the Son the doubts of believers are dissipated, like those of the two disciples who journeyed to Emmaus, while they discover more clearly, and experience more powerfully, the truths of the Gospel." Still they know Christ after the flesh. They are not fully impressed with his divinity. The robe of humanity has not been made transparent for the dazzling radiance of the Godhead to shine through. Jesus is not yet glorified to their hearts, because the Spirit, the Glorifier, has not taken up his abode in them. Hence they are but children; their strength is small; they are weak and unsteady; they have not full assurance. After brief periods of joyful trust, doubts return to shake their confidence. Yet they testify of their love to God gaining ascendency over fear. They no longer utter the sad exclamation at the end of the seventh chapter of Romans, "O wretched man that I am!" With grateful hearts and streaming eyes in view of their deliverance, they exultingly say, "I thank God through Jesus Christ our Lord." Joyful as is their state of freedom when contrasted with the bondage to fear under which they once groaned, they are conscious of an inward vacuity and longing for some object not at first

clearly defined. The study of the words of
Jesus discloses to them the living water promised by him in the last great day of the feast.
" But this he spake of the Spirit, which they
that believe on him should receive ; for the
Holy Ghost was not yet given." " And I will
pray the Father, and he shall give you another
Comforter, that he may abide with you forever." After the object of their desire has
been pointed out to them, they begin to hunger and thirst after righteousness, after the
Holy Spirit, who is the author of all inward
purity. Then they emerge into the " kingdom
of the Holy Ghost," as Fletcher styles it.
They are filled with the Spirit. They now
walk in the light constantly, are consciously
cleansed from all sin, and have joy unspeakable. The Spirit of adoption, formerly indirect and intermittent, has now become the
abiding Comforter ; and to his direct assurance
of sonship he adds that of entire sanctification
and the fullness of Christ's love, " that we may
know the things freely given to us of God."
1 Cor. ii, 12. Fear, which had a painful pre-
dominance in the dispensation of the Father,
and shadowed the brightness of that of Jesus

10

Christ, is now completely banished. No tormenting emotion can abide the presence of the Comforter.

The scriptural proofs of these dispensations are abundant. Listen to Peter, preaching to Cornelius and his staff of officers. "God is no respecter of persons ; but in every nation he that feareth him, and worketh righteousness, is accepted of him."

From the summit of Mars' Hill, the Athenian, passing through the Agora, hears an earnest voice proclaiming to the high caste Autochthones, who boasted of their birth from the soil of Attica, a truth humiliating to their pride of race—"God . . . hath made of one blood all nations of men, and hath determined the bounds of their habitation ; that they should seek the Lord, if haply they might feel after him, and find him, though he be not far from every one of us." The publicans (Roman officials) asked of John, "What shall we do ?" He, seeing that they had no preparation for the dispensation of the Son, and that all that they could then appreciate was the obligation of the moral law, answered, "Exact no more than that which is appointed you." A band of Roman soldiers, utterly ignorant of the prophecies relating to Christ, approach the same great preacher, and demand, " What shall we do?" John, aiming to make them perfect in the dispensation of Gentilism, which consists in doing right so far as known, immediately replies, " Do violence to no man, neither accuse falsely, and be content with your wages." But when John's audience is made up of Jews, he preaches always from one text of Isaiah's prophetic evangel, " Prepare ye the way of the Lord." Here is the dispensation of the Son—" One cometh after me whose shoes' latchet I am not worthy to unloose." Glorious foregleams of the ministration of the Spirit also burst upon John's vision, and he exclaims, " He shall baptize you with the Holy Ghost and with fire."

The official presence and manifest work of the Holy Spirit in the hearts of believers after Jesus was glorified, as totally distinct from his essential presence and secret work in the hearts of just pagans and Jews under the drawings of the Father or the teachings of the Son, is most conclusively announced by Peter on the day of pentecost. " Jesus, being by the right hand of God exalted, and having received

of the Father the promise of the Holy Ghost,
hath shed forth this (plenitude of grace, the
effects of) which ye now see and hear." Since
these Jerusalem sinners had insulted the person of Jesus, the genuineness of their repentance must now be tested by public baptism in
his hated name, before they could be assured
of pardon, a test never required of penitent
sinners afterward. "Be baptized every one
of you in the name of Jesus Christ, for the
remission of sins, and ye shall receive the
gift of the Holy Ghost." Thus these souls
were led rapidly through the dispensation of
the Son to that of the Spirit. The ministry
of Jesus was very brief, possibly typifying the
short interval in the scheme of salvation between the drawings of the Father unto Christ,
and the outpouring of the Holy Ghost upon
the young believer in Jesus. Thus the com-
passionate Father draws the willing soul to the
redeeming Son, who passes it over to the
quickening and purifying energies of the blessed
Sanctifier. The second dispensation was evidently designed to be a transition point only,
and not a stage in the spiritual development.
But contrary to the Divine purpose, multi-

tudes linger all their lives at this point, instead
of passing on to the higher and richer experience of the fullness of the Spirit : while
other multitudes are so "slow of heart to believe," that they linger for years and decades
in that inferior dispensation of the law, the
child-leader, before their tardy feet tread the
threshold of the Great Teacher. To quote all
the Scriptures descriptive of the distinct office
and work of the third person of the Trinity
would be impossible in this essay. Let these
suffice : " Your body is the temple of the Holy
Ghost." " Grieve not the Holy Spirit of God,
whereby ye are sealed unto the day of redemption." " Be filled with the Spirit ; speaking
to yourselves in psalms, and hymns, and spiritual songs, making melody in your hearts unto
the Lord." " Rejoice evermore. Pray without ceasing. In every thing give thanks."

Says Mr. Fletcher, " Without an experimental knowledge of these several states, a
minister can no more lead sinners to evangelical perfection than an illiterate peasant can
communicate sufficient intelligence to his rus-
tic companions to pass an examination for the
highest degree in a university." " As the pru-

dent physician proportions his medicines to the different ages and habits of his patients, so the enlightened pastor, who feels himself concerned for the spiritual health of his flock, sees it necessary to act with equal care and discretion. He preaches the dispensation of the Son to those who, like Socrates and Plato, are longing for a Divine instructor. He leads them either from the law of Moses or from the law of nature to the Gospel of Christ. Lastly, to such as have devoutly embraced this part of the Gospel, he publishes the glorious economy of the Holy Spirit, which was not fully opened till after the bodily appearance of the Redeemer was withdrawn from the world."

It must be borne in mind that the Son and Spirit have always been occupied in secretly influencing the hearts of men. But there was a time when the Son became manifest, making a visible exhibition of his wonderful works. Also, at a certain point in the world's history, the Holy Ghost began to work in a more sensible manner in the consciousness of believers. The mysterious triune personality of God was disclosed to our faith because the advanced stages of spiritual development under the Son and the Spirit could not be realized except through faith in the distinct offices of these persons. To keep these in the faith of the Church in all ages, the names of the three stand in the formula of baptism, and distinct blessings are ascribed to each in the apostolic benediction.

It may be objected that this view of the successive gradations of privilege under the three persons of the Godhead has a tendency to degrade the Father before the brighter glories of the Son's kingdom, and to belittle the Son in the presence of the full splendors of the ministrations of the Spirit. But a little examination of experience, Church history, and the Scriptures, will obviate this objection. They who are brought to the cross of Christ testify to a new and profound appreciation of the work of the Father; while all who enter into the dispensation of the Spirit bear witness that Christ is in an astonishing manner exalted in their estimation. In all ages of the Church we look for the highest spirituality and purity, and the most devout reverence toward the Father, where Jesus has been exalted; and the most ardent love to

Christ where this item of the creed has been emphasized and explained, "I believe in the Holy Ghost." Turning to the Scriptures, we find that the highest honor accruing to the Father is when men honor his Son. To him shall every knee bow, *to the glory of God the Father.* But Jesus is not fully known till the Spirit shows him to our hearts and glorifies him. *No man can call Jesus Lord, but by the Holy Ghost.* Thus each brightening dispensation reflects honor upon the Divine person of the preceding, demonstrating that the Divine Persons are not independent and rival deities, but one in nature and essence, whose different perfections are more clearly manifested to a world of sinners by this threefold development.

The superiority of the ministrations of the Spirit, and its immeasurable wealth of privilege when contrasted with the dispensation of the Son of God in his bodily presence, is expressed by Jesus when he asserts that among them that are born of women there hath not arisen a greater than John the Baptist. Here the wilderness preacher is lifted to a pedestal higher than that of David the king, Moses the lawgiver, or Abraham the founder of the He-

brew nation. Yet he that is least in the kingdom of heaven is greater than he. We are to
understand the kingdom of heaven as St. Paul
expounds it, consisting of righteousness, peace,
and joy *in the Holy Ghost.* It did not consist
in seeing the incarnate Lord, for John saw
him ; nor in gazing on his miraculous works
and listening to his Divine utterances, as did
many unbelieving Jews ; nor in being numbered among his disciples, as were many who
went away and walked no more with him ; nor
in being enrolled among the twelve apostles,
as was Judas Iscariot, who betrayed him. Jesus must have referred to that fullness of spiritual grace and power brought in on the day
of pentecost, to be the permanent inheritance
of all who fully believe the promise of the
Father.

Every soul, however ignorant and uncul-
tured, which is a habitation of God through the
Spirit—every human body which is made a
temple of the Holy Ghost, however weak and
deformed, is greater than he whom the infallible Messiah pronounced superior to all his
predecessors. Such a person may the reader
be if he will by faith enter into the dispensa-

tion of the blessed Comforter, far more glorious than the days when the visible form of Jesus shed its radiance on the earth. "It is expedient—better—for you that I go away; for if I go not away, the Comforter will not come." "Of which salvation the prophets have inquired, testifying beforehand of the sufferings of Christ, *and the glory that should follow.*" Reader, is that glory enrobing your spirit with a vesture of light, so that you are walking in the light toward the inheritance of the saints in light? A dispensation laden with such wealth of privilege carries with it a corresponding burden of responsibility. Light is the measure of accountability. Who of the modern Church, illumined by the sevenfold splendors of the Spirit of truth, will be able to abide the fires of the judgment? Would that these solemn words of Fletcher were sounded from every pulpit in Christendom : "To reject the Son of God, manifested in the Spirit, as worldly Christians are universally observed to do, is a crime of equal magnitude with that of the Jews, who rejected Christ manifested in the flesh."

There are multitudes of nominal Christians

who confidently assert that it is the highest presumption and folly to expect, in modern times, that full dispensation of the Spirit concerning which so many excellent things are spoken in the Scriptures. They brand as a fanatic the man who proclaims to a slumbering Church the presence of the Holy Ghost, ready to raise the spiritually dead, and to transfigure the spiritually living. It is asserted that the era of miracles and the extraordinary gifts of the Spirit are past; not understanding that the Spirit itself is entirely distinct from his supernatural gifts. The Spirit descended upon Mary, the mother of our Lord, and upon several other believing women in the upper chamber; but there is no proof that they were endowed with the gift of tongues, or any other *charisma.* St. Paul himself was not always replenished with miraculous power. A man may be full of the Holy Spirit, and be a temple for his abode, and have no supernatural gift. Love supreme, love made perfect, is superior to all the miraculous endowments. Though I have all faith, so that I could remove mountains, and have not love, I am nothing. Witness Balaam's supernatural prophecy, followed by his violent death among the enemies of God, and the miracles of Judas, quickly succeeded by treason to his Master and wretched suicide.

Another objection which men at ease in Zion raise against the universal outpouring of the Spirit in these days is the fanaticism which it is supposed to breed. This would exclude all spiritual life from the world; for life is liberty, and all liberty has its perils. The prisoners, handcuffed in grated cells, and the dead in silent tombs, are the only two classes of people who are not in peril of the abuse of their physical powers and appetites. That more fanatics and eccentrics start up in a Church filled and thrilled with spiritual life than in a Church in a Laodicean stupor, is no more wonderful than that a free country should give birth to more who abuse their freedom, than an autocratic iron despotism, where none dare to stir. Look at the Roman Catholic Church, where not a breath of spiritual life can be drawn unless it is according to the decrees of the hierarchy, and every pulsation is under the jealous surveillance of the priesthood. The fanaticism of ecclesiasticism, of ritualism, of papacy, of Mariolatry, of indulgences, of penances and

pilgrimages, may flourish there, but not the fanaticism of unscriptural notions concerning the
Holy Spirit. For the Holy Ghost as the witness of pardon, the author of purity, and the
guide of life, comes into collision with the
claims of the priesthood. So the Holy Ghost
must be imprisoned in the apostolic age, and
the Bible must be chained in the cloister or
burned up, because it promotes independent
thought and spiritual freedom. Give us a
spiritual Protestantism, with all its perils of
rationalism and fanaticism, in preference to the
intellectual stupor and spiritual death of such
a system. We must make our election between
these two. Though there may be occasionally
a weak or unbalanced mind carried away into
fantastic extravagances under the copious effusion of the Holy Spirit, as a mighty rushing
wind, the average mind has skill to adjust its
sails to the heavenly gale, and speed its way,
with stable ballast, toward the port of eternal
life. Come, O wind! O breath of God! upon
myriads of becalmed souls, and sweep them
joyfully onward to the haven of rest.

Let us now set up a safeguard against an
abuse of the doctrine of this chapter respect-

ing the three dispensations. If men can be saved by attaining perfection in any one of them, it may be inferred that we may take our choice. Not so. God controls this matter. He allots our place of birth, our education, and surroundings. If it be a pagan country, under the starlight of natural religion, the dispensation of the Father, with no distinctive knowledge of Jesus Christ, we shall be required to be perfect according to the low standard of gentilism. The ground on which the heathen man will be condemned will not be the imperfectness of his life alone, but the fact that his life falls below his creed, poor as that may be. To him the Judge will say, "Ye knew your duty, but ye did it not. You had little light, but you shut your eyes, and refused to use what you had." The moralist, living in Christendom, cannot plead the perfection of paganism. This is a standard far below his degree of light. The sunrise of Christ's incarnation is upon him, showing the path of Christian duty—love supreme to God in his Son, in addition to a perfect morality. Alas! how many will fail at this point. As Capernaum, blessed with the presence, sermons, and miracles of Christ, all misimproved, sinks down in the judgment day below Sodom and Gomorrah, so will the impenitent of Christian lands, with the Bible in his hands—that lamp from off God's throne cast down to earth, lighting up their habitations, making the way of Christian rectitude luminous as a path of light before their feet—sink down under a weight of guilt when the pagan nations shall rise up to condemn them.

Thus the nominal Christian who reads in the Acts of the Apostles of the dispensation of the Spirit more glorious than that of the Son of God, and hears from God's embassador that it is his privilege and duty to be filled with the Spirit, and hears the attestations of unimpeached witnesses that the blessed Spirit of adoption has certified to their pardon, renewed and purified their natures, cannot innocently reject the ministration of the Holy Spirit, because it will cost him a painful effort of repentance, surrender, consecration, and faith to reach this high spiritual altitude. Formalism, ceremonialism, and mere orthodoxy, cannot save him.

CHAPTER X.

PERFECT LOVE AS A DEFINITE BLESSING.

IT took four thousand years to unroll the scroll of the sacred Scriptures—"to import God into knowledge," in the phrase of Dr. Bushnell. The patriarchal and Jewish dispensations were occupied by the disclosure and ineradicable inculcation of the Divine unity upon one nation amid surrounding polytheism. To have taught the trinal personality of God, before the firm establishment of his oneness of substance, might have overtasked mankind in the period of their early theological pupilage. The first words taught to every child in the Jewish nursery for more than three thousand years are these: "Hear, O Israel, the Lord our God is one Lord." Faith in this truth, such as inspired obedience, was saving under the dispensations before Christianity. It is saving now to all who have no higher revelation. What need, then, have we of any clearer and more definite manifestation of the nature of God? Why should he reveal the unthinkable fact of his threefold personality, and require our faith to mount to heights so far above reason? This is a question which the angels might well approach with bashful tread. It is certain that he has not taken me into his counsels. Here I walk by faith. Faith says that the higher revelation of God, and the new requirement of faith in the Trinity, proceed from the gracious purpose to bestow richer blessings upon the believer in a dispensation "rather glorious." Such is the nature of the human soul, and probably of all finite spirits, that faith creates and measures its capacity for spiritual good. By this gateway alone does God enter. Hence it follows that he would make an advanced revelation of himself, requiring a higher upreaching of faith, when he should purpose to fill us with his fullness. It will not now be sufficient to believe in one God, as do the trembling demons. The Son of God, Jesus Christ, in his offices of prophet or teacher, priest and king, and the Holy Ghost, as our regenerator, spirit of adoption, and sanctifier, must be specifically grasped by our faith. Hence we should

11

look for little spirituality where these distinctive truths of the Gospel are little preached, and for much spiritual power and deep religious experience where they are distinctly taught and received with the least intermixture of error, and without disproportionate emphasis upon ritualism. Church history will sustain this assertion. There is always a spiritual decline whenever Christ and the Holy Spirit have a secondary place in preaching; and there is always a revival when the " whole counsel of God," the Father, Son, and Spirit, is faithfully presented in the pulpit. Of many individual believers it may be truthfully said that their spiritual life is feeble and sickly because they fail to grasp Christ and the Comforter in all their distinct offices. Thousands are faintly moving, with languid steps, along the heavenward path, who might run with gladness, surmounting every obstacle and overthrowing every foe by their resistless momentum, if they would only persistently endeavor to "know the exceeding greatness of Christ's power to us-ward who believe." Thousands of sincere souls are harassed and weakened by perpetual doubts, simply because they do not render due honor to the third person of the Trinity by trusting him to do the work of his office, certifying their sonship by "the spirit of adoption." They do not stir themselves up to take hold of this blessed assurance, and to insist that the Divine seal be impressed upon them by the Holy Ghost. They live in constant disregard of the second pungent inference from Wesley's sermon on the Witness of the Spirit, "Let none rest in any supposed fruit of the Spirit without the witness." The natural consequence of this absence of "the spirit of adoption, crying in their hearts, Abba, Father," is a perpetual oscillation between hope and fear, sorrowfully singing :—

> "'Tis a point I long to know ;
> Oft it causeth anxious thought,
> Do I love the Lord, or no ;
> Am I his, or am I not?"

Instead of this they might be exultingly singing :—

> "O love, thou bottomless abyss !
> My sins are swallowed up in thee ;
> Covered is my unrighteousness,
> Nor spot of guilt remains on me :
> While Jesus' blood, through earth and skies,
> Mercy, free, boundless mercy, cries."

I am convinced that this unsatisfactory and unmethodistic experience, too prevalent in our

Churches, is chargeable in part to the failure
of our preachers to specialize this blessing, the
common privilege of all believers. Hear Mr.
Wesley: " Generally, wherever the Gospel is
preached in a clear and scriptural manner,
more than ninety-nine in a hundred do know
the exact time when they are justified." This
is the testimony of a man more competent,
from personal observation, to express a reliable
opinion than any since the apostolic age, for
he visited all his Societies annually; and met
them in class, and put to each member searching test questions which went into the very
core of his being. That was the style of class-
leading in his day. But no such proportion
of conversions, with the direct witness, now
obtains at our altars. The failure is not in the
Gospel, which is a changeless stream of power
emanating from the living Christ, " the same
yesterday, and to-day, and for ever." Where,
then, is the failure? Let every preacher examine his sermons, and see whether he has
made "the spirit of adoption" conspicuous in
his ministry.

Another office of the Spirit is that of purification. He is the Sanctifier. Beginning this

work in the new birth by implanting love to God, the purifying principle, he continues it until perfect love casteth out fear. That this consummation may take place long before death, has never been a disputed question with Methodists. That it was specialized by their great founder, with increasing emphasis, till his dying day, no man on the earth can candidly deny, after reading "Tyerman's Life and Times of John Wesley." That this magnifying of the office of the Sanctifier produced such Christian characters as Bramwell, Hester Ann Rogers, the seraphic Fletcher, and his saintly wife, and many others unknown to fame, but precious jewels in the crown of Jesus, is as certain as the sequence of any effect after its cause.

These results were not the work of chance. There was a distinctive faith which grasped this prize. This faith came from preaching which honored the Sanctifier by dwelling emphatically upon his office, and not by the use of "glittering generalities" gliding smoothly over it like a slurred note in music. It must be borne in mind that the Holy Spirit is the most sensitive person of the Godhead. If blasphemy against him is unpardonable, the slighting of any of his offices must not only grieve him, but also deprive the soul of the blessings which it is his prerogative to bestow. "Grieve not the Holy Spirit of God, whereby ye are sealed unto the day of redemption."

CHAPTER XI.

THE FRUITS OF PERFECT LOVE.

§ 1. *The Joy of the Abiding Comforter.*

THE Gospel is glad tidings of great joy. It was an outgush of song in a sad world —a burst of sunshine after ages of darkness. Paganism to-day is not jubilant, but gloomy and despondent. When, in a Christian land, any class of people discard Christ, their songs die out because their joy has withered. Spiritualism has no exultant songs because it has no gladness in Jesus. It may gather in the tented grove, under the inspiration of waving trees, singing birds, verdant fields, glittering stars, and azure skies, but it confesses that it cannot counterfeit the Christian psalmody which rolls down the ages, lifting the heart of the believer nearer to God. Mormonism, in her mountain-girded valley, sits songless. The habitations of Utah are gladdened by no melodious praise warbled from human lips. Travelers remark this dearth of song in a land smiling with plenty. The explanation is easy. There is no Holy Ghost in their religion. It sows to the flesh and not to the spirit. Free Religion assembles in conventions, and argues, denounces, and blasphemes; but when she tries to sing, her voice is like the gibbering of a ghost in a sepulcher.

Christ Jesus glorified in the soul by the Holy Ghost, is the fountain of true joy. The kingdom of God is "righteousness, peace, and joy in the Holy Ghost." When the blessed Comforter fills the hearts of a people with his joy-inspiring presence, they burst out into spontaneous singing. But where formalism, worldliness, and unbelief have crowded the Comforter out of their hearts, they pay thousands of dollars to a quartette to perform the service which their backslidden souls refuse to render. Hence joy is a very good test, not only of orthodox opinions, but of the strength of our faith in Christian truth, and our personal devotion to Christ. But not all joy is Christian. Joys may be classified as, 1) unnatural, 2) natural, 3) supernatural. The first is the exhilaration resulting from the application of stimulants to the nervous system. Lord Bacon credits drunkenness with intense pleasure. This is the secret of the fatal fascination of the cup. It awakens a delirious, evanescent, and fatal joy, which momentarily lifts up the soul to ecstatic heights, and then plunges it into the depths of despair. The day-dreams of the opium eater, and the serene composure of the slave to tobacco, belong to the class of unnatural and injurious delights. The joy which ends in the scorpion's sting must be ranked as the lowest in the scale of rational satisfactions. Yet all nations and generations have plucked this apple of Sodom and tasted its ashes.

2.) There is a mere animal joy which flows from the healthful condition of the body. The animal spirits overflow in their exuberance. The lambs frisk upon the sunny hillside, and the horse, in the very fullness of life, prances through the pasture with arched neck and nimble foot. So men may be joyful by reason of their good physical condition. There may be not only "no rebellion when the stomach is full," but there may be an outflowing stream of animal joy. Higher than this is the gladness of worldly success, when the corn and the wine increase, the joy of sordid gain, the joy of the miser, the joy of the harvest. Above this is the intellectual triumph of the student, the gladness incident to the victories of mind, the solution of a mathematical problem, or the discovery of the missing truth which was necessary in order to convert an hypothesis into a science. Still higher is ethical joy, the approval of a good conscience pronouncing on a good action. This is no small joy. It is all that many have to cheer their sojourn in this vale of tears. More excellent still is the gladness of beneficence, the joy of awakening gladness in another heart, or of mitigating another's sorrows. Many who are not Christians have learned the secret of this semi-Christian joy, and by a charitable use of money have opened fountains of felicity for themselves along their earthly path. All these kinds of joy are *natural;* they lie on the dead level of the plain of nature. They are transient, and limited to this world.

3.) At the disparity of an infinite distance is the joy of the Holy Ghost. It is *supernatural*—an outgushing fountain from a rock stricken by the rod of a greater than Moses. It is a joy not springing up in the course of nature, but handed down from heaven, and implanted in the believing soul. It is really a miraculous spring opened by the Holy Spirit in the Sahara of the human breast. It may be surprising that the fullness of the Spirit is several times in the Scriptures contrasted with fullness of wine. "Be not drunk with wine, wherein is excess, but be filled with the Spirit." Contrast always implies some point of likeness. This seems to consist in three facts: (1.) Exhilaration and elevation of feeling; (2.) Out of the course of nature; and (3.) By an agent from without the man entering and exciting his sensibilities. The universal appetency of the fallen race of Adam for some external stimulant argues the loss of the true excitant, the Holy Spirit, which filled the hearts of the unfallen pair with satisfying joy, just as He fills now all who regain the Eden of perfect love. Christian joy exists in every degree. There is the joy of penitence, described by the poet as "the sweet distress," "the pleasing smart." There follows the joy of conscious pardon—a radiant angel standing out on the

dark background of condemnation like a thun-
dercloud overcasting all the sky.   The Spirit of
adoption, crying in the heart, Abba, Father, is
the source of gladness above the negative joy
of forgiveness.   Adoption is positive, and en-
titles to heirship with Christ.'   But when we
enter upon the fullness of the Spirit, in the
words of Mr. Wesley, " it will feast our souls
with such peace and joy in God as will blot
out the remembrance of every thing that we
called peace or joy before."   This is strong language, but it is justified by all who have been
led to this banqueting house, and have read on
the banner floating over them the new, best
name of Love—Perfect Love.

> ' O, what a heaven of heavens is this,
>   This swoon of silent love !
>   How poor the world's sublimest bliss
>   Compared with joys above ! "

To portray this bliss by words would be
like representing the rainbow by a charcoal
sketch.   If the meagerness of human language
fails to convey to a blind man the vastness of
that ocean which lies in the hollow of the
Creator's hand, how much more is its poverty
seen when it attempts to set forth to an in-

experienced soul all the plenitude of God himself.

No simple emotion of the soul can be indicated in any other way than by stating the circumstances under which it arises, as the sense of beauty in the presence of the rose, the feeling of sublimity where Niagara pours down its avalanche of waters before our eyes. The heart that has never felt the throb of love and the gladness that follows, as the shadow follows the substance, can never learn it from the most graphic writer in the whole range of literature. It is thus with the joy of the Holy Ghost in the fullness of his abiding presence. It differs from the joy of the justified, from the gladness of the adopted, in degree, if not in kind. These seem like gifts liable to decay, while the joy of the Divine fullness is the possession of the Giver—the perennial fountain of all blessedness. Jesus intimated to the woman begging the mysterious water which he had, that she might not only taste but carry away the well with her. " But the water which I will give you shall be in you a well of water springing up to everlasting life." This promise, rightly interpreted, is, that the love to Christ

and the attendant joy shall become ingrained,
inherent in the fully believing soul as a second
nature ; faith, love, and joy becoming as natural and involuntary as breathing. Hence
permanence is a marked characteristic of perfect love. Mr. Wesley was fifty-five years old
before he became " thoroughly convinced that
it is amissible, capable of being lost."

Yet our discussion of this theme would not
be exhaustive, if several grave errors were not
marked by buoys for the benefit of future
voyagers on this sea.

1. *Do not seek joy.* Seek not the gift but
the Giver. There is a subtle selfishness in crying for joy. If you receive the Giver you will
insure all his gifts. But beware lest you fix
your eye on the gift aside from the Giver.
" God is a jealous God." He must be sought
for his own infinite worthiness. The penitent
sinner may find the gift of forgiveness while
imploring this, without a distinct apprehension
of the supreme excellence of the Divine character. His sins rise like mountains and fill
all the field of his vision. Nor has he had
that spiritual discipline which has disclosed to
him the absolute purity of God in contrast

with his inward depravity. But the believer
has had such a flood of light poured by the
Spirit upon his own inherent vileness and the
spotless holiness of God, that, in his further
approaches, he must be attracted by the in-
comparable beauty of his character, and not by
any mere gift at his disposal. He must utterly
renounce all selfish motives and cry,

> " Suffice that for the season past
>   Myself in things divine I sought ;
> For comforts cried with eager haste,
>   And murmured that I found them not.
> I leave it now to thee alone ;
> Father, thy only will be done !

> " Thy gifts I clamor for no more,
>   Nor selfishly thy grace require,
> An evil heart to varnish o'er ;
>   JESUS, the Giver, I desire,
> After the flesh no longer known ;
> Father, thy only will be done !"

Having anchored a buoy on a rock on which
many have struck in attempting to sail into
the harbor of perfect love, we proceed to place
another on a rock which lies in the very harbor itself.

2. *Do not imagine that the sudden subsidence
of ecstatic joy is the withdrawal of the abiding
Comforter.* You retain him by faith and not

by feeling. The highest Christian experience is subject to variations. Joy, like the tide, ebbs and flows. There are times when the soul, without effort, apprehends the love of God, and joy unspeakable fills, floods, and overwhelms it. Suddenly this bright manifestation is withdrawn, while no testimony of the Spirit is left behind against any act of ours as the cause. While there is no cloud nor doubt, there is no direct assurance. All is a waveless, breathless calm. Then is the time to walk by the lamp of faith, since the sunlight of the direct and joyful witness of God's love is withdrawn. Beware lest you admit the thought that the fullness of God has left you with the cessation of the exultant joy of the Holy Spirit. These alternations of feeling are doubtless regulated by hidden but benevolent laws. They may be requisite for the development of higher faith, when the soul, humbled and hungering, cries out,

> "My heartstrings groan with deep complaint,
> My flesh lies panting, Lord, for thee."

These inexplicable vacations of the manifestation of Divine love may be necessary for the more deliberate examination of our hearts.

As the careful engineer occasionally stops his train in order to click the wheels and prove their soundness, so God may at times interrupt the current of conscious love, to afford us an appropriate occasion for spiritual introspection. The man who walks by faith through these intervals will soon find even a clearer and more joyful outbeaming of the Saviour's countenance to reward his faithful clinging to the Divine promise.

To these cautions an objection may arise in the mind of the reader that we are encouraged by Christ to ask for joy when he says, "Ask and receive, that your joy may be full." The evident design of the Lord Jesus is to indicate one of the blissful consequences of the prayer of faith, rather than its direct aim. Seek ME, and as an incidental result, your joy will be full. Seek ye first the kingdom of God, not in order that food and raiment may be added unto you ; but "all these things shall be added," as an incidental consequence. Another objection is urged, derived from the example of the Son of God, " who for the joy that was set before him endured the cross, despising the shame, and is set down at the right hand of the throne

12

of God." Heb. xii, 2. If Jesus made his own joy the highest end of his actions and sufferings, may not his followers, who are commanded to walk in his steps? This objection is answered by recourse to the original, where we find ἄντι, "instead of," in place of "for," the joy. This reading represents the Son of God, when the alternative was before him of sharing with the Father the worship of angels, and enjoying the glory which he had with the Father before the world was, or of enduring the abasement of the incarnation and the sufferings of Gethsemane and Calvary, as deliberately choosing the cross "instead of the joy which was lying before him" as his inheritance in the immediate future. As Jesus chose the will of God, and not his own will or selfish joy, so are we to walk in his steps, and to pray, not beatify myself, but glorify thyself, O thou adorable Saviour! While it is true that we cannot act in utter disregard of our own happiness, it is also true that we may have a conception of Christ so exalted, and a faith in him so strong, as to identify our joy with his, assured that our highest delight will be conserved while we aim not at it, but at the glory of the Lamb, who is worthy of all honor, and glory, and blessing.

§ 2. *The Tongue Unloosed.*

A confessing mouth always attends a believing heart. As in the world of matter occult forces manifest themselves in their effects, so in the world of mind an unloosed tongue is the infallible result of the hidden Transformer, the Holy Spirit. "Come and hear, all ye that fear God, and I will declare what he hath done for my soul." This declaration, constantly put forth by living men, is a perpetual testimonial to the spiritual medicine advertised in the word of God. A specific held up before the public from year to year, unaccompanied by attested cures, comes to be distrusted and neglected. Hence even the blood of sprinkling, potent to cleanse the heart from all unrighteousness, needs something more than the advertisement of the inspired penman ; it needs the joyful voice of the healed leper, crying, "It hath cleansed me!" The aggressive, conquering power of Christ in this fallen world, and his final triumph over " Satan, who deceiveth the whole world," depend upon the agency of his friends. "And they overcame him by (on account of) the blood of the Lamb *and the word of their testimony.*" Without the blood of the Lamb they could not have answered the accuser, and without their testimony they could not have retained the witness of the Spirit that " Jesus died for me, and that he shed his blood for even me, and that all my sins are blotted out and my nature is renewed." Without both the blood of the Lamb and the word of the testimony the victory cannot be ours; both together form its ground. It is evident that the testimony is to be equal in extent to the cure. Pardon and regeneration experienced are to be attested also. The destruction of inbred sin and the fullness of the Divine life apprehended within are to be attested for the benefit of those still beneath the yoke, and for the glory of the great Emancipator. The chief motive to confession *is to glorify Christ.* If we have not a blessing, it is preposterous to profess in order to receive. It is selfish to profess any state of grace in order to retain it. He who loves Jesus Christ with all the intensity of a sanctified heart will feel a mighty constraint to confess him for his own sake.

There are few, if any, *explicit* professions of holiness or of Christian perfection in the Holy Scriptures. We search in vain for such testimonies as these: "I am holy;" "I am sanctified;" "I am perfect." Even the sinless Son of man, who could rightfully make these *explicit* declarations, chose other ways of professing his spotless purity and faultless perfection. Jesus *implies* his holiness when he puts to the caviling Jews the interrogatory, "Which of you convinceth me of sin?" and when he describes himself as one whom the Father hath sanctified and sent into the world, he said, "I and my Father are one." He asserted his absolute perfection without giving needless offense. He avoided all appearance of boastfulness. St. Paul's professions of entire sanctification, after the same style, are implied and not explicit. To the Thessalonians he says, "Ye are witnesses, and God also, how holily and justly and unblamably we behaved ourselves among you that believe." "For yourselves know how ye ought to follow us; for we behaved ourselves not disorderly among you." To Felix he declares, "Herein do I exercise myself, to have *always* a conscience void of

offense *toward God and man.*" He says to the
Church in Corinth, " Our rejoicing is this, the
testimony of our conscience, that in simplicity
and godly sincerity, not with fleshly wisdom,
but by the grace of God, we have had our conversation (ἀνεστράφημεν, conducted ourselves) in
the world. Giving no offense in *any* thing, but
in *all* things approving ourselves as the ministers of God, by pureness, by the Holy Ghost,
by the armor of righteousness on the right
hand and on the left.". " We have wronged
no man." To Timothy, who had been most
intimately associated with him in public and
private—no man is a hero to his *valet de
chambre*—he confidently appeals, " But thou
hast fully known my doctrine, *manner of life,
purity,* faith, long-suffering, love, and patience."
But the most remarkable implication of the
attainment of the higher life is found in his
letter to the Philippians, wherein, after dis-
claiming the perfection of the resurrection, he
admits that he had attained unto the evangelical perfection of love. " Let *us* therefore,
as many as be *perfect,* be thus minded. Brethren, be ye followers, *imitators,* together of me,
and mark them which walk so as ye have *us*

for an ensample, for *our* conversation (πολίτευμα, citizenship) is in heaven. Rendering the plural *us* and *our* by *me* and *my*, as in Conybeare's version, what have we here but the declaration that the character of St. Paul as an ensample is, in purity of purpose and manifestation, like that of the angels in heaven, who perfectly do the will of God? "Imitate me, for I, amid innocent infirmities and thorns in the flesh, am living the life of a citizen of heaven."

St. John most plainly implies his own purity when he says, "Truly our fellowship is with the Father, and with his Son Jesus Christ." That this implies holiness is evident from the fact of God's holiness, with whom there is a participation. But John does not leave this subject without adding the statement, "If we say that we have fellowship with him, and walk in darkness, (that is, sin,) we lie." It is difficult to resist the inference that St. John records his own experience and spiritual attainments in such hypothetical sentences as these: "If *we* confess our sins, he is faithful and just to forgive *us our* sins, and *to cleanse us from all unrighteousness.*" "If *we* walk in the light, as he is in the light, *we* have fellowship one with another, and the blood of Jesus Christ his Son cleanseth *us* from all sin." " But whoso keepeth his word, in him *verily is the love of God perfected.*" St. John was not a theorizer, but a practical man. He speaks out of the depths of his own experience when he says, " Every man that hath this hope in him purifieth himself, even as he (Christ) is pure." St. John must have had a heart perfectly free from condemnation, and hence from inward sin, or he could not have known the blissful consequences, " confidence toward God," and the ability to pray in such faith as " to receive whatsoever we ask of him." I John iii, 20–22. " He that dwelleth in love dwelleth in God, and God in him. Herein is our love made perfect, because *as he is so we are in this world.*" " Perfect love casteth out fear." This cannot be the conclusion of a syllogism, nor of any logical process, but the utterance of a heart made glad by love so strong as to bind the strong man, fear, and cast him out forever.

St. Peter's implied profession of entire sanctification is found in such expressions as, " Kept by the power of God through faith unto salvation." "Whereby are given unto us exceeding great and precious promises, that by these ye might be *partakers of the divine nature.*" It is certain that Peter was not so inconsistent as to exhort others to climb to heights unscaled by himself, when he says, "Be diligent, that ye may be found of him in peace, *without spot and blameless.*"

§ 3. *The Uplifted Vail.*

It is not by accident that, in the apostolic benediction, the communion of the Holy Ghost comes last. It is the crowning blessing of the Triune God. Without it the "grace of our Lord Jesus Christ, and the love of God," could not be satisfactorily and joyfully known. These might exist as a matter of inference from the gracious dispositions and holy aspirations of the soul. They cannot be immediately known by a knowledge excluding all doubt, except as they are uncovered by the Holy Ghost. " He shall receive of mine and show it unto" you. " He shall testify of me." All views of Christ, without the Spirit's illumination, are mere cold, intellectual conceptions, awakening by his moral beauty such esthetical emotions as arise when we gaze on the marble creations of Phidias or Angelo. To set the soul on fire with love as a consuming passion, this Christ must be brought into personal relations with me; he must be revealed in me by a process wholly inexplicable, but affording absolute assurance, and joy unspeakable. "We have received, not the spirit of the world, but the spirit which is of God; that we might *know* the things that are freely given us of God." No gracious attainment can be otherwise brought into consciousness in the soul of the believer. If the sins of the wicked man are set before him in terrific array, calling for the thunders of wrath Divine, it is the work of the Spirit. If the believer is freely justified through faith in Jesus Christ, the Spirit, as the carrier-dove of heaven, brings down to the condemned culprit the assurance of pardon. The same Spirit pours down light into the hidden depths of the soul after regeneration, and reveals the hideous deformities of a nature not yet wholly conformed to the pattern of Christ's spiritual beauty. Then, by a distinct exertion, he fashions that soul into a form of Christlike symmetry and loveliness, and the great Transformer reports his completed work to the consciousness as something "freely given to us of God." The conscious residence of the Holy Spirit within is the power which gives victory over sin. Sin, whether as an act or a state, cannot consist with the indwelling of the Holy Ghost. Hence he is called "the Sanctifier." They who hold daily communion with him walk the paths of the higher life. They are purified. For how can purity commune with impurity? Hence uninterrupted joyful communion of the Holy Ghost is Christian perfection. Such a soul "rejoices evermore, prays without ceasing, and in every thing gives thanks." How many professed Christians are ignorant of this bliss!

"There is a great deal that is shadowy and dubious about the communion that many have with God. They have no such consciousness of having met and conversed with God, as they have of their communications with men. There has been no bright and animating manifestation of God to their souls. They have not felt the power of his present majesty; nor have his Divine perfections taken hold upon them as by a special revelation. They know that God is revealed in his word as gracious and merciful toward the race of men; but they have not considered that it is the province of faith to single out the believer, and bring him by himself into the presence of his Maker. He is to enter into peculiar and well-understood relations to God. God is his God; he is the child of God; and there must be a conscious acquaintance and intimacy quite distinct from the general goodness of God toward mankind. In order that we may draw nigh to God, we must become *utterly dissatisfied with the vague sort of communion that so many are content with*. We must resolve to be satisfied with nothing less than the bright shining of the Divine presence upon our individual soul. We must believe it attainable, and resolve to attain it at whatever cost.

"Having begun to seek it earnestly, we shall perhaps experience many disappointments. The word of God unfolds itself, it is true, more richly to our souls than it once did, and we get juster conceptions of him. But the

bright and soul-elevating discovery of him
himself, we do not obtain. The more we seek,
however, the more we perceive the importance
of what we seek, and feel that life without this
conscious union of the soul with God, is insup-
portable. We take this conviction as an encouragement from on high, to go on. As we
continue striving in prayer we are led to examine ourselves earnestly to see if there is
any thing in our way of life that is displeasing
to God. We become very scrupulous, very
severe with ourselves; we cut off one indulgence here and another there, and wonder
how we should have formerly been so careless.
Duties that we had not formerly dreamed of,
now discover themselves to us; we find that
we were before very ill-acquainted with the
will of God. These discoveries perhaps only
make us the more unhappy; for we feel that
we need a strength such as we have not, in
order to live the life we are called to. More
and more we see the absolute necessity of
drawing nigh to God and strengthening ourselves in the consciousness of our indissolu-
ble union with him in Christ. Finally, in
some hour long to be remembered, there falls

down, as it were, a great vail, and with joy
unspeakable we behold the light of God's
countenance, and are made glad by the assurance, deeply buried in the soul, that an
Almighty Friend accompanies us along the
journey of life."

This quotation from that garden of spiritual
delights, "Bowen's Daily Meditations," issued
by the Presbyterian Publication Committee,
most graphically describes the process of obtaining full salvation, while delineating the struggles
of a believer to enter into communion face to
face with God. The unrest and dissatisfaction,
the search in the sacred oracles, the increasing
hunger, the heart-searchings, the uncovering
of sins before unknown, the surrender of indulgences, the consecration of all, the glimpses
of the prize which makes all the world look
cheap, further discoveries of corruption within,
and the sense of utter helplessness and need
of the Divine aid, all portray the pathway up
to the plane called the Higher Life, while the
sudden lifting of the vail fittingly describes
the instantaneous uplift to that higher path
where the "smile of the Lord is the feast of
the soul." This search after, and discovery

of, Peniel, the face of God, seen in open enraptured vision, passes unchallenged in a de-
votional book published for the use of a body
of Christians who would lift up their hands
in holy horror if the writer should substitute
perfect love, or Christian perfection, for that
communion with God just set forth as a distinct
attainment by every earnest and persevering
seeker. All the descriptions of high communion with God, whatever sectarian name
they bear, are expositions of this great blessing by the use of different terms. The soul,
fully resting in Christ, instantly recognizes
the great blessing, in whatever guise it may
appear.

> " The o'erwhelming power of saving grace,
>   The sight that vails the seraph's face ;
>   The speechless awe that dares not move,
>   And all the silent heaven of love."

To how many Christian souls is God vailed!
They have need to pray, " Hide not thy face
from me." Many of these do not know that
God is pleased to make communications of
grace which shall be like the removal of a
vail from the face of one beloved and adored.
Such manifestations of grace to others are

believed to be exceptional, that only a few persons of a peculiar and delicate spiritual organization can receive revelations of Christ's love; whereas we are living in a dispensation in which more glorious unvailings of God to every believing soul are possible than was ever enjoyed by Enoch, Abraham, Isaiah, or Daniel. "The light of the moon has become as the light of the sun, and the light of the sun shall be sevenfold." How shall not the ministration of the Spirit be rather glorious? This is our exalted privilege. What are the attainments of a majority of the modern Church? Says Professor Phelps, "Much of even the ordinary language of Christians respecting the joy of communion with God— language which is stereotyped in our dialect of prayer—many cannot honestly apply to the history of their own minds. A calm, fearless self-examination finds no counterpart to it in any thing they have ever known. In the view of an honest conscience, it is not the vernacular speech of their experience. As compared with the joy which such language indicates, prayer is, in all that they know of it, a dull duty. Perhaps the characteristic of the feelings of many about it is expressed in the single fact that it *is* to them a duty as distinct from a privilege. It is a duty which they cannot deny, is often uninviting, even irksome. Yet God's ideal of communion with his saints is this, "I will make them *joyful* in my house of prayer."

13

CHAPTER XII.

SALVATION FROM ARTIFICIAL APPETITES.

JESUS once said, " If the Son, therefore, make you free, ye shall be free indeed." This emphatic " indeed " has in it a deep significance, fathomed only by those who have let down the sounding-line of experience into the depths of this wonderful freedom. These persons attest that they are not only delivered from a sense of guilt and a fear of its penalty ; not only from the dominion, but from the indwelling, of sin within their hearts. They are saved from sinning. They are freed not only from the willful violation of the known law of God, but also from the enslavement of their former tyrannical appetites. The petition in that ancient formula of worship, the " *Te Deum Laudamus*," is answered every day of their lives—" Vouchsafe, O Lord, to keep us this day without sin." Millions of worshipers in liturgical Churches still offer this prayer every Lord's Day. They even go further than this. They pray that the thoughts of their hearts may be cleansed by the inspiration of the Holy Spirit, "that our souls may be washed through Christ's most precious blood, and that we may evermore dwell in him, and he in us." Even beyond this they pray "that our *sinful bodies* may be made clean through his most precious body." The Church for ages has prayed for cleansing from all filthiness of the flesh and spirit. Her mistake has frequently been, in relying on the efficacy of the sacraments instead of the power of the Holy Spirit through faith in the name of Jesus. Yet inward and outward holiness, unmixed and pure, has been aimed at in the prayers of the Church through all the Christian ages. This is no mean argument, proving that Jesus is able to deliver from those inward proclivities toward sin inhering in our bodies, which, like traitors within the gates, are a source of constant annoyance and peril. I refer not only to what is in theology called original sin, or depravity, but also to induced tendencies to sin resulting from pernicious appetites. All the philosophers, from Aristotle to Sir William Hamilton, insist that those

qualities of our nature which have been produced by habit are more invincible than those
born in us. The Bible confirms it. The
Ethiopian's skin and the leopard's spot symbolize, not the impossibility of eradicating natural depravity, but acquired propensities to evil
in those "accustomed to do evil." But there is
salvation from even these. This deliverance is
personal and not generic; it includes the believer himself, and not his seed. I find no such deliverance from depravity as would exempt the
offspring of two such emancipated persons from
sinful tendencies, and hence, possibly, from
any need of atonement. Such a state of grace
is found only in the dreams of fanatics, who
are always going beyond what is written.
There is abundant testimony that Jesus can
emancipate from the degrading and enslaving
yoke of artificial appetites under which universal humanity groans.

How difficult to break the fetters of the alcoholic or narcotic appetite! Yet there are
many who testify that through faith in Jesus
Christ, they were in a moment set perfectly free from fleshly appetites which had enslaved them for years; that the grasp of

those vile demons, opium and tobacco, after scores of years was instantly relaxed when the power of the almighty Emancipator was invoked. The instantaneous victories of King Jesus over king alcohol are too numerous and too well attested to admit of doubt. As Jesus on earth delivered from every kind of disease, so from on high he delivers from every form of sin, saving to the uttermost all who come unto God by him. Since this cleansing of the flesh seems to involve an instantaneous physical change, it comes very near to the miraculous. For this reason there is need of unimpeachable testimony to substantiate our statement. From the " Wonders of Grace," a tract by Rev. W. H. Boole, we quote the following instances:—

" A. C. has been for thirty years a member of the Methodist Episcopal Church ; for the greater part of this time a leader and trustee in a New York Church. His profession was always marked by correctness of deportment and generous zeal, while his cheerful manners won the esteem of all. But he had been addicted to the constant use of tobacco for forty years, until its daily use had become seemingly necessary to health, if not to life. He had made many efforts to rid himself of the doubtful practice, but always failed because of the inward gnawing which its long-continued use had created, and which forced him to begin the practice again. At last, on a certain occasion, in the presence of the writer, he said, ' I have long been seeking a deeper work of grace ; tobacco appears to hinder me ; but I had not supposed it possible to be saved from the dreadful power of this habit until now. Never before have I trusted Jesus to save me from the *appetite* as well as the *use* of it, but now I do,' and, suiting the action to the word, he threw far away from him the tobacco he held in his hand. He still lives, and for several years has reiterated this testimony : '*From that hour all desire left me*, and I have ever since hated what I once so fondly loved.' "

"———— ——— is a prominent member of the Methodist Episcopal Church in the city of Brooklyn, New York. For thirty-five years he has served the Church, giving liberally of his abundant means, and generally ready for every good word and work. From the age of ten he had used tobacco, until the habit had become so deeply rooted he could not endure to be without a cigar in his mouth, frequently rising in the night to 'have a good smoke.' During the thirty years of this manner of life he often felt the bondage of the habit, and resolved against it, but his resolutions invariably failed him. About three years since he became deeply interested in the subject of full salvation, and began diligently seeking for its possession. While pondering what might be the difficulties in the way, he saw that this very doubtful and slavish habit was a bar to his advancement; but so earnest was he for the prize of a clean heart, that he felt altogether willing to yield up the indulgence *if it were possible*. But was it so? He had fought against the passion long and well, yet not once had he conquered. *Who* would deliver him from the body of this death? It was a new idea to him that Jesus saves from the appetite and lust of sin as well as from the act; that he gives strength not only to *strive against* but to *destroy* the power of habit. But no sooner did he apprehend this gospel truth, and read his privilege in the wonderful promise, 'He is able to save them to the uttermost,' than he, all alone, one evening cast himself on Jesus' word, *and trusted him to do it for him.* 'Twas done. Not an hour longer did the desire remain; and his uniform testimony has ever since been, 'It is strange to me that I ever loved the filthy practice.'"

Mr. Boole testifies, "More than a score of examples equally interesting I have witnessed in one year, all occurring in the same community." The author of this book has conversed with several eminently pious men who were instantaneously delivered from the narcotic appetite, one of whom had been a confirmed drunkard, and had twenty years before been delivered in a similar manner from the alcoholic appetite with no subsequent return of the unclean spirits.

But a more dreadful chain is the opium habit in the various forms of its use. In the attempt to leave it off the devotee suffers unutterable agonies. It seems as though a volcano was rending his bowels. His will-power is destroyed. Few indeed, without supernatural aid, ever break this yoke. Some, in the blackness of despair, have committed suicide.

Multitudes increase the dose till nature at last succumbs, and the wretched victim dies with a sense of guilt burning the soul. We quote from the same authority.

" Near the town of Westbrook, Connecticut, there lived an aged woman, seventy-two years old, well known in the community as the ' old opium eater,' who had lived in the daily use of large quantities of this drug for more than twenty-two years. Her daily allowance was enough to destroy the lives of twenty persons not addicted to the habit. Whether she ever had made any previous attempts to break away from the baneful practice, we know not ; but, on a certain day, the writer visited her in company with a brother minister stationed in the town. The subject of her opium eating was introduced, and a close and faithful discussion of the moral aspects of the case followed. The *sin* of the habit was clearly and unhesitatingly exposed, and her unsaved and perilous condition, so far advanced in years, boldly but gently pronounced. Then Christ was presented, able to save to the uttermost—to save from the guilt and the passion of her sinful indulgence. She had listened with evident in-

terest, and the Holy Spirit was without doubt
breathing deep conviction into her soul. As
the last objection to seeking Jesus *now*, trusting in him alone to do all for her, was answered, and the last prop of self-righteousness
removed, this aged sinner, nearly double with
years and a confirmed habit of iron strength,
kneeled down with us to ask Divine mercy
and help. While thus engaged in prayer, 'immediately' the desire left her, and she knew
in herself that she was free from that plague.
The bright Divine evidence of her acceptance
was not received, according to her testimony,
until two weeks afterward; yet the desire for
opium did not *in the interval* return, and she
lived for two years a happy witness of the 'uttermost' power of Christ to save. Her unwavering testimony to the end was, 'I am no
more troubled with any desire for opium than
if I had never sinned in the use of it. Jesus
saves me.'"

We condense one more case from the same
author:—

"—— ——, the subject of this sketch, lives
in Brooklyn, New York. While under treatment for a broken leg he acquired the appe-

tite for morphine, and indulged it ten years.
He breakfasted on it, dined on it, and took a
dose the last thing at night. His daily allowance for several years was fully enough to kill
one hundred persons. In the presence of
several physicians he swallowed enough to destroy two hundred men. He was convinced
of his sin, and tried to break off in vain. Once
he abstained a day and a half until the effects
on body and mind became alarming, and five
physicians were called who prescribed morphine to prevent delirium or death. Thus in-
dulging a year longer, he sought his spiritual
adviser. He was advised to give up morphine.
He replied, 'I shall die.' 'Well, die then;
better so than live in sin and die unforgiven.'
He came forward for prayers in the Church,
and was told *to trust Jesus fully to save him
from his appetite now.* He trusted, and then
occurred a scene never to be forgotten by those
present. The glory of the Lord shone in his
sanctuary; power from on high came upon
this wretched soul whom Satan had bound,
lo! these many years; his very face was illumined, while he poured forth his praises,
exulting in his instantaneous and wonderful

deliverance. It only remains to be added that from that glad hour no desire for his former sin troubled him, no temptation to its indulgence has visited him : he is greatly improved in physical health, and he has experienced no re-action or ill effects from the sudden disuse of the pernicious drug."

At the South Framingham Camp-meeting in August, 1873, a witness, whose testimony was amply corroborated by others from his town, testified that at his conversion two years before, he was instantaneously emancipated from the appetite for rum and tobacco, to which he had been excessively and notoriously addicted. Since the minister could not prevail on this vile drunkard to attend Church, he appointed a meeting in the home of the wretched inebriate. In the sermon Christ was exalted as a savior from all the foul and enslaving appetites which degrade and destroy men. No impression seemed to be made upon the bloated, blear-eyed tenant of that hovel. But, awakening in the night, the preacher's words were applied by the Spirit to his heart. He saw his hopeless slavery, and he saw his great Deliverer. He called

upon him in faith, and even before he had
arisen from his bed, he was enabled to say
with the poet,

> "Long my imprisoned spirit lay
>   Fast bound in sin and nature's night ;
> Thine eye diffused a quickening ray ;
>   I woke ; my dungeon flamed with light ;
> My chains fell off, my heart was free—
> I rose, went forth, and followed thee."

He declares that all desire for tobacco and
alcoholic drinks was taken from him in the
twinkling of an eye, and that it has not returned for an instant, even amid the fumes of
these poisons.

Verily our Jesus is " mighty to save."

It will be seen that these deliverances were,
in several of these cases, wrought in the moment of the justification of the persons concerned. The explanation is that they were
distinctly apprehending thus much of the evil
of their nature, and were trusting Christ for
deliverance from this galling yoke. If all their
inherited depravity had been as clearly seen
as were these acquired defilements, and their
faith had laid hold of Jesus as able " to cleanse
from all filthiness of the flesh and the spirit,"

there is reason to believe that their complete sanctification would have been accomplished when they were justified.

In this power of Christ to bind and cast out the strong man of appetite, what encouragement is afforded to the Christian world to attempt to save the countless hosts of drunkards and moderate drinkers of alcoholic beverages— the estimated ten millions of Mexicans and South Americans who defile and destroy themselves with coca juice; the hundred millions of Hindoos chewing betel; the two hundred and fifty millions of Asiatie hasheesh eaters; the four hundred millions enslaved to opium; and the eight hundred millions who bow beneath the galling yoke of that filthy tyrant, tobacco.*

* Methodist Quarterly, 1859, p. 191.

CHAPTER XIII.

THE FULL ASSURANCE OF FAITH.

§ 1. *Salvation from Doubt.*

"I know not what it is to doubt;
My heart is ever gay."—*Faber.*

THE most surprising fact which came to the knowledge of Jesus was the weakness of his disciples' faith. Descended from heaven, written all over with proofs of his divinity, and bearing the great seal of God in his right hand—the miracle-working power—he stood unrecognized in the world. A little band of a dozen or more attach themselves to his fortunes, and avow faith in him; but often their perception of the wonderful beauty of his character was so dim, and their glimpses of his divinity were so brief, that they relapsed into distressing doubt, and were on the point of abandoning him forever. We often wonder at their skepticism and spiritual stupor, as if we, standing in their place, would have had eyes to pierce the clouds of doubt, and to behold and adore the full-orbed sun in its first rising upon the world's darkness; but we are by no means sure that if we had been the companions of Christ's earthly wanderings, listened to his words, and witnessed his works, we should have escaped the oft-repeated rebuke, "O ye of little faith! wherefore do ye doubt!" Should Jesus to-day step into our Christian assemblies, and tell us his view of our spiritual condition, he would find a sentence in his gospels just adapted to the state of the modern Church, "O ye of little faith."

We have somewhere met with a quaint, but exhaustive classification of mankind in respect to Christ; namely, believers, half-believers, make-believers, and unbelievers. There is no fifth class. Nor can they be reduced to three. Some persons deny the existence of half-believers. They assert that there are no degrees of faith; that it is not possible that a soul should be in such an equivocal attitude toward Christian truth; that there is either full belief or unbelief. But half-believers have existed all along the history of the Church; and they throng our churches to-day, and they make up the majority of disciples now as they did in the days of the Son of man. It is interesting to trace the boundary between half-believers, or doubters—we use the term synonymously—and unbelievers. Unbelief has no positive element of faith, and hence is always the ground of condemnation. It is always fatal to right practice. The unbeliever cannot perform Christian duties with any sincerity, for there is no motive power. Unbelief is spiritual paralysis, voluntarily induced and retained. Its inner essence and culpability lie in the obstinacy of the will against the truth. The secret reason why the intellect does not assent to the truth is, because the will refuses to obey. Unbelief has always a moral and not an intellectual cause. It arises, not from a lack of evidence, but from an unwillingness to follow wherever the truth may lead. Hence, Jesus applies his antidote directly to the will when he would prescribe an infallible remedy.

" If any man wills * to do His will, he shall know of the doctrine, whether it be of God, or whether I speak of myself."

* See the Greek. Our version has obscured the distinct element of volition.

14

Perfect consecration is the doorway out of the most inveterate unbelief. This is also the perfect cure for doubt. There is this difference between unbelief and doubt. In all doubt there is a positive element of faith toward which the soul moves, when it is met by a counter current of objections and difficulties. These two opposing forces—faith and doubt—distract the soul; but if the result is progress toward Christ, the doubt, though it has weakened, has not destroyed, the Christian. The positive element in it has triumphed. Jesus always upbraided doubt, but he never sends the doubter to hell, because it is possible for the will to be in an attitude of obedience despite the doubts. It is possible for a Christian to live on the right side of doubt; that is, to act as if he had no doubts. When Naaman was told to bathe seven times in Jordan, his reason immediately questioned the efficacy of this prescription for the leprosy. At first he was a positive unbeliever, and turned his face toward Damascus; but at the suggestion of his servants, and in view of the greatness of the benefit and the simplicity of the remedy, he was induced to turn the head of his cavalcade toward the despised Jordan. He was still brimful of doubt, but he had faith enough to move him in the right direction. He dipped himself once, and examining his skin, found no change. His doubts increased with each plunge; but he still had faith sufficient to go on till the seventh plunge, when his flesh became like a little child's. This is living on the right side of doubt. He went to the Jordan a doubter, and was healed, instead of going to Damascus an unbeliever, to linger out his days in abhorred loathsomeness.

In Bunyan's immortal allegory there is a scene which strikingly portrays unbelief, doubt, and faith. Christian and Pliable tumble together into the Slough of Despond. Pliable wallows till he gets out " on that side of the slough which is next to his own house ; so away he went, and Christian saw him no more." This is living on the wrong side of doubt, and going into the darkness of confirmed unbelief. Christian " struggled to that side of the slough which was farthest from his own house, and next to the wicket gate." He lived on the right side of doubt, and reached the Celestial City, while Pliable per-

ished in the City of Destruction. Christian did
nobly, but he might have done much better.
There was another pilgrim, named Faithful,
who, on coming to the same slough, looked
carefully, and found "substantial steps placed,
even through the very midst of this slough,"
and walked in safety upon them. These steps
are the Divine promises, and this character,
Faithful, represents all perfect believers in
Christ Jesus, lifted by faith above the quag-
mire while planting their feet upon the immu-
table granite of God's word.

Such a life is possible. It begins with the
moment when the half-believer "knows the
exceeding greatness of his power to us-ward
who believe" fully in "the working of his
mighty power, which he wrought in Christ,
when he raised him from the dead." This is
salvation from doubt. There are witnesses on
earth to-day who testify to this salvation as
the blessed experience of years, yea, scores of
years. Harassed and weakened by doubts,
they opened the Bible and found it a vast
magazine of promises. Among these, one
promise rose like Mont Blanc, and fixed their
gaze : it was "the Promise of the Father,"

the Comforter, who should glorify Christ by a
revelation of his power to save. They appropriated this great promise of the greatest gift
that men can wish, or heaven can send, and
suddenly their feet were lifted from the plane
of their past experience, and planted on that
serene and cloudless summit, where each might
sing :—

> " Rejoicing now in earnest hope
> I stand, and from the mountain top
>   See all the land below ;
> Rivers of milk and honey rise,
> And all the fruits of Paradise
>   In endless plenty grow."

It is not surprising that many, believing the
testimony of their brethren and sisters, are
earnestly crying,

> "O, that *I* might *at once* go up ;
> No more on this side Jordan stop,
>   But *now* the land possess ;
> This moment end my legal years,
> Sorrows, and sins, and *doubts*, and fears,—
>   A howling wilderness."

But many are kept back from seeking salvation from doubt by the suggestion that this
whole question of assurance is determined by
our mental and physical constitutions. They
say that this salvation is for the sanguine, the

ardent style of minds, with whom faith is easy. But bilious and phlegmatic temperaments, when they fully trust in Jesus, the complete Saviour, are just as easily lifted to the sunlit summits of assurance, and they become far more stable in their experience. Read the Acts of the Apostles, and you will find that after the pentecostal outpouring of the Spirit, there was great joy, betokening that the shadows of the night of doubt were dispelled by the rising of the day-star within their hearts. New Testament Christians are abounding in joy as soon as they receive the Holy Ghost in full measure. Temperament makes no difference.

§ 2. *The Psychology of Christian Assurance.**

Man's cognitive or knowing powers are few in number. Through his senses or perceptions he knows the qualities of matter. By

---

* If the reader abhors metaphysics, he would do well to skip this and the following chapter. Yet we have tried to practice the advice of our college preceptor, Dr. Olin: "Students, if you put metaphysics into your sermons, be sure that you make them luminous." We trust that much skepticism will be dispelled by showing that a degree of certitude in spiritual knowledge, higher than even that of material things, is attainable by every believer in Jesus Christ.

his internal perception he knows also the inner world. By his faculty of relations, discursive or elaborative power, he infers the unknown from the known. But lying back of these faculties, and existing before them all in the order of nature, but not in the order of development, is the power of original suggestion, the faculty of intuition. This term, from the Latin *intueor*, "look directly at," is used to designate the ability of the mind under certain conditions to gaze immediately upon certain truths independent of the perceptive or the elaborative faculties. These truths have various designations, as first, self-evident, or intuitive truths, first principles, native notions, etc.[*]

The notions grasped by this faculty are space, time, cause, substance, right and wrong, personal existence, personal identity, the axioms of mathematics, etc. When the mind is brought into activity by the presentation of the external world to the senses, or by sensation and perception, these notions start into being as if from the very groundwork of the mind. They may be known by the following

[*] Sir William Hamilton's "Metaphysics," p. 514.

criteria: 1. *Incomprehensibility*—We do not comprehend how or why the thing is. 2. *Simplicity*—It cannot be resolved into several other notions or cognitions. 3. *Necessity*, and consequent *universality*—The non-existence of a first cause cannot be conceived; hence it is said to be necessary, and, of course, universal. 4. *Comparative evidence* and *certainty*—This strictly pertains to the thinking subject rather than to the primary truth. The mind has the highest degree of certitude in contemplating these truths.

The interesting question now arises, whether the notion of a personal God is given by intuition. The intuitional Deists of India, constituting the Brahmo Somaj, teach that the idea of God, and all other religious truths, are given by the faculty of original suggestion, intuition, or pure reason. Hence a revelation is a superfluity. The American transcendentalists agree with these Asiatic philosophers in ascribing to man, as innate in his soul, all truth necessary to his proper religious development. But neither Scripture, experience, nor observation justifies this system. The notion of cause is given by this faculty, and, by implication, a first cause. But this is not a personal God. It is disputed that the notion of right and wrong given by the ethical sense, added to that of first cause, develops the notion of a personal God. If it could, the notion would violate the second criterion, and, consequently, would not be a primary truth. And yet if God is ever known, it must be through intuition that this knowledge is reached. The analysis of the human soul discloses the anomalous fact that it has a faculty for a class of ideas of which it is destitute. The only explanation of this anomaly must be found in the absence of the proper conditions under which this kind of truths is developed. The abstract notion of space can never arise in one born blind till he gazes upon objects in space.

We believe that the distinction between right and wrong arises only after intercourse with human beings in whom rights inhere. Hence the wolf-reared men found at different times in India evinced no moral sense. Now the lacking requisite for spiritual perception is the presence and illumination of the Holy Ghost in the soul. This was the natural and normal state of the unfallen man in Eden. God was immediately apprehended as a personality through a sense of his love flowing like a river through Adam's consciousness. There was an interior light, the Holy Spirit, within the human spirit. Sin extinguished that light, and the religious intuitions ceased, leaving a yearning—a painful yet ill-defined—sense of want, unrest, and forebodings of ill, sufficient to produce a blind activity of the religious nature. St. Paul has truthfully portrayed this condition: "But the natural man receiveth not the things of the Spirit, for they are foolishness unto him; neither can he know them, for they are spiritually discerned."

In marked contrast is the clear vision of the believer. " Eye hath not seen, nor ear heard, neither have entered into the heart of man, the things which God hath prepared for them that love him. But God hath revealed them unto us by his Spirit. Which things also we speak, not in the words which man's wisdom teacheth, but which the Holy Ghost teacheth, comparing spiritual things with spiritual," or, more properly, " explaining spiritual things to spiritual minds." The soul, when thus filled with the light of the Spirit, immediately apprehends the existence of God in Christ, and his great love to me, individualizing me in his regards, and also it has an intuitive conviction of immortal life. " For we *know* that if the earthly house of this tabernacle be dissolved, we have a house not made with hands, eternal in the heavens." That the person thus coming into communication with the believer in this exalted state of spiritual illumination is Jesus Christ, apprehended as the Supreme Deity, is evident from the testimony of all advanced believers. Christ stands forth before them, the chief among ten thousand, and the one altogether lovely. They speak of an ineffable joy and assurance arising from an inexpressible love to him. Their language is,

> " On Christ, the solid rock, I stand ;
> All other ground is sinking sand."

He is, as never before, the sovereign of their hearts. His divinity impresses itself upon the soul, which, despite all former doubts, now cries out, " My Lord and my God." How exactly does this experience harmonize with the Scripture, " No man can say" (truly from the heart, not dogmatically from the head) "that Jesus is the Lord, but by the Holy Ghost."

Not only does experience assert that Jesus is Lord, but the Son of God expressly assured his disciples that the Paraclete should *glorify* him, "for he shall receive of mine, and shall show it unto you."

Thus the humblest, most illiterate mind, by the exercise of perfect faith in Jesus, grasps the only key to the fortress of unbelief, the citadel of anti-Christ—modern Rationalism, the sum of whose faith, or rather unfaith, is, the only God is the Father; Jesus Christ is dead and gone in the same sense that Julius Cesar is in his grave, and influences this world only through history. That key is the immediate, intuitive knowledge of Jesus as a living and almighty Saviour, reigning within the soul without a rival. The question has been asked, whether this knowledge of Christ is independent of the testimony of the evangelists, and of the women who saw Jesus alive after his death? We reply, that their testimony is the appointed means used by the modern believer to the attainment of the end, an inward manifestation of Christ. He who climbs up the stairs leading to the dome of St. Peter's, uses every stair to increase his elevation. But he is not using every stair when he stands upon the summit of the dome, and the magnificent landscape of the Eternal City, the Campagna, the Apennines, the Albanian hills, and the Mediterranean, lie in entrancing beauty before his eyes. So faith in the statements respecting the historic Christ, constitutes the staircase up which we mount to reach the summit of Hermon, where that historic Christ is gloriously transfigured before our spiritual vision. In an important sense, the testimony of the believer of to-day is independent of the record of the evangelists, and is a new confirmation of its truth. The fact of the resurrection rests upon historic proofs. The fact that Jesus lives a king, and reigns over the believer, rests on intuitive evidence.

The contents of that assurance afforded by the spiritual perceptions are, CHRIST JESUS OUR LORD. Dogmatic truths are not discovered in their abstract form. They are concrete in Him, the Alpha and Omega—pardon, purity, life eternal. He is made unto us wisdom, sanctification, and redemption.

It remains to prove that this apprehension of Christ sustains all the tests which are the peculiar criteria of intuitive knowledge. It is *incomprehensible*. We can give no account of the rationale. It lies beyond the range of our powers. The Scriptures assert that the manifestation of Christ is by the medium of the Holy Ghost. But he himself is not apprehended. The eye does not apprehend the light, but the object manifested by the light as a medium. We do apprehend the personality of Jesus, but not that of the Divine torch-bearer who pours illumination upon the spiritual eye. The trinal distinctions of the Divine Persons is not manifested, nor their separate offices in the salvation of the soul.* Christ

---

* We do not deny that some souls have been brought into communion so intimate as to distinguish the persons of the Trinity. There is indisputable testimony on this point. The Marquis De Renty, the most spiritual mind which France has produced, professed " to carry about with him an experimental verity of the Holy Trinity." Rev. Thomas Collins, an eminently successful Wesleyan preacher, who dwelt ever on the serene summits of perfect love, whose words were thunderbolts to the hearts of sinners and worldly professors, had a similar power of discriminating between the persons of the Trinity. Hester Ann Rogers, Lady Maxwell, William Bramwell, John Smith, and Charles Perronet, intimate that they have communion with each Divine Person distinctly. We are of the opinion that these are exceptional and abnormal experiences, notwithstanding that Dr. Owen, in his quarto on Communion,

fills the vision. The source of the light in which he stands radiant is not cognized. By faith in the words of Jesus we know it is the Holy Spirit.

The knowledge has the second characteristic, *simplicity*. It cannot be resolved into constituent elements. Though concrete, it is not complex. The fullness of blessing in Christ is the fullness of an indivisible person, not of a thing separable into its elements.

The third criterion is *necessity*, and hence, *universality*. The testimony of advanced believers under the illumination of the abiding Comforter is full on this point. The non-existence of Christ's love to them is something as unthinkable as the annihilation of space.

teaches that the earliest and purest Christian ages held that this experience is attainable by all advanced believers. The Scriptures which come the nearest to a promise of such an experience are John xiv; 17, 23. It is a fair interpretation of the first that under the illumination of the Comforter, revealing and glorifying Christ in the believer's consciousness, his supreme Deity shall be demonstrated: " Then shall ye know that I am in my Father." The second text assures the believer that the Father and the Son shall come and abide with him. But to only a few is the telescopic power given to resolve this double star into two distinct orbs. To every other retina turned toward it the two appear as one.

He is to them all and in all. They find him the center of their thoughts, around which they revolve by the constraining power of his love. He fills all things, all their thoughts. Praise and prayer to him are involuntary, and unconsciously offered, even while the in-intellect and the hands are busy with the cares of life, so perfectly has Christ's personality pervaded theirs. " I will make my abode in you." The criterion of *universality* accompanies, of course, *necessity*. If a notion is necessary it must be universal. The only exception is, where the conditions of any intuitive notion do not exist. The abstract idea of space does not exist in a person who has never had eyesight.

To the trained mathematician there are intuitive truths relating to numbers and quantities which do not exist in the savage. Dr. M'Cosh teaches, that the intuitional faculty is capable of cultivation. Hence the *universality* exists wherever the proper conditions are found. It is just so with the knowledge of Christ in high Christian experience. *It is universal with those who have perfect faith in Jesus.* That a majority of the inhabitants of the world, including some great writers on mental philosophy, are destitute of this intuitive apprehension of Christ and the joyful assurance of his love, does not disprove this criterion, for the majority do not perform the conditions, they do not fully trust Christ. It gives great pleasure to state that the experience of perfect love sustains the fourth test of primary truth—*certainty*. Of nothing is the mature believer under the holy unction more certain, than he is that his Redeemer lives. Doubt, which haunted the beginning of his Christian life, has been dispelled by the rising of the Sun of Righteousness. The darkness is past, the true light now shines. He can sooner doubt the solid earth or the shining sun than his sonship to God, and joint heirship with Christ.

> " O love, thou bottomless abyss !
>   My sins are swallowed up in thee ;
> Cover'd is my unrighteousness,
>   Nor spot of guilt remains on me :
> While Jesus' blood, through earth and skies,
> Mercy, free, boundless mercy, cries."

The conclusion to which we have arrived is, that in his unfallen state, man had and fully exercised the power of intuition Godward, and

15

spiritual truth flooded his soul as the sun-beams fill the rain-drop.   Sin shrouded the soul with a pall of blackness, excluding the glorious sunlight ; but perfect faith in Jesus Christ removes the pall, and the long-lost light again fills all that spirit.   The soul, amid the intensity of this spiritual illumination, enjoys an assurance of salvation which could not be increased were that fact written by Gabriel in letters of fire across the arches of the sky.   No amount of testimony, human or angelic, can increase the certitude of the soul lit up by the presence of the Comforter.   We do not need lanterns to see the sun rise.   He brings his own self-revealing light.

§ 3. *The Spiritual Manifestation of Christ not Illusory but Real.*

I speak wisdom (philosophy) among them that are perfect.
—ST. PAUL.

There is in many minds, even among be-lievers, a grave misapprehension of the grounds of certainty with respect to spiritual things. It is tacitly conceded that there is more room for doubt with respect to Christian experience than there is in the affairs of this life.   It is

the purpose of this chapter to demonstrate
that this concession is unnecessary, and to
show that we may, under the full illumination
of the Holy Spirit, as certainly know God in
Jesus Christ as we know any facts in this
world. Let us take the fact of the existence
of an external world. Ordinary minds regard
an outer world as a certainty the highest possible for the mind to entertain. But when we
begin to look for the ground of this certainty
we find ourselves afloat on a broad sea of con-
flicting opinions on which we are so tossed
that our indisputable certainty becomes very
uncertain, and in some minds vanishes altogether.

The two grand divisions of opinion are,
1) that our consciousness of external objects is *mediate*, and, 2) that it is *immediate*.
Philosophers adhering to the first view reason
thus: The mind, imprisoned in the body,
cannot travel out óf it and grasp external objects. It must always remain in its appropriate sphere. It is conscious only of what is
taking place within itself. It is unextended,
and cannot grasp matter which has extension.
It is immaterial, and cannot lay hold of the

qualities of the material world. Yet in some way we are quite sure of an external world. But how? Here we find philosophers dividing again into two classes: 1. That there is a third thing between the material object and the immaterial mind, which constitutes the medium of perception. What this third something is, it puzzles the philosophers to tell. If it is material, it is in need of a medium itself in order to come into contact with the mind. But if it is purely immaterial, the mind in cognizing it is gaining no knowledge of matter, and hence no certainty.

2. The other way of explaining this difficulty is to assert that in perception we perceive neither the material objects nor their images, called by the ancients, " skins of things," the *media* above described, but we perceive only certain modifications of our own minds which we are perpetually mistaking for external objects. Both classes of these philosophers are Idealists. Their fundamental assumption is, that only the mind itself can be immediately known as an ultimate fact in consciousness. The logical sequence is, that the external world is a groundless and unnecessary assumption. This

is pure idealism. But some, the hypothetical Realists, who start with the same assumption, try hard to save the external world from vanishing into cloud-land by making it an *inference* from the third thing spoken of, or from the modification of itself. But an inference is not worth any thing unless certain proved premises lie back of it. In this case the logical premises are lacking, and we have no certainty of the existence of any thing external to mind. The material world is logically annihilated by the philosophy which assumes that in consciousness the *ego*, or self, is all that is immediately known. Yet this is the philosophy which is dominant in Germany to-day, and is widely prevalent throughout civilization wherever the modern school of the *natural Realists* or *natural Dualists* does not prevail.

This school, of which Sir William Hamilton is the chief, assumes that both the self, or *ego*, and the not-self, or non-*ego*, are immediately known in consciousness. This is the second grand division of philosophers. They are called Realists. Sir William Hamilton boldly enlarged the sphere of consciousness to include not only the modifications of mind, but the outward object which produces the inward change. According to him, I am not conscious of the idea of this writing desk as a third thing between the material desk and the purely spiritual mind, but I am conscious of the desk itself. Hence the Hamiltonians—a minority of these philosophers—are certain of an external world; the rest of them are either in great perplexity on this subject, or they have settled down upon the airy foundation of pure Idealism, and are content with the belief that matter is a stupendous illusion. I do not say that a majority of mankind are in this predicament, for happily the mass of the human family are not metaphysicians, they have not ventured to turn over the corner-stone of their knowledge to see what it rests upon: they have the good sense to act upon their experience of realities as natural realists, and have no difficulties with the grounds of their knowledge. We shall proceed to show that Christians act in the same way with their knowledge of spiritual realities. They are spiritual realists, those of them who have become acquainted with the Spirit of truth, or the Spirit of reality, as it might be correctly translated. We will now endeavor to show the philosophic grounds of certainty in regard to the spiritual manifestation of the Son of God to the perfect believer.

The subtle suggestion is sometimes presented that this whole matter of Christian experience is all illusory—a phenomenon of our own minds under the influence of causes wholly within itself. The thoughtful believer is sometimes annoyed by the thought that God has nothing to do with inward religious emotions—that what seems to come from without, and to move so marvelously within the soul, assuring of pardon and cleansing from sin, really arises from the hidden depths of our own mysterious nature while intently contemplating religious ideas, and that there is no manifestation of God at all as an objective existence.

To this we have two answers. In the first place, if this illusion leaves permanent beneficial effects upon the character, gives victory over sin, fills the soul with love toward God and the purest philanthropy, destroys the fear of death, and adorns and beautifies the spirit with all excellences, it is infinitely better than any reality to be found on earth, and it should be earnestly coveted and diligently sought by every person.

2. But we may know that God manifests himself in Christian experience by the testimony of consciousness—the same testimony that assures us of the existence of the external world. To demonstrate the existence of the material world, as we have shown, has been for ages " the puzzle of philosophers," as Tyndall styles it, many contending that the sphere of consciousness is limited to the operations of mind itself, and that it cannot directly cognize any thing external. The most that it can do is to infer that its sensations have an external. unknown, and forever unknowable cause. Those who. deny the correctness of this inference deny the existence of matter, and resolve it into ideas. With idealists, the *ego* only exists; the mountain, river, and plain are only so many different modifications of the *ego*, or self. At length Sir William Hamilton arose, and cut this metaphysical knot by boldly enlarging the sphere of consciousness to include the outer world. So we reply that the soul illumined by the Holy Spirit is conscious, not only of its own subjective religious exercises, but of God, their

external cause, impressing himself mysteriously upon the Spirit. In other words, we may have, when our perceptions are quickened by the Holy Spirit, the same knowledge of God as we have of the external world. Christians in advanced experience universally testify that they know God.

It is fundamental in philosophy that consciousness cannot lie. To deny this would be to nullify mental science by throwing discredit upon the source of it facts. For it is a law of evidence that one proved falsehood destroys the credibility of a witness. "*Falsus in uno, falsus in omnibus*"—false in one instance, false in all. Consciousness testifies in Christian experience that a power from without the soul enters in and subdues all things to itself, and that this power is a person, since it does the work of a person, certifies to the penitent believer his pardon, and awakens an intense love toward the worker—an affection directed toward persons only. That this person is Christ, or rather, the Holy Spirit revealing him, is also directly apprehended by our spiritual perceptions in a manner wholly inexplicable to reason. But it ought not to be strange that He who created the infant with power to interpret its mother's smile should endow the human spirit with power to recognize its Creator's presence.' But there are persons who cannot accept Sir William Hamilton's widening of the sphere of consciousness to include the external world. It is not our purpose to defend any system of philosophy. If you admit the certainty of an external world as attainable by the mind without its direct cognition by consciousness, you must assume that it is an irresistible inference from modifications of mind through sensation and external perception. In other words, the sudden pain which shoots through the nerves to the sensorium carries with it the feeling of certainty that some cause outside of the mind, some thorn or needle, is the cause of this sensation. In like manner, we argue that certainty which the Christian feels, that the changes occurring in his experience are not from some cause from within, but from without, and that this cause is not material but spiritual in its nature. We are endowed with the ability to discriminate between the objective and the subjective. If it were not so we could not distinguish our perceptions from the images of our fancy. In like manner we are enabled to discriminate between religious emotions having an objective cause, and mere subjective phantasies. Hence, advanced Christians, especially, speak with the utmost assurance of their communion with God, and of the joy of the Holy Ghost. The Christian under the full illumination of the Spirit, as certainly knows God as either the Hamiltonian or the non-Hamiltonian may know matter. Consciousness testifies to no greater certainty in the apprehension of the external world than she does in the knowledge of Christ. The direct intuition, or the inference, if it be an inference, amounts to an absolute certainty in both cases.

But we utterly despair of convincing the Idealist of the agency of God in Christian experience, since he invalidates the testimony of consciousness to the existence of any thing except the operations of his own mind. He resolves into the omnivorous *ego* the earth and sky, and the God who fills them. To attempt to prove to the Idealist the agency of God in regeneration and sanctification by assuming that he is immanent in the human soul would be only confounding the subject with the object, and affording the premises from which Pantheism, with all its disastrous moral sequences, is the logical inference. This book is written for people of common sense, who believe that consciousness attests that we live in a world of realities, and not of illusions. To such persons we would say that the field of internal Christian experience affords the groundwork for a philosophy as positive as any based upon the facts of physics or civil history. The moral and religious intuitions furnish us with utterances as authoritative as those which arise in the field of pure intellect. Of course the advocates of Positivism, and the other various forms of Materialism, will not expect the Christian to demonstrate the reality of the work of the Divine Spirit from a stand-point so low as the denial of the separate existence of the human soul, and the rejection of the Divine personality. For if the universal testimony that the *ego*, the thinking subject, is not the body, but a distinct substance, be discarded, it is scarcely reasonable to suppose that the attestations of millions of Christians to a supernatural change wrought in their consciousness, and transforming their characters, will be received by these miscalled philosophers. For that only is a genuine philosophy which recognizes all the facts in the world of mind, and constructs some rational hypothesis for their explanation. The facts for the truth of which Christian believers vouch are as stubborn as any in the domain of science. It is certainly very unscientific to refuse to put them to the test of experiment, and to discredit the testimony of the vast body of competent witnesses who had done so, with the assertion that they are deceived or deceiving.

In our reference to these systems of philosophy it is not our purpose to prove one or disprove others, but simply to show that if any of them admit a certainty of any one fact in the outer or the inner world, the facts of Christian experience are just as certainly known, resting on the same basis—the testimony of consciousness. The Christian can give just as good an account of his experimental knowledge of Jesus Christ, as the philosopher can give of his knowledge of the external world.

It is to be regretted that the writers on mental philosophy have with so great unanimity

deemed the psychology of Christian experience
unworthy their notice.* We know of no better
explanation of this fact than the absence of a
marked spiritual experience of conscious salvation in the hearts of these writers. If they had
been made conscious " partakers of the Holy
Ghost, and had tasted the powers of the world
to come," they would not have failed to describe the marvelous phenomena attendant upon
that transformation of the entire man which is
called a "translation from darkness to light, a
new creation, a resurrection from the dead."
No modification of mind is more sharply defined in the consciousness, and more tenacious-
ly grasped by the memory. Hence these religious transitions and uplifts of the soul present an attractive field for the lover of intellectual science.

Rauch, in his Psychology, has devoted a
chapter to religion, styling it "a *peculiar* activity of God in the human soul, differing
from all his other operations, by which it is
converted, renewed, and purified, by a power
which manifests itself to the consciousness,

* President Finney and Professors Upham and Mahan are
conspicuous exceptions.

needing no other light." He writes like a man of Christian experience, or like a candid philosopher who attaches importance to the testimony of multitudes who have had such an experience. But Cousin has touched upon this subject, in one of his lectures, in a far different spirit from Rauch, indicating his utter ignorance of the spiritual power of the Gospel in affecting transformations of the character. With him Christianity is not a glorious life within the soul, but a set of facts and a list of dogmas apprehended by the intellect. Cousin's fundamental error, his πρῶτον ψεῦδος, lies in this proposition : " The only faculty of knowledge is reason." All the negations of Rationalism lie folded in this acorn. The Infinite Being can never be " the direct object of love." " Such a love cannot sustain itself save by superhuman efforts, which terminate in folly." All this would be true were there no supernatural Agent to "shed abroad the love of God" in the believer's heart, and to attest directly to my soul that he loves me, even me. With an utter destitution of the spirit of true philosophy, this celebrated psychologist slurs over all Christian experience within, as the dreamy vagaries of mysticism, " chimerical and

mischievous," overlooking entirely the amazing
activities and heroic labors and sacrifices which
have made all the Christian centuries illustrious,
and none more brilliant than the missionary
century in which he lived. To refute the declaration that "reason is the only faculty of
knowledge," we quote the utterance of another
French philosopher, whose fame will outlive
that of Cousin. Pascal says, " The things of
this world must be known in order to be loved,
but Jesus Christ must be loved in order to be
known."   This is only another form of the inspired utterance of St. John, teaching that the
heart is a faculty of knowledge : "Whosoever
loveth not knoweth not God, for God is love."
As a painting is known only through the eye, a
symphony through the ear, and an odor through
the smell, so God is known only through the
heart in holy love. We may hear words about
a painting, we may read the notes of the music,
we may discourse about an odor, and we may
reason about God, but we can have a knowledge of none of them except through the appropriate faculty.

A description of Niagara awakens no emotion, but a view from beneath Table Rock

overwhelms the soul with emotions of sublimity. The cataract is now for the first time known, because the right perceptive faculty is applied. We do not *know* God when reason apprehends a first cause, and conscience demands an executive of the moral law. He may still be a nondescript impersonality. The wrong faculties are in exercise. To know him as a *person* we must know him through that department of our nature which always has a person for the object of its activity. Our affections go out only toward persons. When the heart voluntarily moves toward God in perfect love, the soul is deluged with that flood of joyful emotions which announce the advent of the personal God in the consciousness. This is the only "God-consciousness" of which we are capable. It is one thing to have notions about God, and it is quite a diffent thing to *know* him.

John Stuart Mill, the great logician and oracle of Materialism, has most signally failed in his attempt, not to invalidate the testimony of Christians, but to explain their unanimous assertion that the Holy Spirit abides within them, "to witness God's eternal love." His

16

interpretation of the experience of believers in
Christ is, " that it is neither more nor less than
ascribing outward existence to the inward creations of our own faculties—to ideas or feelings
of the mind—and believing that, by watching
and contemplating these ideas of its own making, it can read in them what takes place in
the world without."   Hence the witness of the
Spirit is, to him, an illusion, and communion
with God is a pleasing hallucination, and victory
over death through faith in Jesus is the happy
delusion of the sailor dreaming of safety while
approaching the rocks, lured by a false light.
But is Mr. Mill competent to philosophize on
this subject?   Have his spiritual intuitions
been called into activity by the quickening
Spirit?   If not, then he is reasoning as wisely
as one born blind who asserts that colors are
purely subjective, " the inward creations of our
own faculties."   So long as consciousness is
the source of all the facts of psychology, and
the basis of all correct conclusions, just so long
will one spiritually blind be incompetent either
to testify or to theorize truthfully respecting
spiritual experience !

In 1866 an operator at Valencia sat at the

end of the broken cable while search was made for the other end in the depths of the Atlantic. While he was, at midnight, intently watching the delicate magnet disturbed by the influences of the sea, suddenly the tiny spot of light flashed out the words, "God save the Queen." How many metaphysicians as great as Stuart Mill would it take to prove to that operator that this message was not from the other world, mind answering to mind in clear, majestic thought, but that it was a lucky combination of the incoherent pulsations of the sea? Just as many such philosophers will it require to prove to the new-born soul that the "Abba, Father," suddenly resounding in his soul, originates in the depths of his own nature, and that it is not the voice of Him who sitteth on the throne above and sends down assurances of pardon and adoption to penitent believers below. Mr. Mill's groundless assertion will become an argument worthy of consideration when he has demonstrated—

1. That he has had a similar Christian experience, and that it bore the marks of an origin purely subjective and internal.

2. That just such experiences arise in the

devotees of false religions when intently contemplating Buddha, Brahma, Jupiter, Woden,
Thor, or any African fetich, as are attested by
believers in Jesus Christ.

3. That these experiences are attended by
a moral transformatioñ, a victory over sin, an
assurance of the Divine favor, and an adornment of the character with the whole constellation of Christian virtues, love, joy, peace,
long-suffering, gentleness, goodness, fidelity,
meekness, and temperance.

Until these propositions are proved, Christians are not to be charged with folly for
persisting in a faith which works by love, puri-
fies the heart, overcomes the world, brings life
and immortality to light, and enables the believer to cry, " O death, where is thy sting? O
grave, where is thy victory?"

We have made the statement that the Holy
Ghost communicates no theological truth. He
adds no article to the Apostles' Creed, but he
gives reality to the truths lying cold and inop-
erative in the intellect. The vague becomes
definite, the obscure becomes clear, the distant
is brought nigh. Especially is Jesus Christ presented as a *real*, *living*, and DIVINE PERSON.

It is the great mission of the Comforter to disclose the Deity of Christ. "He shall take of mine and show unto you." If the Son of God were a creature, the Spirit of truth would reveal him as a creature. What is the universally attested fact in that high Christian experience, the conscious abiding of the Comforter? It is the manifestation of Christ as a living, loving, and almighty Saviour, able to save to the uttermost. Henceforth all speculative difficulties subside. As spiders' webs are swept away by the mighty rushing wind, intellectual objections to the Deity of Christ are wiped out by the pentecostal breath of God, the ever-blessed Spirit. This result of the coming of the Comforter to the disciples was distinctly foretold by Jesus. "At that day ye shall *know that I am in my Father.*" This immediately became the subject-matter of the Apostles' preaching. "And he hath given to us the ministry of reconciliation; to wit, that *God was (is) in Christ* reconciling the world unto himself."

It is the coming of the Comforter which is the only power that can lift the yoke of Rationalism from the skeptic's soul. Logic fails. There are in the human mind naturally strong procliv-

ities toward Unitarianism. We long to carry
our knowledge up to unity. We delight to discover τὸ ἕν in τὰ πολλὰ, the one in the many—
one principle binding up into unity many phenomena. This tendency of our minds lies at
the basis of classification and induction. If allowed its full scope in theological speculations
it ends in Deism—in plucking the crown of
Divinity from the head of Christ. Hence our
love of unity is a prolific source of error. Says
Sir William Hamilton, " To this love of unity
—to this desire of reducing the objects of our
knowledge to harmony and system—a source
of truth and discovery if subservient to observation, but of error and delusion if allowed to
dictate to observation what phenomena are to
be perceived—we may refer the influence which
preconceived opinions exercise upon our perceptions and judgments, by inducing us to see
and require only what is in unison with them.
'What we wish,' says Demosthenes, 'that we believe.' 'What we expect,' says Aristotle, 'that
we find : ' truths which have been re-echoed by a
thousand confessors and confirmed by ten thousand examples." Not only does the natural man,
devoid of spiritual illumination, strongly drift

toward Unitarian views of Christ; but the Christian Church, under high intellectual culture and low spirituality, tends in the same direction. Hence the only salvation of orthodoxy is in the baptism of the Holy Spirit—the anointing that abideth and teacheth—poured by the Divine hand upon the mass of believers. "What the world needs is not a mere teacher to communicate something *about* God, but *to know God himself* by his own personal manifestation to each heart."

This personal and loving manifestation of God to the soul required two steps: First, the incarnation, to bring God into the sphere of our sympathies in that most affecting way in which he is presented by the manger, the garden, and the cross. But born into the world a helpless infant, unfolding in physical, mental, and spiritual power under the laws of normal development, subject to the limitations and ills of humanity, his Godhead was not so conspicuous as his humanity. The Divine glory which he had with the Father before the world was, was eclipsed by the robe of clay in which it was wrapped. Only a subdued brightness gleamed through the earthly vesture. But the time came when it was expedient for Jesus to take the second step, when his deity should burst forth, a full-orbed sun upon this dark world. To this end Christ withdraws the visible, material form, in order that it may no more divert the eye from the full splendors of his Godhead (Godhood). He goes up on high and is glorified, and sends down the proof in the gift of the Comforter, whose great mission on earth is to "*glorify*," exalt, deify, the Son of God by a revelation of his divinity in the inmost consciousness of every one who loves him. This undoubted, assured knowledge of Jesus Christ as "God over all, blessed for ever," emboldened the apostles to preach, and to suffer shame joyfully, for his sake. This knowledge is described by St. John as comprising "all things." "But ye have an unction from the Holy One and ye know all things." All spiritual truth is centered in Jesus Christ. To know him by the anointing is to know "all things pertaining to life and godliness." To know Christ is to know the law, for love is the fulfilling of the law. "And ye need not that any man should teach you." The highest and most trustworthy cognitions are those of the intuitions. The logic of Aristotle and Bacon cannot reach up to this knowledge of the Divine Jesus revealed in the very sanctuary of the soul by the Holy Spirit. Gal. i, 16. We cannot agree with Dean Alford, that those strong expressions of St. John are "so many ideal statements on Christian perfection," implying that believers in his day did not "have in living and working reality what they had in the ideal depth of their Christian life." We cannot conceive of an assertion more positive and explicit of the perfect spiritual knowledge possessed by those whom he addresses in this epistle. They had what St. Paul craved for the Ephesians, "the love of Christ which passeth knowledge," or intellectual comprehension or logical statement.

CHAPTER XIV.

THE EVIDENCES OF PERFECT LOVE.

IN addition to the direct witness of the Spirit to the completeness of his work, (1 Cor. ii, 12,) we have the following corroborative evidences which may be appropriately styled the fruits of the Sanctifier :—

1. EASY VICTORY OVER SIN.—In the justified state there is victory, but after intense and painful struggles. Yet sometimes, in moments of weakness, sin takes the soul so by surprise that it is brought into condemnation. Victory on hard-fought battle-fields, with occasional defeats, is the usual experience of regenerate souls. But after the fullness of Christ's love is shed abroad in the soul, temptation greatly loses its power. An invisible shield quenches the fiery dart. The soul, surrounded by "the munitions of rocks," understands what it is to be "kept by the power of God through faith." It has but to utter, " Get thee hence, Satan," and the Tempter flees in confusion.

It may take time for the entirely sanctified person to unmask Satan, to disrobe him of the angel's robe of light. Jesus had no such necessity. His omniscient eye glanced instantaneously through all disguises. But the souls of men, though they are all aglow with love to God, have no such intuitive insight into the moral character of all acts. They must fall back upon their judgments. Abstract right may be an intuition, and, at the same time, right in an act may require careful deliberation or application of the reasoning faculty. This may cause delay and anxiety to know the path of duty, but no struggle to overcome inward antagonists to perfect rectitude. Just here is a good place to explain the singular phenomenon of two perfectly sanctified persons, like Paul and Barnabas, disagreeing in their conclusions. Their judgments of what is expedient differ, while both are actuated by perfect love to God and man. The impulse toward the known right is equally strong in both. They would die at the stake before they would swerve from the purpose of righteousness. But their original intellectual capacities, education, and circumstances, which all have an influence upon their judgment, differ so greatly that they innocently arrive at widely different conclusions. This accounts for the fact, that professors of entire sanctification are sometimes severely criticized by non-professors of this grace for doing deeds which the superior moral training of their critics would not let them do. For instance, the laws of one country may not regard as property the fruits growing wild in the field. The appropriation of such is as free to all as the sunshine and the rain. Another country may define such fruits as the property of the land-owner, and punish the unlawful appropriation as theft. An emigrant from the former land to the latter, though perfectly upright in his purposes and holy of heart, might without apostasy be convicted of theft unwittingly committed. Here is the appropriate field for the charity that "thinketh no evil." It was possible by Divine grace for Abraham to obey the command, "Walk thou before me, and be perfect," while it would have been impossible, even with God's help, to walk before men and be perfect in their estimation.

2. ONENESS WITH CHRIST.—The advocates of an advanced Christian experience insist, with

great unanimity, that there is a well-defined
line separating it from the former Christian
life. We are often called on to state the
specific difference—to draw the line between
these two religious states; hence the attempts
to discriminate between the new birth and
entire sanctification are some of them conclu-
sive, and others unsatisfactory. We are not
whetting our theological razor to assist at this
hair-splitting; we need less theorizing and
more exemplification—less dogma and more
experience.

Are there men and women now on earth
living the so-called "higher life?" There
are saints treading the earth day by day, vic-
tors over the world and sin, "dead indeed
unto sin," and "free indeed" from its very indwelling. It was not so with their former
Christian state. Can they tell us what is the
most conspicuous line running through their
consciousness, separating these experiences?
The unanimous testimony is, that it is a
sense of oneness with Christ, contrasting most
strongly with the former feeling of duality, or
twoness, if we may coin a Saxon word, instead
of borrowing from the Latin. We have heard

of a converted Indian who came to the missionary one day in great distress, saying, "There are two Indians inside of me—a good and a bad." He expressed what all Christians feel in their initial spiritual life. There is a painful distraction. The secret is, that self is still alive, and disputing with Christ the throne of the soul. Self has not learned the difficult lesson of perfect and joyful submission. There is an inward schism between the spiritual and carnal forces. The prayer of the psalmist has not been offered in faith, "Unite my heart to fear thy name."

Octavius, who had been a triumvir, thought it for the interest of peace that the world should have but one ruler, and, styling himself Augustus, he became that ruler by the defeat of Mark Antony. It was found that a three-men power, or a two-men power, only provoked strife. It is certainly for your soul's peace, my dear reader, that you should henceforth have but one sovereign. The one-man power is what you need—the God-man. Which will you have for your king? Jesus, or the Barabbas of Self? Which will bring in genuine, eternal peace? The Prince of Peace. He is able to dethrone and extinguish self as a foe to his reign.

"But can I not have perfect peace under his rival?" Yes, but not till Jesus is banished from his realm, and the Holy Ghost, his representative, has withdrawn, and conscience, God's vicegerent in the soul, has been dethroned. Then you would have the awful blessing of peace—the alarming tranquillity which presages the earthquake—the peace of an unwaking, endless stupor. Endless? No; death will dispel it, and set the worm, remorse, to gnaw forever. Do not, my Christian friend, try this way to peace. Jesus, the great peacemaker, is in thy heart, and offers to establish your perfect peace on an eternal foundation. He wishes to rule supreme; he has been thrust aside by self, and with sorrow has he protested against the usurpation of another, knowing the miseries to which you will be reduced. You may not be distinctly conscious of a power in you, rivaling and antagonizing the Lord Jesus; you have lived so long in the atmosphere of self that you do not recognize its presence. The hidden self will come forth from his hiding-place into the sunlight if you begin in earnest and in detail to consecrate all to Christ. You will hear a plea for this little self-indulgence, for that small interest to be untouched by King Jesus; you will find a shrinking back from giving him full range through your whole being; he may uncover some secret idol.

That shrinking, dear reader, is self. You don't feel the shrinking now, because you are not earnestly attempting entire consecration. You are enjoying a kind of false peace. Self has sent a flag of truce to Christ, not intending an unconditional surrender, but a compromise. "Immanuel may reign over all my being, with certain trifling exceptions. I think that my sense of propriety is a little superior to his, therefore I wish to reserve the privilege of self-direction in some matters wherein others, by blindly following Christ's directions, have lost the good opinion of some cultivated people, and even made themselves unpopular. Then, again, there are certain principles of commercial morality which tend more directly to wealth than the high and impracticable ethics of the Sermon on the Mount. I always deemed it unfortunate for the success of Jesus

Christ's moral code that he had not a business education—that he had not worked his way up from a journeyman carpenter to a master builder, and become a millionaire by his shrewd management. He never rose in business because he was an impractical theorizer. Hence, there are some points in which his ethics have become a little obsolete : at any rate, almost every body thinks so, and there must be some good ground for their opinion ; therefore, it is not prudent to submit without reservation to his will ; it is not the short cut to riches nor to honors."

To the reader who has not been made perfectly one with Christ in will and desire, let me say, If you lay your ear close to the lips of Self, and listen to his soliloquy, you will find such whisperings of distrust respecting Jesus, whom you have theoretically acknowledged as "God over all, and blessed for evermore," and invited to dwell in your hearts, and exercise a general oversight over you. Alas, the number of such Christians is not small. They are the majority in nearly all our Churches. They are good and conscientious, and in the main dutiful, and are limping along toward

17

heaven. The great defect in their experience is, that they are not completely one with Christ. There are points on which they cannot trust him; he is held back from completing his own ideal in their lives, because they interfere and insist on the alteration of his plans. He does not abandon them, but continues working, sad to see his own splendid and perfect plan marred by the impertinent antagonism of Self. The consummation which he most devoutly wishes, is to see this officious intermeddler nailed to his cross. The crucifixion of Self is the painful birth of the soul to the higher life —the life of perfect oneness with Christ. He who has entered into this rest will find the most difficult petition in the Lord's prayer—— "thy will be done"—the easiest for the tongue to utter.

3. Hence THERE IS NO APPREHENSION OF FUTURE ILL, and there is perfect contentment with our providential circumstances. We rejoice evermore, pray without ceasing, and in every thing give thanks. We thank God for our disappointments, not before they come, because we do not know then that they are in the will of God. But when they are thus

known, the soul which is in full trust receives them joyfully.

> " Ill that He blesses is our good ;
>   Unblessed good is ill ;
> And all is right which seemed most wrong,
>   If it be his sweet will."

4. INSATIABLE DESIRE TO COMMUNICATE THE LOVE OF CHRIST TO UNBELIEVERS and to imperfect believers, with corresponding efforts to convince them of sin, and bring them to Christ. The anointed soul has full sympathy with David Brainerd, the missionary : " I long to be a flame of fire continually glowing in the divine service, preaching and building up Christ's kingdom to my latest, my dying hour." This desire springs up in the experience of pardon, but it does not become a passion inflaming all the soul like a mighty furnace, till love fills its utmost capacity. The feet of Jesus were ever hasting toward lost men. His mighty heart was ever yearning over the spiritually blind and dead. It is natural that the fullness of love to Christ should bring us into sympathy with this dominant passion of his holy soul, and that our footsteps should ever after be toward the perishing. There is a grave

mistake somewhere when a person imagines
that he has mounted up to the plane of the
"higher life" and feels no quickened impulse
toward sinners dying in their sins around him.
That ecstasy of delight must be spurious which
inclines its possessor to sit still and selfishly enjoy the raptures of divine love, instead of going forth to communicate and widely diffuse
the joy.

5. INCREASED BENEFICENCE, ENLARGED LIB-
ERALITY, inevitably follow the blessing of perfect love.   The purse must be consecrated to
the advancement of Christ's kingdom when the
heart becomes the abode of the Sanctifier.
But it must not be expected that there will be
an indiscriminate outpouring of our money to
all good causes.   The judgment will still be exercised in determining the best channel through
which our benefactions may be poured.   Some
may magnify the importance of Christian education, while others may deeply feel the wants
and woes of the pagan world.   One may reserve all his gifts for the poor, and another
be inclined to schemes of Church extension.
Now if this diversity of generous impulses does
not find expression secretly in obedience to

the directions of our Saviour, there is afforded ample occasion for misjudging one another in respect to our liberality. Hence, groundless complaints have been made against some of the holiest persons. It is not to be expected that we shall all see alike in these matters. Here is the appropriate field for that charity which " hopeth all things."

6. AN ASTONISHING INSIGHT INTO THE HOLY SCRIPTURES and a daily HUNGER for the word of life. Gospel truth ceases to be vague and shadowy. It becomes real. A mysterious power unvails its meaning, and applies it to the soul. There is a voice within which attests the objective truth. An invisible interpreter attends the reading of the sacred page, and " we discover wonders in God's law." These new beauties, unfolding evermore, so commend themselves to our hearts—they yield us so much strength and comfort—that we are never again troubled with doubts of the inspiration of the Bible. The hungry man, when he finds bread that perfectly satisfies and nourishes him, has no difficulty with the sophistry which would prove that it was made of chaff and not of wheat. The higher life takes root

in the deeper knowledge of God's word. It lives by every word which proceedeth out of the mouth of God. Its possessor becomes a *homo unius libri*, a man of one book. Elegant literature, though sparkling with rhetorical gems, affords no more nutriment to such a soul than the frostwork on the window satisfies the cravings of the wearied laborer. He may occasionally read Dickens or Scott, just as he may, for a few moments, look upon the beautiful tracery of the frost artist, but he feeds on the Gospel of the Son of God. The novelists and airy poets become more and more dusty on his shelves, while the Bible becomes more and more soiled and worn.

7. The IMPULSE TO CHRISTIAN ACTIVITY has changed from DUTY to DELIGHT. " I will *run* the way of thy commandments when thou shalt enlarge my heart." Instead of dragging himself to duty, there is a free, spontaneous impulse moving him to render with gladness any possible service to his Master, not from fear of the law, but from love to the Lawgiver. There is a point between the earth and the moon where gravitation changes. A projectile from earth, passing that point into the superior at

traction of the moon, freely moves to meet it with ever-increased velocity. Thus the believer, lifted by the power of the Holy Spirit out of the attraction of the world, under the stronger attraction of Christ, gravitates upward. He no longer needs a whip and spurs to urge him, but the magnetism of love draws him sweetly, yet mightily, onward toward the King in his beauty.

> " Sink down, ye separating hills ;
>   Let sin and death remove ;
>   'Tis love that drives my chariot wheels,
>   And death must yield to love."

8. HUMILITY IS MARVELOUSLY INCREASED. Pride, the primal sin and last to surrender, is extinguished. Love made perfect humbles the soul to the dust. When the Comforter makes his abode in us, our language is, " Lord, what is man, that thou art mindful of him ? and the son of man, that thou visitest him ? I am not worthy of the least of thy mercies. I am dust and ashes." Yet Satan may take advantage of this very humility to tempt the soul to a more subtle, yet more baneful kind of pride—spiritual pride. He will sooner or later suggest, " You are a peculiar favorite of heaven, few are so

highly blessed, it is very proper that you should put a corresponding estimate upon yourself. You ought to prize yourself for what you really are." The presentation of such a temptation is no proof that the person does not love God with all his heart. But to yield to this suggestion is certainly to cast one down from the pinnacle of perfect love.

9. A CHRONIC FAITH. I use this word *chronic* to distinguish the abiding faith attending this blessing from the evanescent and spasmodic faith in lower states of experience. The one is the continuous flow of a fountain sending up its steady and copious stream, the other is the intermittent gush of the suction pump, ceasing when the force is no longer applied. In the one the divine element is predominant, in the other the human. Humanity is always inconstant. God is a changeless, perennial stream of power. It was of the continuity of this faith inwrought by the Holy Spirit poured out after Jesus should be glorified, that he spake, when, standing in the temple, he cried, " If any man thirst, let him come unto me, and drink. He that believeth on me, out of his in-most soul shall flow rivers of living water." All

his victories, all his graces, all his activities, all
his beneficences, and all his testimonies, are
rivers pouring forth from this well-spring of un-
dying faith. In the justified state faith frequently gives way to doubt, but in the state of
entire sanctification doubt is permanently excluded. Hence, from the prominence of this
fact, the experience is denominated by some,
the full assurance of faith.

10. JOY AND POWER are usual fruits of this
blessing. But the joy may be intermittent,
and the degree of power may not be productive of marvelous effects in the estimation of
man. Great apparent success may not attend
our efforts. From some persons the fruits of
their labors are wisely hidden in this life. But
no loving soul is powerless in the sight of God.
Measured by human standards, ministers with
very little faith, and some with no grace at all,
have been the apparent instruments in the
promotion of great revivals; whereas the great
day will disclose the secret spring of that power in the closet of some obscure, yet fully
consecrated believer, whose public utterance
seemed to fall powerless from a stammering

A transitory joy may exist where the heart is not fully purged. A perfectly holy soul may, from the influence of the mortal body, be at times devoid of rapturous joy. Hence, this is not an infallible evidence of entire sanctification.

11. A VIVID RECOLLECTION OF THE SUCCESSIVE STEPS. "If your soul has passed the barrier between you and this full salvation, my dear brother, you can mark the period when your inward corruptions were a burden intolerable to be borne; when you desired deliverance from them more than any thing besides; when you resolved, in the strength of God, to seek this great salvation; when it began to appear near at hand; when you were able to consider it as present, and claim it as your own. You can recollect the revolution which then took place in the whole train of your views and feelings. How gloriously resplendent appeared the character of God, the cross of Christ, the way of holiness! How easy it was to believe, to love, to obey; how small you seemed to yourself; how worthless all your best performances; how the world receded from your view, and heaven and glory appeared

to come down to earth; how you desired that this heavenly state might be the common privilege of all Christians, and how you immediately began to talk of the great things God had done for you." *

Reader, does this mirror your experience?

* Peck's Christian Perfection.

CHAPTER XV.

TESTIMONY.

"I testify the Gospel of the grace of God."—St. Paul.

A PHILOSOPHER has said, "The experience of our rational being is of interest to all who become cognizant of it." This is because we are so constituted as to be similarly affected by like causes. Let half a dozen of persons, far gone with pulmonary consumption, publish to the world their complete cure by the same remedy, and the glad news would flash across the continents and beneath the seas, irradiating with hope myriads of sick chambers. Hence the value of testimony. Justice, in her walk through the earth, leans upon this staff. The entire science of medicine and art of healing have been founded upon it. The pharmacopœia has been filled through the attestations of cures. Who can better authenticate the healing than the healed patient? Who better than the cleansed soul can certify his spiritual transfiguration, and the power by which it was accomplished?

Experience is one of the chief elements of evangelical power. On critical occasions St. Paul, the master logician, when liberty, or even life, hung on the balance of a Roman governor's will, and some most persuasive argument was needed, told the simple story of his conversion from being a persecutor to a preacher of the faith he once destroyed. In fact, his commission, three times renewed, was not to preach but to testify. "When the omnipresent Jesus," as Bishop Simpson graphically describes him, "standing as picket-guard for the little Church at Damascus," took Saul of Tarsus prisoner, he said to him, " I have appeared unto thee for this purpose, to make thee a minister and a *witness* both of these things which thou hast seen, and of those things in the which I will appear unto thee." Ananias assured him that he should be a "*witness* unto all men;" and years afterward, while slumbering in the castle of Antonia, a prisoner, the Lord Jesus stood by him and said, "Be of good cheer, Paul, for as thou hast *testified* of me in Jerusalem, so must thou bear *witness* also at Rome."

Testimony is the most cogent argument. A herald is useful to make proclamation of the law, and of the will of the court, but, make way! here comes one more important to the ends of justice—an unimpeachable witness. All jurists tell us that one word of authentic evidence outweighs ten thousand words of professional pleading. The witness must speak, the plea may be dispensed with. The testimony can go to the jury without the argument, but it will be folly to send the argument without the testimony. We fear the modern Christian Church is making this sad blunder, when, respecting the question of full salvation in this life, she listens more attentively to the speculations of theorizers than to the declarations of witnesses attesting that Jesus is a complete Saviour.

It is not often, as we know, that the witness and the advocate are, in our courts, combined in the same person. But all jurors know how much more weighty are an advocate's words, when, summoned from the bar to the witness-stand, he, with uplifted right hand, solemnly swears to the facts. There is now no professional quibbling, no insincere and cunning speech. O if every Christian pulpit could be for only one Sunday converted from

an advocate's stand to a witness box, and each
anointed preacher should say, "Come, and hear,
all ye that fear God, and I will declare what
he hath done for my soul," what a stir there
would be in the unbelieving world! We verily
believe that they would give the verdict of
truth to the Man of Calvary, "and falling down
would acknowledge that God is with us of a
very truth." The great want of the age is a
witnessing Church and ministry. The want
lying back of this is something to speak of—
an overwhelming visitation of the Divine Spirit.
"The Church of Christ, as it is visible in the
world, exhibits nowadays much of the aspect
worn by the nation of the Jews in the time of
our Saviour; there is, with an almost universal
profession of Christianity, much Sadducean
infidelity and licentiousness, as well as much
Pharisaic display and outside godliness. It is
only a few who, in hope of being like the Lord
at his appearing, are now purifying themselves,
as He is pure. There has been a great falling
away from the faith—from the living, world-
conquering faith. The nut-shell of orthodoxy
remains, but the kernel of vital godliness has
shrunk almost into a thing of naught. Indi-

vidual and local revivals testify that the gift
of the Spirit has not been withdrawn from the
Church; but the gift was made to the Church
as a whole, and has not the Church *as a whole*
resisted, and grieved, and well-nigh quenched
the Spirit?"*   To awaken and quicken the
whole Church, every anointed soul is called to
testify with tongue and pen to the reality of
the Divine anointing, attainable now by all
who seek for it with the whole heart, trusting
in the promise of the Father for the mighty
outpouring of the Holy Spirit.   In all humility,
and solely for the glory of Christ, the marvelous work of the Holy Spirit is put on record.
Surely he who has had this experience has
been led by a way which he knew not!   But
the path is known now, and the retraced foot-
prints may encourage some desponding soul :—

> " Footprints that perhaps another,
>   Sailing o'er life's stormy main,
>   A forlorn and shipwrecked brother,
>   Seeing, may take heart again."

In November, 1870, a college professor, after
an earnest and persistent struggle, entered into
a spiritual enlargement utterly inconceivable

* Memoir of Hewitson.

before, a permanent spiritual exaltation and fullness which found an outlet through tongue and pen. Distant friends were notified by private letters. One of these was addressed to Gilbert Haven, editor of "Zion's Herald," who assumed to publish it to the world with an editorial preface, entitling it, THE FULL-NESS OF BLESSING. The preface by the editor is retained :—

" Much is said about the Higher Life ; less is felt of its great fullness. An experience is worth a thousand theories. The following letter, written for private eyes, is worthy of note as a testimony to this Divine filling of the soul by the Holy Ghost. The writer is one of the first scholars and writers in the Church, holding high official position in one of her colleges, a man of great sobriety of temper and evenness of character. He has been a steadfast, devout Christian for many years. An anthracite coal he would be called by all his acquaintances. An anthracite coal on fire this letter shows him to be. Many who are incredulous as to the possibility of such experiences would not doubt the credibility of this witness, nor should it be doubted of many others.

13

"That there is a Pauline experience of the heights and depths of grace divine, that the Holy Ghost can now fall on the believer in fullness of power, it is impossible to doubt in the face of multitudinous testimony from all ages and branches of the Church. May this experience win many to a like consecration of faith and power. The familiarity of its style arises from its privacy. It will not make it any the less attractive. There is also a deprecatory vein as to past experience and efforts which his many admirers will not accept as quite the fact, his word having often been with power.—*Ed.*

"'I have experienced a most marvelous manifestation of the love of Christ to me. O the unsearchable riches of Christ! Do you know how unspeakably precious Jesus is when you trust him fully? My experience was never marked. I never could tell the day of my conversion. My evidence was chiefly an inference, rarely the direct testimony of the Spirit. Hence my utterances have been feeble and destitute of power. But all this is gone by. God has so certified this blessed Gospel to my soul, that I shall no more blow the trumpet with an uncertain sound.

"'Rev. Mr. Earle spent four days here a month ago. The spirit of his preaching, and his success, and his remarks at his farewell on what he styles "the rest of faith," set me thinking and praying, and confessing the coldness of my heart, and my satisfaction in past days with the mere perfunctory performance of Christian duty. I began to pray for the baptism of the Spirit to enable me to carry on the revival which has broken out in the village. God answered my prayer most graciously. I am at times so overwhelmed with the love of God that I cannot stand the pressure on the earthen vessel, and have to beg God to stay his hand.

"'The joy is indescribable. I am a free man in Christ Jesus—"free indeed;" free from the fear of man. I can approach any person anywhere. I am free in my utterance. My mouth is opened, my heart is enlarged toward sinners. I can't help preaching. As the boy said of the whistle, "It whistles itself." Every body is astonished at the complete and wonderful transformation through which I have passed. There is a new meaning to the hymns of Charles Wesley—especially

to " Wrestling Jacob," which I always admired
æsthetically, but was never in experimental
sympathy with.   O how real the promises are!
I have been treating them like our irredeem-
able greenbacks, not representing gold to-day,
but payable in coin at some indefinite future
time.   I have found out, to my unspeakable
joy, that God never has suspended specie pay-
ment; that behind every word of promise
there is gold coin in the treasury of heaven.

"'I can't interpret the blessing; whether
it is the second or third, it certainly is the
greatest that I ever received.   IT STAYS.   It
is very strange that my mouth should be
filled with laughter, and my tongue with
praises—the coolest and least demonstrative
man in the Methodist Episcopal Church.

"'Last Thursday, November 17, I think I
went where Paul did when he heard things not
lawful, not possible to utter.   My whole being, soul and body, was pervaded with the indescribable joy of the Holy Spirit.   The nervous sensations were delicious, a thousandfold
more than any I ever experienced before.   I believe that on that day—though the Divine influence had been descending for two weeks—my

great Joshua brought me in, and allotted me a
portion in the mountain of God. If I should
derive my theology from my feelings I should
have to adopt one of the five points of Calvin,

" But this I do find,
We two are so joined
He'll not live in glory and leave me behind."

" ' The same feeling appears in " Wrestling
Jacob ; " after his victory he exclaims :—

" Nor *have I power from Thee to move ;*
Thy nature and Thy name is Love." ' "

This private letter, published anonymously,
having been ascribed to another, who would
have the ungracious task of disowning a work
of grace unless the author should avow himself, made it necessary to publish the following
CHRISTIAN EXPERIENCE :—

" I have been content with a daily confession with the mouth, and private letters to my
friends, carefully refraining from any appearance of seeking to be lionized in the public
prints. But my friends urge me to run this
risk for the strengthening of my brethren in
this age, when a subtle skepticism respecting
Christian experience is poisoning and paralyz-
ing myriads of professed followers of Christ.

At my conversion, thirty years ago, through
weakness of faith, the seal of my justification
was impressed so slightly, that the word Abba,
my Father, was scarcely legible ; yet, in answer
to a mother's prayers in my infancy, consecrating with conscious acceptance her son to the
Christian ministry, I was called to preach, but
called with a ' woe unto me,' instead of an
' anointing with the oil of gladness.'   I will not
dwell upon the unpleasant theme of a ministry
of twenty years almost fruitless in conversions
through a lack of an unction from the Holy
One.   My great error was in depending on the
truth alone to break stony hearts.   The Holy
Spirit, though formally acknowledged and invoked, was practically ignored.   My personal
experience during much of this time consisted
in

> ' Sorrows, and sins, and doubts, and fears,
> A howling wilderness.'

But an evangelist extraordinary power to awak-
en slumbering professors and to bring sinners
to the foot of the cross, came across my path.
I sought to find the hidings of his power, and
discovered that it was the fullness of the Holy
Spirit enjoyed as an abiding blessing, styled by

him 'the rest of faith.' I was convicted. I
sought earnestly the same great gift, but could
not exercise faith till I had made public confession of my sin in preaching self more than
Christ, and being satisfied with the applause of
the Church above the approval of her Divine
Head. I immediately began to feel a strange
freedom daily increasing, the cause of which I
did not distinctly apprehend. I was then led
to seek the conscious and joyful presence of
the Comforter in my heart.

"Having settled the question that this was
not merely an apostolic blessing, but for all
ages, 'He shall abide with you forever,' I took
the promise, 'Verily, verily, I say unto you,
whatsoever ye shall ask the Father in my
name, He will give it you.' The '*verily*' had
to me all the strength of an oath. Out of
the '*whatsoever*' I took all temporal blessings,
not because I did not believe them to be
included, but because I was not then seeking them. I then wrote my own name in
the promise, not to exclude others, but to be
sure that I included myself. Then writing
underneath these words, 'To-day is the day
of salvation,' I found that my faith had three

points to master: *the Comforter; for me; now.*
Upon the promise I ventured with an act of
appropriating faith, claiming the Comforter
as my right in the name of Jesus.   For several
hours I clung by naked faith, praying and repeating Charles Wesley's hymn,—

> 'Jesus, thine all-victorious love,
> Shed in *my* heart abroad.'

I then ran over in my mind the great facts in
Christ's life, especially dwelling upon Gethsemane and Calvary; his ascension, priesthood, and all-atoning sacrifice.   Suddenly I
became conscious of a mysterious power exert-
ing itself upon my sensibilities.   My physical
sensations, though not of a nervous temperament, in good health, sitting alone and calm,
were like those of electric sparks passing
through my bosom with slight but painless
shocks, melting my hard heart into a fiery
stream of love.

"Christ became so unspeakably precious that
I instantly dropped all earthly good—reputation, property, friends, family, every thing—in
the twinkling of an eye, my soul crying out,—

> 'None but Christ to me be given,
> None but Christ in earth or heaven.'

He stood forth as *my* Saviour, all radiant in his loveliness, "chiefest among ten thousand." Yet there was no phantasm, or image, or uttered word, apprehended by my intellect. The affections were the sphere of this wonderful phenomenon, best described as 'the love of God shed abroad in the heart by the Holy Ghost.' It seemed as if the attraction of Jesus, the loadstone of my soul, was so strong that my heart would be drawn out of my body, and through the college window by which I was sitting, and upward into the sky. O how vivid and real was all this to me! I was more certain that Christ loved me than I was of the existence of the solid earth and shining sun. I intuitively apprehended Christ.

" My college class were just then discussing the subject of the intuitive cognitions. I began to apply Sir William Hamilton's tests of these, namely, that they are simple, incomprehensible, necessary, and universal. The last adjective, of course, could not apply to the intuitive belief of one individual, though subsequent observation abundantly demonstrates that all believers who fulfill the conditions required for awakening the spiritual perceptions have the

same intuition of Christ.* But my consciousness testified that my certainty of Christ's love
had the three first-named characteristics, that it
was to me even a necessary truth, the contrary of
which was as unthinkable as the annihilation of
space. The last remarkable peculiarity remained
more than forty days, after which I had hours in
which I could conceive the contrary of the proposition, ' Christ loves me.' On such occasions
my firm conviction of his love was not an intuition, but an inference from my past experience, together with the absence of any feeling
of condemnation. I no longer doubt Wesley's
doctrine of the direct witness of the Spirit as
distinct from the testimony of my spirit dis-
cerning the fruits of the Spirit and inferring his
presence and work. I cannot to this day read
the promises without feeling a sudden but delightful shock of an invisible power sweetly ap-
plying them to my heart.

"Thus much I think is due to those who would
study this manifestation of the Spirit from the
stand-point of theology and mental philosophy,
a point of view I myself have often wished that
remarkable experiences could be seen from. But

* See chapter on the Psychology of Christian Assurance.

language is wholly inadequate to express a manifestation of Christ which did not formulate itself in words, but in the mighty, overwhelming pulsations of love. The joy for weeks was unspeakable. The impulse was irresistible to speak of it to every body, saint or sinner, Protestant or Papist, in public and in private. At the time of this writing, seven weeks from the first manifestation, the ecstasy has subsided into a delicious and unruffled peace, rising into ecstasy only in acts of especial devotion. I find no fear of man, nor of death. I can no longer accuse myself of unbelief, the root of all sin. What may be in me, below the gaze of consciousness, I do not know. I must wait till occasions shall put me to the test. It would not be wise for me to assert that all sinful anger—there is a righteous anger—is taken away till I have passed through a college rebellion, or something equally provoking. If sin consists only in active energies, I am not conscious of such dwelling in me. If sin consists in a state, as some with truth assert when they describe original sin, I infer that I am not in such a state, from the absence of sinful energies flowing therefrom, and more especially from the indwelling of the Holy Spirit. This has been accompanied with such a feeling of inward cleanness, that I doubt not that the Purifier has taken up his abode in the temple of my heart. But the direct testimony of the heavenly Guest is *love*, LOVE, all-consuming LOVE, flaming in the heart of Jesus—*love to me*. I feel that sin cannot abide the flames of this furnace kindled to such an intensity about me. If others should insist that it is the direct witness of entire holiness, I could not dispute the assertion, so assured am I, beyond a doubt, that, by the grace of Jesus Christ, I have lived to see the death of the old man, the extinction of ' all filthiness of the flesh and spirit.'

" My personal friends do not need to be informed that the doctrine of entire sanctification, as a specialty, has not been my hobby, but rather my abhorrence, in consequence of the imperfect manner in which it has been inculcated and exemplified. Hence, if there is any thing in this experience confirmatory of that doctrine as a distinct work, considering my former attitude toward this subject, my testimony is something like that of Saul of Tarsus to the truth of Christianity. If I have any advice to give

to Christians, it is to cease to discuss the sub-
tleties and endless questions arising from entire sanctification or Christian perfection, and
all cry mightily to God for the baptism of the
Holy Spirit. This is certainly promised to all
believers in Jesus.

" O that every minister and layman would inquire the way to the upper room in Jerusalem,
and there abide till tongues of fire flame from
their heads ! "

After walking in this marvelous light for the
space of a year, the following testimony of
the same person was published in order to
magnify the grace of our blessed Lord Jesus
and the power of the Holy Spirit.

A YEAR WITH THE COMFORTER.

" If ' the greatest debtor to grace may speak
first,' I arise to testify to the unsearchable
riches of Christ, and to the ' rapturous height
of that holy delight,' which the abiding Comforter bestows upon me, even me. It is a
year this blessed 17th of November since

'Down from on high the blessed Dove
Did come into my breast,
To witness God's eternal love—
This is my constant feast.'

"Such an anniversary cannot be permitted to pass by without the grateful erection of a stone of help, a monument of praise to God, 'a spectacle unto angels and to men.' So glorious was the visitation of the Spirit, and so joyful was my soul while entertaining the carrier dove of heaven, bearing the glad evangel of Christ's boundless, fathomless love, that both tongue and pen were kept busy in spreading the ineffable joy. That testimony seems to require another, lest any person, from my silence, may suppose that the fire then kindled has quickly burned out, like a basket of shavings, and left me in darkness.

"There is another reason why I wish to reappear for a moment on Christ's public witness-stand. The 'new departure' which the doctrine of full salvation has recently taken, is remarkable for the prominence which it gives to testimony, to the exclusion of speculative theories. The movement so providentially and powerfully begun will lose its momentum just in proportion as it becomes disputatious, and substitutes wrangling for witnessing.

"Never before were there so many believers, of every denomination, honestly and earnestly

calling for light on the subject of the higher
life. Therefore, let every one who has a
heaven-lit torch now lift it high, and keep it
aloft, that all may see the light and rejoice
therein. 'Blessed be God, even the Father of
our Lord Jesus Christ, the Father of mercies,
and the God of all comfort, who comforteth
us in all tribulation, that we may be able to
comfort them which are in any trouble, by
the comfort wherewith we ourselves are comforted of God.' Let there be laid before the
Church, especially before souls panting after
'all the fullness of God,' the exact transcript
of each Christian consciousness under the illumination of the Holy Ghost, so far as language
can be a vehicle of that which 'passeth knowledge,' and not only will souls in trouble be
comforted, but there will be accumulated a
mass of facts out of which some analytic
mind—some theological Sir William Hamilton—may do what all systemizers have hith-
erto failed to do, construct out of the Bible
and experience a consistent and symmetrical
science of Christian perfection.

" When preconceived theories modify testimony, its value is proportionally diminished.

This serious defect inheres in the statements of many, who, under a dogmatic bias, have unconsciously shaped their expressions to suit the demands of a supposed orthodox ideal. I suppose that it is not possible for me to divest myself entirely of the influence of opinions, and to detail in unmixed purity the changes which the transforming Spirit has wrought in my consciousness. Of this the reader may be assured, that as a witness on a most important question I will endeavor to speak the truth, the whole truth, and nothing but the truth. Let him who values his theories more than the truth, not expect me to color my statements to suit the complexion of his opinions.

"In some important particulars my recent experience contradicts my own lifelong beliefs. Sharply defined transitions after regeneration, sudden uplifts in the divine life, had been excluded from my creed as unphilosophical and unnecessary. I had never, though I had read such things in Christian biography, really believed it possible for a soul to tabernacle on earth a whole year without a cloud, or a doubt, or a temptation, other than an occasional momentary thrust of the adversary, easily parried

with the shield of faith. Twelve months ago
I should have received with utter incredulity
the statement that any one could utter, mentally or orally, a doxology to Jesus three hundred and sixty-five days long, with no inter-
mission save that of sleep, and that balmy
sleep itself would often flee from the presence
of a sweeter delight, the luxury of praise. I
find my mistake corrected, that the witness of
the Spirit, in its higher manifestations, is intermittent. The reverse is true. It is intermittent in its lower manifestations; in its
highest it is constant. All the philosophies I
find at fault in the assertion that the human
mind cannot endure the strain of high joy for
a long period; and that the more intense, the
more evanescent it is.

"I have from the first moment till this hour
been impressed with the permanence of this
blessing, as if a ceaseless fountain had been
opened in my soul. See John iv, 14; vii, 38, 39.
The voice of Jesus to my inward ear is:—

> ' Mine is an unchanging love,
> Higher than the heights above,
> Deeper than the depths beneath,
> Free and faithful, strong as death.'

19

"Whatever this confidence may be called—whether the full assurance of faith or the full assurance of hope—as defined by Wesley in Tyerman's Life, vol. ii, page 491, I am convinced that it is attainable by all, though not necessary to saving faith. God has reserved to himself the prerogative of doing "exceeding abundantly above all that we ask or think" in the outpouring of his wondrous love, and the exhibition of the exceeding greatness of his power to us-ward who believe."

"I have been catechised respecting the mental state, or act, immediately previous to the coming of the Comforter, whether there was a specific act of faith. I reply, that my soul had been for three weeks the furnace of intense desire, and it had been during that period in the attitude of trust. I was, at the moment preceding the great blessing, reviewing Christ's earthly life, and noting the grounds of faith which it affords, as I had often done before. I did not at that time put forth a distinct and specific energy of faith differing from that attitude of voluntary trust, in which I had been for several days.

"I am convinced that a hungry, longing, ear-

nest soul, in the general attitude of trust, may
be surprised, as I myself was, by the sudden
unction of the Holy One. At no time did I
believe that I received the desired blessing till
I knew that it was mine. The promise in Mark
xi, 24, was not opened to my faith then as it
is now. I did for several days, either orally or
mentally, assert that Christ is true, and that
he is now offering the very boon which I crave.
At length I reached a point where I was assured, beyond a doubt, that he would speedily
come into blissful realization. Over and over
again did I pray the hymn :—

‘ Jesus, thine all-victorious love,’ etc.

“ Pausing at the epithet ‘all-victorious,’ I
begged the mighty Saviour to conquer me
wholly, and thoroughly reconstruct me from
top to bottom, from center to circumference,
and to leave not one disguised rebel lurking
within. That prayer was graciously heard.
So thorough was the conquest, that not one
masked Ku-Klux has come forth from his
hiding-place to torment my loyal soul, and to
render a second war of extermination necessary. To be sure, I have not been tested by

passing through a college rebellion, as I cautiously intimated a year ago, and I begin to think that I never shall pass through this ordeal, if the Comforter dwells in the hearts of us professors. For there is always more or less pride at the bottom of both parties to every war.

"A year ago I said that I did not know what was below the gaze of my consciousness. I still say the same, adding the testimony that the varied changes and perplexities through which I have since passed have failed to reveal any proof that Jesus is not king over the domain of my unconscious, as he is over my conscious, self. I have been questioned respecting my religious state previous to the Divine anointing, by persons interested in confirming the theory that I had then, for the first time, experienced the joys of pardoned sin. To them I reply, that I believe myself to have been in the pre-pentecostal state. It is objected that this is impossible eighteen hundred years after the effusion of the Holy Ghost. Perhaps those who doubt my testimony will accept that of so eminent a theologian and deeply experienced a Christian as the 'seraphic

Fletcher." He says, vol. iii, page 171 : 'Converted sinners, or believers, are either under
the dispensation of the Father, under that of
the Son, or under that of the Holy Ghost,
*according to the different progress they have
made in spiritual things.* Under the dispensation of the Father believers constantly experience the fear of God, and, in general, much
greater degree of fear than love. Under the
economy of the Son, love begins to gain the
ascendency over fear. But under the dispensation of the Holy Spirit, perfect love casteth
out fear.'

" This quotation abundantly justifies the assertion that I was in the pre-pentecostal state
of Christian experience. I believe that I
dwelt a long time in the dispensation of the
Father, a shorter period in that of the Son,
and that now, at length, by the grace of God,
I have entered that of the Holy Ghost. In
the first, I enjoyed the first element of the
kingdom, righteousness or justification—*dikai-
osune*—the act of the Father; in the second,
peace, the legacy of the risen Jesus ; and in
the third, joy, the endowment of the Holy
Ghost. To those who object to this assign-

ment of distinct blessings to the persons of
the Trinity, we would quote the apostolical
benediction, where the same distinction is
made, the communion of the Holy Spirit
always being the climax.

"Thus much theorizing seems necessary to
make good my assertion respecting my previous experience. A more practical question
some soul propounds to me, 'How to keep
the blessed Comforter?' He will keep himself, and you too, if you will let him. 'Kept
by the power of God through faith,' the human
and Divine agencies beautifully blend. He is
not so capricious as many imagine. He is
in no haste to leave any bosom, after so long
an endeavor to get an invitation to enter it.
Nothing but sin can dislodge him. The soul
which holds him by faith will be upheld by
him.

That beautiful device, a hand grasping the
cross, with the motto, '*Teneo et teneor*,' 'I
hold, and I am held,' expresses it all. Every
day, yea, almost every hour, I find myself repeating the couplet :

> "Thy grace can full assistance lend,
> And on that grace I *dare depend*,'

" The unwise query has been raised why I write my sermons if I am conscious of the indwelling of the Holy Spirit, the fountain of spiritual light. There is a vast difference between the *grace* and the *charisma*, the theopneustic gift of the Spirit conferred on the soul for the purpose of making it the organ or medium of revelation to the human race. The grace of the Spirit, while it floods the soul with light on its personal relations to God, communicates no dogmatic truth. Though it assists in the study and application of revealed truth, it does not modify the intellectual faculties, any more than it changes the manual dexterities of the craftsman. Hence, the Holy Spirit affords no dispensation from hard work. He is not bestowed as a premium to laziness. The preacher will yet be under the necessity of laboriously preparing the beaten oil for the sanctuary. But he will find this toil wonderfully alleviated by the removal of all inertia, and of every antagonism within himself, and by the sweet delight of the labor of love. Often, with his Master, he will exclaim, ' My meat is to do the will of Him that sent me.'

" Let me say, in conclusion, that my spiritual life is no longer like a leaky suction pump, half the time dry, and affording scanty water only by desperate tugging at the handle, but it is like an artesian well of water, ' springing up unto everlasting life.'

> " ' The fountain of delight unknown
> No longer sinks beneath the brim,
> But overflows, and pours me down
> A living and life-giving stream.'

" The Scriptures are sweeter than honey. Prayer and praise are a delight ; the closet with the door closed is paradise regained ; the glory of Christ has become the all-absorbing passion of my soul. Never before could I appreciate the paradox of Pascal, ' The things of this world must be known in order to be loved, but Jesus must be loved in order to be known.' My only apology for the use of the pronoun in the first person singular, instead of the impersonal and editorial *we*, is, that I have been relating *my* experience.

> " ' Glory to God the Father be,
> Glory to God the Son,
> Glory to God the Holy Ghost,
> Glory to God alone.

" ' I need not go abroad for joy
Who have a feast at home ;
My sighs are turnéd into songs ;
The Comforter is come.' "

EXPERIENCE OF A PASTOR—FOUR YEARS ON WINGS.

" They shall mount up with wings as eagles."

To ascribe praise to our Lord Jesus, to glorify the Father, and to honor the ever-blessed Spirit, the promised abiding Comforter, in order that all other believers may be induced to trust fully in the Triune God, I give public testimony. There is, in the estimation of some persons, the feeling that such a testimony shows a lack of good taste, an absence of that refinement and delicacy of sensibility which instinctively shrinks from exposing to public view the inmost chamber of the soul where Christ reveals his unutterable name. I have always had sympathy with this feeling; but I have learned with the great Apostle to " count all things but loss for the excellency of the knowledge of Christ Jesus." Was St. Paul immodest in the frequent narration of his experience? Then let me, for Jesus' glory, share in such shamelessness. During twenty-eight years I plodded wearily along the uphill path of spiritual life ; but four years ago the Holy Spirit endowed my soul with wings, and bade me mount upward with mine eye fixed upon the open gate of heaven. But even a bird of paradise may become weary in her long flight toward her native home, and fold her pinions and rest on some lofty mountain peak. In the " higher life " there is danger of dropping down from the wing to the foot again, unless the strength is constantly renewed by waiting upon the Lord. Faith is the atmosphere which bears up the soul. If the atmosphere becomes rare the eagle naturally sinks earthward. My soul has neither sought nor found an earthly object to rest upon. There is no weariness nor faintness. The air of the regions through which I pass is very bracing ; it buoys me up. Nor have gusts of adversity beaten me from my course, for God has permitted the head-winds of persecution to test the strength of my wings.

Socrates, in the Gorgias of Plato, is represented as saying, " If I happened to have a golden soul, do you not suppose that I would be glad to find the very best touchstone which men use in the testing of gold, which I might apply to my soul to be assured that it was well cared for, and that no other ordeal was necessary?" If the soul is golden, the touchstone to demonstrate its genuineness is indispensable. God, in wisdom and goodness, very soon provides every one of his golden-souled children with some infallible touchstone. Perfect love will not long go untested. In my year with the Comforter, I had not been called to suffer distinctly for Christ from the opposition of that hostile spirit which nailed him to the cross and slew his apostles. The lion was not dead, but asleep. He awoke and glared upon me with fiery eyes, and gnashed upon me with his cruel teeth. My soul was calm as a summer's evening, But when it pleased the blessed Master that I should be numbered among " the souls of them that were beheaded for the witness of Jesus and for the word of God "—to suffer reproach and vilification for the advocacy of an earnest Christianity against a proud and world-pleasing formalism—then it was that the river of joy which flows from the throne, clear as crystal, flowed through my heart as never before. It was a new experience—the quintessence of delight. My soul

bathed in an ocean of balm, which not only removed every pain, but made each wound the
avenue of positive and ineffable joy, new in
kind and in degree. The shouts of burning
martyrs are no longer a mystery. I stagger
no more at the account of the saints, " who
took joyfully the spoiling of their goods." •It
does not now require an extra effort of faith to
receive the promise of Jesus, *"Blessed* are ye
when men shall revile you, and persecute you,
and shall say all manner of evil against you
falsely, for my sake." I will no more question
the possibility of obeying this command to the
persecuted, " Rejoice and be *exceeding* glad,
for great is your reward in heaven." The jubilant song from the Philippian jail is a phenomenon as natural as the warbling of the bobo-
link in a June morning. The wonder, how
the beaten apostles could go forth from the
council "rejoicing that they were counted
worthy to suffer shame for his name," is all dispelled. No surprise to me are the words of
Faber :—

> " The headstrong world, it presseth hard
>   Upon the Church full oft ;
>   O then how easily thou turn'st
>   The hard ways into soft."

Yet in this exultation of soul I have had one intense, all-consuming, and sometimes distressing, desire for spiritual power in such measure as shall break hard hearts all about me. As a preacher, my daily and hourly prayer has been the cry of St. Paul, "that utterance may be given unto me" commensurate with the greatness of that salvation with which I have been personally saved. I have seemed to be plunged into the mid-ocean of the sweet waters of Divine love with a voice too feeble to reach the ears of my thirsty fellow-men wandering with parched tongues in distant Saharas, and to draw them to this shoreless, fathomless immensity of living waters. The great wonder and grief of my life during these four years has been the stolid unbelief of impenitent sinners, and the manifest skepticism of multitudes in the Church when the richness and fullness of the provisions of the Gospel are presented for their acceptance. Yet I find that I am not alone. Some sinners were hardened under the appeals of the great Apostle to the Gentiles, who had been caught up into the third heaven and heard things not lawful for him to utter; and some believers were so "beguiled with the

enticing words of man's wisdom" as to loath
the preaching of God's word "in demonstration of the Spirit and of power." I have
made this observation in order to guard
against an error into which many are falling,
who confound purity with power, and expect
every fully-saved soul to become, in Christian
efficiency, a Wesley, a Whitefield, or a Finney.
Both purity and power are attainable by faith
in Christ, but the degree of the latter seems,
like various kinds of intellectual power, to be
dispensed in a sovereign manner by 'the self-
same Spirit, dividing to every man severally as
he will.' In no marked degree has the endowment of power to convert sinners been divided
unto the writer, though he has coveted it with
intense desire, with strong cries and tears.
Yet the withholding of this gift has not for
a moment interrupted the repose of his soul
in the blood of Christ, or shaken his tranquillity and peace, or diminished the "joy unspeakable and full of glory." In his power
to edify believers and " to perfect the saints,"
and in the impulse to constant toil for Christ
in proclaiming distasteful truths, he gratefully
acknowledges a wonderful increase.

CHAPTER XVI.

SPIRITUAL DYNAMICS.

THE relation of the baptism or fullness of the Spirit to the efficiency of the believer, is a subject of intense interest to all Christians. Though much has been said on this question, there remains much more to be uttered, especially in view of the errors into which many good people have fallen. It is generally supposed that the copious effusion of the Spirit upon the believer to his utmost capacity will render him like an electric battery, emitting such shocks of power that sinners will instantly tremble, and fall down and cry for mercy, as did the thousands under the pentecostal preaching of Peter. Such phenomena do sometimes occur in modern times, but they are exceedingly rare. We are convinced that these large measures of power in individual believers would be more common were the whole Church full of faith in her glorified Head. But even then all would not be en-

dowed with equal measures of spiritual power,
all not having suitable spiritual capacity.

Soon after Rev. Dr. Finney's conversion
he received a wonderful baptism of the Spirit,
which was followed by marvelous effects. His
words uttered in private conversation, and forgotten by himself, fell like live coals on the
hearts of men, and awakened a sense of guilt
which would not let them rest till the blood
of sprinkling was applied. At his presence,
before he opened his lips, the operatives in a
mill began to fall on their knees and cry for
mercy, smitten by the invisible currents of
Divine power which went forth from him.
When like a flame of fire he was traversing
western and central New York, he came to
the village of Rome in a time of spiritual
slumber. He had not been in the house of
the pastor an hour before he had conversed
with all the family, the pastor, children,
boarders, and servants, and brought them all
to their knees seeking pardon or the fullness
of the Spirit. In a few days every man,
woman, and child in the village and vicinity
was converted, and the work ceased from lack
of material to transform, and the evangelist

passed on to other fields to behold new triumphs of the Gospel through his instrumentality.

Another rare instance of extraordinary spiritual power is that of Father Carpenter, of New Jersey, a Presbyterian layman of a past generation. A cipher in the Church till anointed of the Holy Ghost, he immediately became a man of wonderful spiritual power, though of ordinary intellect and very limited education. In personal effort, hardened sinners melted under his appeals and yielded to Christ. Once, in a stage-coach going from Newark to New York, he found six unconverted men and one believer his fellow-passengers. He began to present the claims of Jesus, and so powerfully did the Spirit attend the truth that four were converted in the coach, and the other two after reaching New York. At his death it was stated that by a very careful inquiry it had been ascertained that more than ten thousand souls had been converted through his direct instrumentality. The following is a well-authenticated instance of his power, under God, of reaching difficult cases:—

20

"An excellent and conscientious woman had fallen into a delusion of Satan that she had blasphemed the Holy Ghost, and was beyond the reach of God's mercy. For twelve years this dreadful incubus had crushed her soul. She could never be persuaded to detail the circumstances under which she supposed that she had committed the unpardonable sin. Father Carpenter, hearing of her sad condition, went to her house, insisted on the disclosure of the facts, with the declaration that he would not leave the house till he died if she persisted in her silence, and thus succeeded in opening her lips. Seeing that Satan had fastened the fiery dart of a lie in her soul, and kept it there for many years, and that no human power could pluck it out, in the presence of the distressed woman he boldly addressed Satan thus:—'O thou father of lies, thou accuser of the brethren! O thou god of this world, who dost blind the minds of men and hide from them the face of Jesus Christ! O thou tempter of the Son of God, thou roaring lion, thou murderer from the beginning! wherefore hast thou kept this daughter of Abraham, lo, these twelve years?

In the name of Jesus, come out of her, and let her go in peace!' Under this bold rebuke of the devourer the snare was broken, and the good woman came out of the captive's cell shouting praises to God for her deliverance." Here is a degree of spiritual power rarely seen in the Church.

But it is evident that there have been believers just as full of the Holy Spirit, who have had no such power to reach and save others. No man in modern times had larger views of Christ and of Christian privileges in the dispensation of the Spirit than Samuel Rutherford, who lived in Scotland in the seventeenth century. His "Letters," the joy of all advanced believers, are full of Christ. The superlatives in the English language are exhausted to express his supreme love to the adorable Son of God, " a rose that beautifieth all the upper garden of God—*a leaf of that rose, for smell is worth a world.*" " If it were possible that heaven, yea, ten heavens, were laid in the balance with Christ, I would think the smell of his breath above them all. Sure I am that he is the far best half of heaven ; yea, he is all heaven, and more than all heaven ;

and my testimony of him is, that ten lives of black sorrow, ten deaths, ten hells of pain, ten furnaces of brimstone, and all exquisite torments, were all too little for Christ if our suffering could be a hire to buy him." Here is the testimony of one whom "Christ led up to a notch of Christianity that he never was at before;" whose experience in the highest altitude of the "higher life" was one constant outgush of rapturous praises. Yet in his ministry no extraordinary power was manifest.

Two years after being settled at Anworth he writes: "I see exceedingly small fruit of my ministry. I would be glad of one soul to be a crown of joy and rejoicing in the day of Christ. I have a grieved heart daily in my calling." This is not a solitary case. Many eminently holy men have failed to produce immediate effects in the conversion of sinners. The fault was not with the thoroughness of their consecration, nor in their faith. They walked with God, and were filled with the Spirit; but the power to fasten saving truth upon multitudes of souls was not given to them of God. They do wrong to write bitter words of self-condemnation, and to bewail in tears the absence of this kind of power. God gave to Rutherford another kind of efficiency, which is to-day working in the Church, training believers up to the " measure of the stature of the fullness of Christ." It costs more to keep a soul in the love of Christ than it does to bring him to Christ. It is, therefore, really a higher gift. The great work of the ministry is the " perfecting of the saints," and the power that effects this, though not so conspicuous in the eyes of men, may be more excellent in the sight of God.

Evangelistic or converting power is by no means commensurate with strength of faith and fullness of the spirit or outgushing emotional experience. Unusual success in this direction requires that there be, in addition to entire consecration to God, a peculiar constitution of the sensibilities, and a personal magnetism sanctified by the Holy Ghost. It is not derogatory to the Creator to say that he endows men with this magnetic power for this very purpose, not that it may be prostituted to selfish or Satanic uses, but that it may be subsidized by the Holy Spirit and used as a spiritual force to push forward

Christ's kingdom. Instead, therefore, of vainly
struggling for a gift not designed for us, let
us employ to the utmost the gift of which we
are possessed, even if it does not glare like a
meteor upon the gaping world, nor cause our
names to resound through the trumpet of
fame.

Our theory of spiritual dynamics is this:
The Holy Spirit sheds abroad love in the
believer's heart. Love is power. This power is always efficient to conquer sin, and in
its higher degrees to overcome self. But its
effect upon others is modified by our temperament and mental constitution. Some are
designed by nature to be, when surcharged
with the Spirit, like galvanic batteries of a
thousand-cup power, electrifying vast multitudes with the shock of saving Gospel truth;
while others, endowed constitutionally with a
smaller capacity for the exercise of immediate
suasive influence, are more largely gifted in
the direction of a well-balanced intellect,
adapted to instruct and edify believers—the
chief function of the pastoral office. See Eph.
iv, 11-13. The history of the Church, both
apostolic and modern, sustains this view. Peter

was the preacher on the day of pentecost, not by chance, but by Divine purpose. Thomas could not have been substituted with the same results. His feebler grasp of truth, smaller spiritual caliber, and inferior personal magnetism, could not have been the channel through which the floods of spiritual life and power were borne to the multitude of dead souls. The quick and generous impulses, the inflammable sensibilities, the re-invigorated faith and ardent love of Peter, recently graciously restored to a sense of the love of Jesus, were the divinely-appointed aqueduct through which the first full outgush of the water of life should deluge the thirsty earth. Nor would Philip, with his materialistic turn of mind, nor even John, with his contemplative and subjective cast, though aflame with love to Jesus, have been just the man to carry the Gospel to the head-quarters of Cornelius, and be the medium through which the Holy Ghost should fall upon all his household. It was the providential arrangement that both Jews and Gentiles should receive the first outpouring of the Spirit through Peter, because he was the best medium of this great blessing.

Modern days have witnessed the career of great evangelists—Whitefield, Wesley, Finney, Caughey, and Earle—through whom multitudes have been aroused from the sleep of sin and awakened to newness of life, to be afterward under the care of thousands of less conspicuous but not less useful "pastors and teachers," having also for their work other gifts and energies of the Spirit. While, therefore, every one should earnestly covet the best gift, he should not rest satisfied till he has received the grace of the Holy Ghost in the plenitude of his purifying and inspiring efficacy. Then he should thankfully employ the gift bestowed, and not in vain repinings covet the more showy gift of his fellow-laborer in the Lord's vineyard.

In conclusion, we cannot be too well on our guard against the mistake of inferring great grace from great apparent usefulness, and *vice versa*. Men with very little grace, and some with none at all, have been very successful in awakening slumbering sinners; while holy men, in the most intimate communion of the Holy Ghost, have toiled on for years in labors apparently fruitless. I say *apparently*, because the whole chain of sequences is badly tangled, and it is impossible to trace the invisible footsteps of each man's influence. Paul may plant, and Apollos water, but God giveth the increase. He may see more fidelity and sacrifice in the humble water-carrier than in the dignified seed-bearer, and proportion his rewards accordingly.

The chief effect of the spirit-baptism is to secure strength of impulse and continuity of effort in the worker himself. Love makes all toil for its object a delight, and furnishes a motive for constant activity in behalf of others. We have recently heard a venerable bishop quoted as saying that "a revival may occur at any place where there are God and a Methodist preacher." We understand by this that every preacher, who is as holy and as believing as he ought to be, may, at will, at any time and in any place, see the simultaneous conversion of sinners. The necessary inference is, that all who do not constantly witness this are living in a cold and semi-backslidden state. This inference is afflicting thousands of Christian ministers who enjoy the fullness of the abiding Comforter. Both the inference and the assertion from which it is drawn are untrue. The great work of a preacher in a certain place may be almost wholly within the Church, to save those who are but slightly healed, and to fill the membership with spiritual power to such a degree that they may act with saving efficacy on the impenitent long after he has passed from that to another field of labor, or to his final reward. God has varieties of work and different agencies, and it is just as foolish for the hand to say to the foot, "You might be a hand if you only had faith," as to say, "I have no need of thee." When we hear such extravagant assertions we are inclined to say "Amen" to a wish recently expressed in our hearing, "O for a baptism of common sense!"

We cannot conclude without exposing and refuting the widely prevalent and mischievous error of estimating the usefulness of a preacher solely by the number of penitent seekers who crowd his altar and receive baptism at his hands. This great and glorious work may be done while neglecting to instruct and build up believers, leading them on from first principles, the milk for babes, to that advanced experience of the perfected believer who requires strong meat for his spiritual sustenance. Thus his

Church may be increasing in quantity and decreasing in quality at the same time. The real power of a Church may decline under a revival preacher. He may be repeating the folly of the priest who undermined the temple in his eagerness to get coal to keep its altar fires burning. Methodists especially cannot be too often told that the hidings of spiritual power are not found in the last census report. " Not by might, (*a host* in the Hebrew,) nor by power, but by my Spirit, saith the Lord." Zech. iv, 6. The people who, in these modern times, have largely taken the appointing power in their own hands, should understand that in clamoring for a preacher who may make the greatest stir in their community, and secure the largest rental of the pews, and in passing by the man through whom the highest spiritual purity and power of the Church may be attained, they are not wise. A Church whose members are all aflame with the fullness of the Spirit will always afford a healthful attraction to the unconverted, and will always be making aggression upon the unbelieving world. " Star preachers " are the poorest possible substitute for a sanctified Church.

CHAPTER XVII.

STUMBLING-BLOCKS IN THE KING'S HIGHWAY.

THE largest of these lies before the very gate of this highway:—1. Full salvation, as an experience, is begirt with *speculative difficulties*. Metaphysical quiddities perplex and bewilder many believers, and they never emerge from the fog into the clear atmosphere of truth till their hearts are filled with all the fullness of God. The purified heart clarifies the head. We can never philosophize ourselves into that "perfect love" which "casteth out all fear that hath torment."

Faith is the only door through which God enters the soul. Cease philosophizing and take up the great work of believing. "This is the work of God, [which God approves,] that ye believe on Him whom He hath sent." No sinner would ever find Jesus if he should stubbornly seek him with the lantern of reason, refusing the lamp of faith. No imperfect believer can grasp Jesus as the complete Saviour

so long as he leans upon speculative reason
as a supplement of his defective faith.   Pride
of intellect, the subtilest form of pride, is keeping thousands of Christians from that higher
knowledge of God which is obtained only by
climbing up the ladder of faith.   It is not necessary for the penitent sinner to be able to define repentance with theological exactness before he repents of sin, nor to have unquestion-
able views of the atonement in its relations to
God and to man.   All that he is required to do
is, to abandon every other hope and plea, and
to cry, "For me, for me, the Saviour died."
It is not necessary for any soul to discriminate
intellectually between regeneration and entire
sanctification, or between the stream of love
shed abroad by the Spirit of adoption and the
ocean of love which the abiding Comforter
pours around the purified soul, in order to enter upon this great salvation.   As it is enough
for the penitent to know that he is guilty, and
Jesus can pardon, so it is enough for the longing Christian to know that he is hungry, and
that there must be perfect satisfaction somewhere in the universe correlated to that intense
and painful appetency.   It is sufficient for him

to know that God is a satisfying portion, and to insist that he should completely satisfy our spiritual cravings, as he has abundantly promised.

We find in some honest minds a theoretical difficulty which constitutes a stone of stumbling in the way of their seeking full salvation. It is the notion that the grace of perfect love is of the nature of a *charism*, or special gift of the Holy Ghost, dispensed by the Father according to his own will, and hence not attainable by all believers.

Are there not instances in which the fullness of the Spirit, or perfect love, is dispensed in a sovereign manner without compliance with the usual conditions? We dare not say that there are not; for, (1.) We read in the Scriptures of one who was to be filled with the Holy Ghost from his mother's womb. (2.) We believe that the souls of infants, defiled by inborn depravity, are, without faith on their part, entirely cleansed before death by the blood of sprinkling because they are included in the new covenant which is ratified by that universal atonement which saves all souls which do not willfully reject it by unbelief. (3.) For the same reason we believe that all justified souls, all persevering believers in Jesus Christ, who, through imperfect apprehension of the "exceeding greatness of his power" "to save to the uttermost," are painfully conscious that they are not cleansed from all inward unrighteousness, are, before death, entirely sanctified by the sovereign will of Him who stands pledged "to finish the good work which he has begun" in them, and "to present them faultless before the presence of his glory with exceeding joy."

Nevertheless we must be careful not to fall into the great error of supposing that a blessing sometimes sovereignly bestowed is *not* attainable by all who seek it in the way prescribed in the Holy Scriptures. We are not to suppose that because God fed Elijah by the ravens, and the Israelites with manna from heaven, the ordinary and regular mode of obtaining supplies by sowing and reaping is no longer available to the human race. Says Mr. Wesley, "God's usual method is one thing, but his sovereign pleasure is another. He has wise reasons for hastening and retarding his work. Sometimes he comes suddenly and unexpectedly, sometimes not till we have long looked for him." Yet Wesley strongly and constantly urges all the justified to press forward and grasp this greatest prize this side of glory, saying that " it is neither wise nor modest to affirm that a person must be a believer for any length of time before he is capable of receiving a high degree of the Spirit of holiness."

The arbitrary bestowment, in rare instances, of the Holy Spirit in the fullness of his power for the accomplishment of some great work in the spiritual kingdom, has led our non-Arminian brethren in past days to regard this high blessing as a *charism,* a special gift, not attainable by every earnest seeker. Not a few Arminians who repudiate, with great zeal for the honor of the impartial God, the insinuation that the graces of repentance, pardon, and adoption are dispensed only to a favorite few elected to life from eternal ages, are, on purely Calvinistic grounds, excusing themselves from strenuous and persistent endeavors to obtain entire sanctification by imagining that only those receive full salvation before death whose constitutions were peculiarly constructed for its reception. This as effectually para-

lyzes effort as the old doctrine of the con-
tinuance of inbred sin till Death, the great
sanctifier, comes to the aid of Jesus. To exhort a thousand to seek the higher life because it is possible that one of that number
—the ratio fixed by this theory—has the inherent qualities necessary for its attainment,
sounds very much like advice to invest in
a lottery ticket which has one chance in a
thousand of drawing the prize. But this experience of perfect love is not a race, where here
and there one of a thousand lawful racers receives the crown. The blessed Jesus has for
every head, even in the present life, a diadem
resplendent with those precious stones called
by Mr. Fletcher "a spiritual constellation
made up of these gracious stars—perfect repentance, perfect faith, perfect humility, perfect
meekness, perfect self-denial, perfect resignation, perfect hope, perfect charity, for our *visible* enemies as well as for our earthly relations, and, above all, perfect love for our *invisible* God, through the explicit knowledge of
our Mediator, Jesus Christ." This crown, O
ye generation of worldly professors, ye busy
tribe of muck-rakers, intent upon your straws,

21

the Angel of the New Covenant, the adorable
Son of God, is holding over each of your heads
and begging you to wear as the badge of your
present sonship and future kingship unto the
Lord God Almighty. Look up, and see and
grasp this crown designed to adorn your earthly life before that life has vanished like a vapor,
and you have irretrievably lost the crown of
graces on earth fitting for a more resplendent
crown of glory on high.

Some good Christian people are alarmed at
what they deem the incipient fanaticism of
those who testify that, through the abiding of
the Sanctifier in their hearts, they feel no proneness to sin. This is another stumbling-block
which should be removed. We apprehend
that a little attention to the meaning of the
terms "prone" and "proneness" will remove all
cause for alarm. Turning to Webster's Dic-
tionary we find that prone signifies " bending
forward, inclined, not erect, headlong, running
downward ; applied to the mind or affections,
usually in an evil sense, as prone to intemper-
ance." Wesleyanism has always taught that
the believer may be graciously delivered from
that sin which is described in the seventh of

Romans as "another law in my members warring against the law of my mind, and bringing
me into captivity to the law of sin which is in
my members."

There is no difference on this point between
the advocates of the theory of gradual sanctification and those who preach the possibility
of an instantaneous deliverance from this proneness to sin. There would be just ground for
alarm were any persons in the present state of
probation proclaiming that they had attained
a condition of grace in which they were no longer liable to sin. There is a very great difference between the possibility of sin and proneness to it. Adam in Eden came from his
Maker's hands with no proclivity toward disobedience, yet there was that possibility of sinning which is implied in free agency. The
same is true of the angels in their first or pro-
bationary estate. But the entirely sanctified
soul is neither angelic nor Adamic, but is human, with all the disabilities of powers crippled
and dwarfed by sin. Hence, his liability to sin
is grounded on both his free agency and on
these disabilities. If you ask how a perfectly
holy soul may sin, you strike upon the vexed

question with which theologians and philosophers have wrestled for ages—the origin of sin.
To give a reason for sin is to justify it. Sin is
the most unreasonable thing in the universe.
Yet it is possible for the holiest soul in probation to perform that unreasonable act. The
most that grace can do for us here is to enable
us to abstain from sin—"*posse non peccare*," as
the old theologians express it. We may ap-
proximate, but in this world shall never reach,
the state of inability to sin—"*non posse peccare.*"
Practical inability to sin is attained in that
fixed state of character in which holy souls will
exist after death, when all the motives are so
manifestly preponderating toward virtue that
sin is a glaring act of suicide, from which the
recoil is as immediate as that of a sane man
from precipitating himself down a precipice.
We have used the word practical to indicate
the certainty of the continued obedience of
souls after probation, confirmed in holiness, and
yet, as free agents, theoretically free to fall.
There is another Latin formula by which the fathers used to express the awful state of character
toward which impenitent sinners are all hastening, lurid foregleams of which we see in the

present life—"*non posse non peccare*," inability not to sin. May not this self-induced and culpable inability to obey the law of God be the ground of the final sentence to everlasting punishment?

An exhaustive discussion of the relation of a completely sanctified soul to the possibility of sinning, involves the theory of temptation. Some teach that sin enters the soul when the sensibilities are stirred by the cognition of the forbidden object by the intellect. We are not of that class. The activity of the emotional nature in the presence of its proper objects is just as inevitable as that of the perceptive faculties. An apple presented to the gaze of a hungry child necessarily awakens, not only a perception, but a desire. This desire is as innocent as the impression on the retina, or the cognition in the mind. Sin comes in when the will indulges the desire, or even fosters it against the remonstrance of conscience. Yet this state of excited sensibility in the presence of a forbidden object is full of peril, for here is where sin is conceived. "Lust when it is conceived bringeth forth sin." Into this region the Sanctifier enters, and does his work, by exterminating every incentive to sin which is culpable *in itself*, such as pride and malice; by preventing the improper excitement of the innocent sensibilities, and by reinforcing the will, and inclining it to obey the mandates of the moral sense, the eye of which is now purged from the film of sin. The abiding Comforter is, therefore, the keeping power within the soul The vigilance enjoined by our Saviour is obligatory upon the entirely sanctified, and consists in that habit of faith which holds the soul in communion with God, and links it to that spiritual force which gives it constant victory, "being kept by the power of God through faith unto salvation." Hence we indirectly, yet most effectually, watch against all sin, while we maintain that believing attitude of soul which retains the Holy Spirit in the fullness of his purifying and keeping power. A rupture in the continuity of this life of faith is the breach through which the forces of Satan enter and recapture the city of Mansoul. He has already passed over the boundary between Christian discretion and fanaticism who imagines that St. Paul did not write for him, " Let him that thinketh he standeth take heed lest he fall," and that

our Saviour did not have in view the highest
state of grace attainable under the Gospel
when he said, "What I say unto you, I say
unto all, watch."

> " Hang on His arm alone,
>   With self-distrusting care,
> And deeply in the Spirit groan,
>   The never-ceasing prayer."

We cannot commend the scruples of those
who say that they have reached a religious experience in which they cannot join with the
congregation in the use of every hymn in our
excellent collection. I can blend my voice
with that of every worshiping assembly in
singing hymns expressive of every phase of
experience. I can sing the language of the
penitent, because, though conscious of forgiveness, I wish to remember with gratitude the
miry pit from which my feet have been taken.
I would not for my closest devotion select,—

> " What peaceful hours I once enjoyed !
>   How sweet their memory still !
> But they have left an aching void
>   The world can never fill : "

yet I sing these words in order to increased
thanksgiving to God for filling this " aching

void." For the same reason, while conscious that all the currents of my soul have been graciously made to flow heavenward, I may properly sing, "Prone to wander." In public no one worships for himself alone, but for the benefit of all the congregation.

2. There are also *practical difficulties*. How may I consecrate all to the Lord, and yet retain the control over all? How, for instance, can I surrender all my property to God and still retain some of it for life's uses? The question is pertinent. No man can live without appropriating something to his own personality. Property is one of the great natural rights with which we have been invested by our Creator. We could not exist without it. What are we to do when we consecrate possessions to the Lord? Not to shovel our money into the streets, or to pour it indiscriminately into the treasuries of the nearest elecmosynary institutions, but to become Christ's stewards for the faithful custody and expenditure of this property, making it accomplish the greatest possible good in the well-being of men and the glory of Christ. So much as we can spare from our business and

the proper maintenance of our families we must make immediately productive for good in some department of Christ's service, for the Lord at all times condescends to use consecrated substance. But so much as is requisite for the conduct of our business and decent support of those dependent on us may be retained and administered solely for the glory of Him who gave himself for us. Here we must depend each on his own judgment under the illumination of the word and the Spirit of God.

How may I know that I have laid all on the altar? Self generally rallies on some one point—defends itself in some last ditch. When that is surrendered, the struggle is felt to be over. We know that we have yielded and hung out the white flag, the token of our capitulation. Besides, with all honest souls God is under covenant to reveal to them the state of their hearts. It is the office of the Holy Spirit to hold up a mirror and to furnish a lamp with which we may see our exact visage.

CHAPTER XVIII.

GROWTH IN GRACE.

WE are exhorted to grow in grace and in the knowledge of Jesus Christ. Some tell us that we find the true philosophy of Christian growth by reversing this order, and putting the knowledge of Christ first, as the means of increasing in grace. But the order of the apostle—grace first and knowledge second—is the most philosophical. We grow in the knowledge of Christ through the heart, and not through the head. We do not know Jesus till we love him, and the more we love the more intimate our knowledge of him. The more we familiarize ourselves with the perfect character of Jesus, the more we shall admire him, just as by studying the works of Angelo we come to admire him the more. But admiration is not love. It kindles no furnace-glow in the affections; it impels the soul onward through no losses and labors, self-denials and persecutions, to the martyr's stake. As the

character of Christ folds its splendors beneath
the long and earnest gaze of the student, he
may be growing esthetically by familiarity with
so many moral beauties, and he may become
more perfectly grounded in his theological
beliefs respecting the Divinity of the man of
Nazareth, and yet he may, in his own heart,
be refusing to receive and to enthrone him as
his rightful king.

We advance a step further, and say that
growth in grace, while accompanied by increasing power to abstain from actual sin, has no power to annihilate the spirit of sin, commonly called
original sin. The revelation of its indwelling
is more and more perfect and appalling as we
advance from conversion. Hence, in Calvinistic writings especially, we find that the measure of true piety is self-abhorrence. The more
entire the consecration, the more vile in their
own eyes do eminent saints appear. This
standard of piety is a peculiarity of all the truly devout souls who were taught to believe
that there is no power to deliver from inborn
depravity this side of the grave. To these
persons a piety which is not self-loathing and
self-condemning is as contradictory as a piety

which is not penitent. But the sinless Jesus
exhibited the marvelous proof of an impenitent
piety. May not they who have washed their
robes in the blood of the Lamb stand forth,
even on earth, as specimens of a piety which
glorifies God without self-vilification? Does
God get the highest revenue of glory from us
while we perpetually proclaim that the blood
of Christ fails to reach the root of evil in our
natures? If not, then the self-loathing style
of piety, like that of David Brainerd in his
early ministry, who saw so much corruption in
his heart that he wondered the people did not
stone him out of the pulpit, is a mere initial
and rudimentary form, reflecting not the highest honor upon its Author.

But the fact remains undisputed, that in all
Christian experience, whether under Calvinian
or Arminian doctrines, growth in grace reveals
and magnifies that remaining inward corruption
which it has no power entirely to remove. In
the advanced yet not entirely sanctified believer,
the spiritual perception is keener, the sensibility
to sin more delicate, and hence more painful. It
is the experience of the Christian world through
all ages that the converted soul never outgrows

this taint in its texture and substance. So strong is the belief of the Church on this point that many have asserted that the cure of the spirit of sin is impossible in this life. On the other hand we have the testimony of thousands, that by faith in the all-cleansing blood of Jesus Christ they were instantaneously, completely, and permanently delivered from all those inward proclivities toward sin which formerly gave them so much pain, so that they can indorse the testimony of the now translated Cookman two years before he " swept through the gates,"—" I, Alfred Cookman, am washed in the blood of the Lamb." Here are two classes of witnesses—the whole body of imperfect believers, attesting the presence of inward corruption which they do not completely outgrow, and a goodly number in full trust in Christ, affirming with lip and life that they were instantaneously delivered from " the body of this death." Both classes witness to the same truth—depraved inclination in the justified soul is not outgrown by spiritual development, but killed by the power of the Holy Ghost through a specific act of faith. But this spiritual development by growth is the necessary preparation for this destruction of inborn sin. The power of the Holy Spirit is exerted only through faith, and this faith is possible only when we are conscious of a need of cleansing from all inward tendencies to sin. This consciousness is awakened by the increasing clearness of our spiritual perceptions under the illumination of the Holy Spirit. As Dr. Tyng says, "There is no´ calendar containing the length of time necessary for the conversion of the sinner," so there is no limit in time for this preparation for the work of entire sanctification. It may be an hour after regeneration, or the soul may be so slow in apprehending its privileges in Christ Jesus that years and decades may roll by before " faith grasps the blessings she desires."

We do not deny that incipient believers may, and do, in their gradual spiritual unfolding, mortify and diminish the remains of sin lingering in them after justification. What we affirm is, that the complete eradication of inbred sin after this period of decay is by the direct energy of the Sanctifier, whose interposition is specially invoked. This is his great office in the economy of salvation. His glory he will not give to another. " The Lord your God is a jealous God." The Spirit of Truth will not let growth or development usurp his function and wear his honors. Hence the moment of entire sanctification is usually attended by an unmistakable demonstration of the power of the Holy Ghost, marking it as the most marvelous and memorable event in the soul's history this side of glory. We do not deny that there may be successive operations of the Holy Spirit, or baptisms culminating in the grand *finale*—the extinction of sin and the fullness of God.

Says Rev. J. Fletcher: "Should you ask how many baptisms or effusions of the sanctifying Spirit are necessary to cleanse a believer from all sin, and to kindle his soul into perfect love, I reply, that the effect of a sanctifying truth depending upon the order of the faith with which that truth is embraced, and upon the power of the Spirit with which it is applied, I should betray a want of modesty if I brought the operations of the Holy Ghost and the energy of faith under a rule which is not expressly laid down in the Scriptures." "If one powerful baptism of the Spirit ' seal you unto the day of redemption, and cleanse you

from all [moral] filthiness,' so much the better.
If two or more be necessary, the Lord can repeat them." " I may, however, venture to
say, in general, that before we can rank among
perfect Christians we must receive so much of
the truth and Spirit of Christ by faith as to
have the pure love of God and man shed abroad
in our hearts by the Holy Ghost given unto us,
and to be filled with the meek and lowly mind
which was in Christ. And if one outpouring
of the Spirit—one bright manifestation of the
sanctifying truth—so empties us of self as to
fill us with the mind of Christ and with pure
love, we are undoubtedly Christians in the
full sense of the word."

Says Mr. Wesley: " The generality of those
who are justified feel in themselves more or
less pride, anger, self-will, and a heart bent to
backsliding. And till they have gradually
mortified these, they are not fully renewed in
love. God usually gives a considerable time
for men to receive light, to grow in grace, to
do and to suffer his will before they are either
justified or sanctified. But he does not invariably adhere to this. Sometimes he ' cuts
short the work.' He does the work of many

years in a few weeks; perhaps in a week, a day, an hour. He justifies or sanctifies both those who have done or suffered nothing, and those who have not had time for a gradual growth either in light or grace. God may, with man's good leave, do the usual work of many years in a moment. He does so in a great many instances. And yet there is a gradual work before and after that moment. So that one may affirm that the work is *gradual*, another that it is *instantaneous*, without any manner of contradiction."

The entire sanctification of all persevering believers before death, without a conscious act of faith, is hinted at in the above quotation. The grounds of our faith in this particular are the Divine promises unto those who are in covenant relations with God. He stands pledged to the persevering believer to bestow upon him eternal life: " This promise involves all the qualifications requisite to admission to a holy heaven. Being confident of this very thing, that he which hath begun a good work in you will perfect (Greek) it until the day of Jesus Christ." Phil. i, 6.

22

CHAPTER XIX.

OBJECTIONS ANSWERED.

M Y DEAR FELLOW-BELIEVER IN CHRIST:
You have honest objections to the experience of entire sanctification as a distinct blessing. Let me help you to remove them. You may be stumbling over the glaring imperfections of some who profess to be walking in this higher path of Christian life. In the first place, remember that impenitent men are using the same argument against all our endeavors to turn them to Christ. You invariably tell them that Christianity is liable to be counterfeited by hypocritical professors; that all valuable things are exposed to base imitations; and that the most valuable is the most exposed. Please apply your own logic to yourself when reasoning on the question of the higher Christian life.

Again, the Holy Spirit, in his most intense illumination, does not insure infallible moral judgments. John Newton, while master of a slave-ship, blinded by the darkness of his times, said that while enjoying intimate communion with God, "he never had the least scruple as to the lawfulness of the slave-trade;" and the seraphic piety of George Whitefield did not deter him from pleading before the trustees of Georgia for the introduction of slaves, on the ground of "the advantage of the Africans." Hence a man whose heart is full of love, and whose intellect is darkened by ignorance, may appear unconscientious to one favored with high moral culture.

You should constantly bear in mind this fact, that a man can never appear above the criticism of his fellow-men. Did Jesus Christ, the absolutely sinless man, escape hostile criticism? Was he not accused of being a demoniac, a wine-bibber, a Sabbath-breaker, a Beelzebub, and a subverter of the law? The difficulty was not in Jesus, but in his green-eyed critics. Perhaps this is the solution of your perplexity about the imperfect exemplifications of the love "that passeth knowledge." God once said to Abraham, "Walk *before me* and be thou perfect." He did not command him to be perfect in the estimation of fallible men. Suppose that Abraham had interpreted the command to include men as well as the heart-searching Jehovah? He is commanded to go to Mount Moriah, and to offer Isaac in sacrifice. He goes and exhibits to God a heart perfectly obedient, as proved by the severest test. God is satisfied. But suppose that some of Abraham's jealous neighbors wonder what the mysterious three days' journey means, and that they follow on the patriarch's track afar, and, at last, they see him actually seize his son and cruelly bind him hand and foot; and then, O horrible! he draws out from his belt a great sheath knife, and raises it on high and attempts to plunge it into the throbbing heart of innocence. But something seemed to prevent the wicked purpose—the spies are too far away to see what it was—but they saw enough of Abraham's harsh conduct in his family to satisfy them that his profession to be an especial "friend of God" is a stupendous piece of hypocrisy. "Perfection on earth," say they, "is all a myth; we have proved it." Yet, while this damaging misconstruction of Abraham's conduct is whispered from one to another of the neighboring Canaanites, the patriarch is in the enjoyment of the inward testimony that his ways please Jehovah; he walks before him and is perfect. It may be thus with many a living friend of God, maligned of men, while approved of Heaven.

False professions of this blessed experience should be expected, and due allowance should be made by all candid minds. But where there is a secret disrelish for an experience so high, it is natural to magnify such instances out of all due proportion to the number of the genuine professors, as wicked men magnify the hypocrisies in the Christian Church till they hide the multitude of true Christians.

Are you stumbled at the fact that many seek the fullness of Divine love and do not find? Do not many feebly seek regeneration and fail? There are no instances of persons seeking with their whole heart, with an unappeasable hunger and a tireless persistence, who have not received this greatest of Divine benefactions. In the distribution of his spiritual blessings God is no respecter of persons. "Every one that asketh receiveth."

Fanaticisms have attended the profession of this high grace. True. Extremists and

unbalanced minds have abused justification by
faith.   Yet this doctrine resounds in all our
churches.   In all attempts to promote experimental godliness there is danger that some
one may go astray from the path of sobriety.
Our Protestantism, which accords to every
soul the right of studying the Bible and of ac-
cess immediately to God without the intervention of a Latin-mumbling priest, must run the
risk of more or less abuse of freedom, and
eccentricity in doctrinal belief.   There is no
cure but the iron railroad track of papal infal-
libility prescribing the exact grooves in which
all religious thought and devotion shall run.
The remedy is a thousand-fold worse than the
evil.   The fanaticisms which have attended
the people who have devoted themselves
wholly to Christ, and who have been filled
with the fullness of the Spirit, have been
greatly exaggerated by the imaginations of
unsympathizing enemies.   They are not half
so disastrous as the heresies that spring up in
a cold and worldly Church, void of the Spirit
of Truth.

Again, the people who profess holiness are
generally unpopular.   They are secretly hated.

A very accurate observer of human nature has suggested the reason. He asks and answers this question: " Are we not apt to have a secret distaste to any who say they are saved from all sin?" Answer: " It is very possible we may, and that upon several grounds ; partly from a concern for the good of souls, who may be hurt, if these are not what they profess ; partly from a kind of implicit envy at those who speak of higher attainments than our own; and partly from our natural slowness and unreadiness of heart to believe the works of God."* This answer could very easily be intended to include other reasons for this distaste. A holy life is a rebuke to all unholiness. Jesus was a perpetual rebuke to the Jews. In the intense light of his pure life, their spots and stains were made manifest through the whitewash of ceremonialism. Their hatred of the light was turned against the light-bearer, and Jesus of Nazareth was the best-abused man of his times. In this respect the servant must not expect to be above his Lord. A person entirely dead to the world, and thoroughly alive unto Christ through every fiber

* Wesley's " Plain Account of Christian Perfection."

of his being, will make all conformers to this world so uncomfortable that they will begin to hate him, and to pick all manner of flaws in his life. They are not willing to give up their idols, and holiness comes to kindle a destroying fire among them. They are averse to strenuous effort, to earnest wrestlings with God at Peniel, and hence they dislike those who point to the sunlit heights of life above the clouds, and urge them to mount up thither, as disturbers of their repose. Again, since all love to God is in antagonism to the spirit of this world, the higher the degree the more intense that antagonism.

Another reason may be found in the activity of Satan, who seeks to plunder the Gospel of that element which gives it the highest efficiency in its warfare with his kingdom. He blinds the eyes of them that believe not, lest the light of the glorious Gospel of Christ shine unto them. He succeeds so well with unbelievers that he applies the same method to believers, blinding their eyes to their highest Gospel privilege, the fullness of the Spirit, lest the light of this blessing should gladden their eyes, strengthen their hearts, and intensify their zeal against his kingdom. Says John Wesley, in a letter to a Christian woman respecting her preacher, in 1771: "I hope he is not ashamed to preach full salvation, receivable now by faith. This is the word which God will always bless, and which the devil peculiarly hates; therefore he is constantly stirring up both his own children and the weak children of God against it." Hence the difficulty which the great Head of the Church has in keeping this doctrine in the pulpit. It dropped out of the English pulpit, and Methodism was raised up to bring it back. Wesley, true to the great light, "the grand *depositum* intrusted to the Methodists," found his preachers inclined to abandon this precious theme. Even now, after the inquiry on this subject among the laity has become so general, the majority of preachers pass over the subject like a slurred note in music, as if it was a demi-semi-quaver in the jubilant song of our Christianity, and not its very key-note.

Some believers may be warped by the influence of those who are mistaken in their profession of this blessing. Many, quickened and gladdened by some manifestation of the

Saviour's love, jump to the conclusion that they are entirely sanctified through the fullness of love, shed abroad in their hearts, and, under injudicious advice, rush into a declaration of full salvation before they have the witness of the Spirit to this great work. (1 Cor. ii, 12.) Such persons soon become what Mr. Fletcher styles "land-flood" or freshet "professors," left high and dry by the evanescent emotions of which they are the subjects.

The injudicious presentation of this blessing by some of its advocates has contributed to the eclipse of faith in its reality. Mount Sinai, instead of Mount Calvary, has been taken for the pulpit, and the terrors of the Lord have been denounced upon the Lord's children, although heirs of God, and joint. heirs with Jesus Christ. Let not this offend you. The wise counsel of the founder of Methodism has not always been heeded in preaching on this subject, "Always by way of promise; always drawing rather than driving." Thus injudicious advocates have awakened prejudice. All these causes combined have almost wrested this doctrine as a great vital, practical truth from the pulpits of Christendom, and driven it into select meetings in parlors; from the candle-stick to the bushel. O Lord! how long, how long, must this precious light be hidden from the faith of thy people?" Speedily lift it up from under the bushels to the candlesticks, there to shine till its splendors blend in the brightness of thy coming!

Are you afraid that if you embrace Jesus as a whole Saviour you will lose your broad sympathy for the whole body of believers and become clannish? Are those who have found full salvation inclined to clannishness from choice or from necessity? Is there not such a chilly temperature in many Churches that ardent believers can no more dwell safely in them than they can in a sepulcher? They prefer the light and warmth of a sympathizing Christian fellowship. Suppose, now, that all the Church were rejoicing in the increased grace given to each victorious soul, and, as in the case of St. Paul who had been caught up to the third heavens, they were glorifying God in him, we should hear no more of the segregation of those who are fully saved, than we hear in the New Testament Church of the withdrawal of the Spirit-baptized from the neophytes who had not yet received the Holy Ghost since they believed.

My dear brother or sister in Jesus, the fault may be more in your prejudice, your apathy, your love of the world, and lack of consecration to Christ, than in the souls drawn together by the mighty magnetism of love to Christ, the ruling passion of their bosoms. Do you not suppose that the Jews accused the disciples of clannishness when they persisted in their ten days' upper-room meeting before pentecost, and afterward in their breaking bread from house to house? The cure for the fault-finding Jew would have been to secure the pentecostal blessing, and feel the mighty attraction of Christian love. Your remedy is, to attain that perfect love which will bind you to all believing souls with a threefold cord.

But this intense fellowship, which has been stigmatized as clannishness, may be one of the strong scriptural evidences of Christian purity. Hear what St. John says will invariably result when a number of fully-consecrated souls walk arm in arm with Jesus, robed in the spotless linen of his righteousness: " But if we walk in the light, as he is in the light, *we have fellowship one with another*, and the blood of Jesus Christ his Son cleanseth us from all sin." Those in whom the bond of Christian communion is so weak that Church sociables must be resorted to for the promotion of Church feeling in the absence of true spiritual sympathy, which died with the forgotten prayer-meeting and the disbanded class-meeting, may well wonder at the mysterious magnetism which draws together devout persons, and holds them with hooks of steel, without ice-cream, oysters, segars, or other sensuous attractions of the club-room.

Let that Church which is vexed with a clique devoted to the higher Christian life take the following course, and the clique will be killed and buried beyond hope of resurrection. Let them no longer forsake the assembling of themselves together, but exhort one another daily, while with one accord and in one place they seek to be filled with the Spirit. Then let them give free expression to His voice within them, not by a hired quartette, but by speaking to themselves " in psalms, and hymns, and spiritual songs," making melody in their hearts to the Lord. (Eph. v, 18, 19.) Let them evince the genuineness of the Spirit-baptism by a life ever victorious over the world through faith in Jesus Christ, a beneficence which comes from " first giving yourselves unto the Lord," and a daily practice in harmony with the moral code of the Gospel. Under such treatment clannishness would speedily disappear, and the longest-lived " holiness meeting" would not survive a month. Again, you are stumbled by professors of a full trust in Christ, who still keep their purse-strings closely drawn. The secretaries of our various benevolent societies do not make this indiscriminate charge against those who have professed to find Jesus a complete Saviour. They know that recently, in consequence of the revival of this doctrine and experience, living springs of beneficence have been opened which are pouring constant streams into the Lord's treasury. Here and there a narrow-minded man has not been brought up to the standard, either because his intellect has not been sufficiently enlightened or his heart copiously anointed.

But you see no reason why you, after a score of years in the average Christian life, should rein up your soul to this one definite aim—full salvation through the blood of Jesus Christ—and go through a mighty struggle to attain that which only a minority of the justified profess to receive before they are laid on the bed of death. You think that if such a glorious experience had been designed for you you would have been led into it long ago, especially since in your daily prayers you have constantly prayed for the fullness of the Spirit. It may be that a subtle skepticism has kept you from vigorous efforts to grasp this great prize, which you might have seized in any day of your past Christian life, if you had sincerely believed in Christ's power to do this work, and distinctly aimed at it with all the intensity of spirit of which you were capable. The fact that you have gone so lông without this pearl of great price is a reason why you should now earnestly seek it; that thus both your own happiness and your usefulness to your fellow-beings may be increased, and your God honored. The heaven on earth of heart purity cannot be entered by chance. There must be a definite aim uniting all the forces of the soul. "And ye shall seek me, and find me, when ye shall search for me with all your heart." Jer. xxix, 13.

CHAPTER XX.

AN ADDRESS TO THE YOUNG CONVERT—THE HIGHER PATH.

M Y BROTHER OR SISTER IN CHRIST JE-
SUS:—Permit an older soldier to offer
a few words of advice to a new recruit in the
army of the Lord. An ancient writer has
wisely said, that there have been from the beginning two orders of Christians. The one
live a harmless life, doing many good works,
abstaining from gross evils, and attending the
ordinances of God, but waging no downright
earnest warfare against the world, nor making
strenuous efforts for the promotion of Christ's
kingdom, nor aiming at special spiritual excellence, but at the average attainments of their
neighbors. The other class of Christians not
only abstain from every form of vice, but they
are zealous of every kind of good works. They
attend all the ordinances of God. They use all
diligence to attain the whole mind that was in
Christ, and to walk in the very footsteps of

their beloved Master. They unhesitatingly trample on every pleasure which disqualifies for the highest usefulness. They deny themselves, not only of indulgences expressly forbidden, but of those which by experience they have found to diminish their enjoyment of God. They take up their cross daily. At the morning's dawn they cry, "Glorify thyself in me this day, O blessed Jesus!" It is more than their meat and drink to do their heavenly Father's will. They are not Quietists, ever lingering in secret places delighting in the ecstacies of enraptured devotion ; they go forth from the closet, as Moses came from the mount of God, with faces radiant with the divine glory; and, visiting the groveling and sensual, they prove by lip and life the divineness of the Gospel.` Men tremble before them as Satan in Paradise Lost, when he first saw the sinless pair in Eden, "trembled to behold how awful goodness is."

Next to the power of Jesus, the living Head, these earnest believers preserve and perpetuate the Church from age to age. The secret of their strength is, that they, by the guidance of the Spirit, found the King's high-

23

way up the summit of Christian holiness. They strove, they agonized to plant their feet on that sunlit height. They have left the first principles of the doctrine of Christ, and have gone on to perfection.

They have accompanied St. Paul in his wonderful prayer in the third chapter of Ephesians, " till they know the love of Christ which passeth knowledge," and are " filled with all the fullness of God." Says Mr. Wesley, whose greatness the Christian world is just beginning to appreciate, " From long experience and observation I am inclined to think that whoever finds redemption in the blood of Jesus—whoever is justified—has the choice of walking in the higher or the lower path. I believe the Holy Spirit at that time sets before him the ' more excellent way,' and incites him to walk therein—to choose the narrowest path in the narrow way—to aspire after the heights and depths of holiness—after the entire image of God. But if he do not accept this offer he insensibly declines into the lower order of Christians; he still goes on in what may be called a good way, serving God in his degree, and finds mercy in the close of life through

the blood of the covenant." This is on the
condition that he is a persevering believer.
But this lower path lies so near to the broad
way, that many are almost insensibly lured
into it, and go down to destruction with the
thoughtless throng who enter in at the wide
gate. Would you, young Christian friend,
place the best possible safeguard against such
a spiritual catastrophe? Take the higher
path; consecrate all to Christ; seek full salvation through his blood, which cleanseth from
all sin. This is the divinely-invented safeguard of the Christian life.

> " Jesus, thine all-victorious love
>   Shed in my heart abroad ;
> Then shall my feet no longer rove,
>   Rooted and fixed in God."

These two paths lie before your feet, young
convert. Choose you that one in which you
will walk—the higher or the lower, the safer
or the more perilous. Let one who has tried
both give you the benefit of his experience :—

The lower path seems easier, but in reality
it is far more difficult. The sultry heat produces languor, and the noxious vapors induce
stupor, making it exceedingly difficult to keep

walking, even though the road is compara-
tively level. The beautiful bowers of ease
tempt the drowsy traveler to lie down and
sleep. To sleep is to lose heaven, as, alas! multitudes of the lower-path travelers have done.

Let their whitened bones, scattered along
this path, be a warning to you to seek the upward path. It appears to be steep and rough;
but the few who have tried agree in testifying
that the atmosphere is so bracing and ex-
hilarating that they seem to be lifted up the
mountain by an invisible hand. Such a flood
of life courses through their veins, such electric
vigor shoots through their limbs, that they are
not inclined to turn aside to the pleasure-ar-
bors which Satan has unwisely located here
and there near this way. The way itself is
the highest pleasure on earth. The pilgrims
run and are not weary. The Hebrew psalmist explains this paradox: "I will run the way
of thy commandments when thou hast enlarged my heart." Along the higher path the
joy of the Holy Ghost pours, a river deep and
wide; while along the lower it is a brooklet,
more than half the year dried up by the torrid
sun, Through the clear Italian atmosphere

of the higher path, the celestial city is ever in view to the eye of faith ; but clouds frequently settle down upon the pilgrims in the lower path, bringing perplexing doubts respecting the issue of their journey. The upward way leads to "an abundant entrance," while the pilgrims in the other road are haunted by distressing fears lest they shall come short of being even " scarcely saved."

Christian reader, a fellow-pilgrim to the New Jerusalem has had this experience in these paths. His testimony could be affirmed by many thousands, the brightest names that shine on the pages of Church history. Have such names as St. Paul, Madame Guyon, Fletcher, Bramwell, James Brainerd Taylor, no weight with you in deciding the question of which path?

Having chosen the higher path, do not be discouraged by the obstacles in the way of your entering and walking therein. You are not to remove them by your own strength. You have an almighty and complete Saviour, " able to save unto the uttermost all who come unto God by him." With a submissive will and believing soul, " pray that you may know the exceeding greatness of his power to us-ward who believe."

Pray, and faint not. Take into your closet
Charles Wesley's great dramatic lyric of a
struggling and victorious soul, "Wrestling
Jacob," and pray its words till the intensity of
the expressions kindle your soul with earnestness and unconquerable persistence. Let your
faith grasp some one of Christ's many precious
promises, and use it as a key. Then will the
iron gate across the king's highway swing back
upon its hinges, and the path never trod by
the lion's whelps shall lie before you.

Dropping all figurative language, let me say
to you plainly, that you may enter upon the
higher Christian life by simple faith in Jesus
Christ as your complete Saviour. As you
have received Jesus, so walk in him. You received him at the first by faith; you are to
receive by faith "the measure of the stature
of the fullness of Christ." Repentance was
the indispensable condition of justifying faith;
you could not believe without giving up your
sins. Consecration is the necessary qualifica-
tion for sanctifying faith; you cannot believe
till you give up self.

But you may say, "I did this when I was
converted." You then, like a conquered rebel,

threw down your weapons and surrendered yourself as a prisoner of war. Now that you have been pardoned and made a citizen, Christ gives you the privilege of showing your loyalty to his government by pouring all your substance into his treasury as a freewill offering, and of volunteering soul and body in his conquering army. The difference between the two acts of consecration is the difference between surrendering with reluctance and volunteering with gladness. The subsequent service is marked by more or less servility in the one case and joyous freedom in the other. The one is a servant, the other is a son. It is true that all who are born into the divine family are sons by adoption; but many forget their sonship, and begin to work for wages. They become legal in spirit, trusting to the merit of their works, and thus put a yoke upon their necks. But the full measure of Christ's love, shed abroad by the Holy Spirit, makes free indeed. Service is no longer a drudgery, but a delight. The motive to obedience is no longer fear, but love—not the dread of the law, but affection toward the Lawgiver.

Let me illustrate the difference between

law-service and love-service by the conscript
and the volunteer soldier. The impulse which
thrusts the former into the field is fear of the
law reinforcing his feeble patriotism. When
the news comes that his name has been drawn
out from the wheel of fortune, and that the
strong arm of the law has seized him to push
him into the front of the battle, his cheeks
turn pale and his heart sinks within him.
Nevertheless, he puts on the military uniform,
and shoulders his knapsack, though it seems
to weigh a ton. Reluctantly he leaves the old
homestead, and wearily journeys to the conscript camp, strongly tempted to slip away
from the officer and escape from the country;
but the fear of the law, and his weak love for
his native land, overcome this temptation.
He murmurs at the hardness of his rations,
discomforts of the camp, the severity of the
discipline. Yet he bravely does his duty.
The law, like a bayonet behind him, drives
him into the battle, where he fights like a hero.
Yet he does not enjoy the privations and
perils of the service. He cannot overcome its
irksomeness. Every hour he wishes that he
could avoid the disagreeable duties of a sol-

dier's life. He sees the volunteer enduring the weary marches with patriot songs, and with cheerful smiles rushing into battle as to a banquet. He sees him brought back mortally wounded, borne on a stretcher, blessing the old flag of his regiment as it fades away from his glassy eye, and thanking God for a country worth bleeding and dying for. The conscript notes with shame the contrast between the spirit of this volunteer and his own cold, apathetic, reluctant service, and hides his blushing face from his comrades with the earnest, unspoken prayer for the inspiration of nobler feelings toward his country. Let us suppose that the prayer of the conscript is heard, and that a baptism of patriotism descends upon his soul. Now his country stands before him as the chief among ten thousand nations, and the altogether lovely. He gladly grasps his rifle and runs with eager delight to the thickest of the fight to drive back the rebels who are trampling beneath their feet the glorious old flag, the emblem of the object dearest to his heart, and for the honor of which he would gladly pour out his heart's blood. He has passed through a crisis in his military life. A new motive power has taken up its abode behind his will—love instead of fear—and it throws a halo about the hardest tasks, changes suffering into enjoyment, and transfigures death itself into an envied martyrdom. He is a new man. The temptation to desert, which once cost him a struggle to resist, never troubles him now. His rations are wondrously palatable, and his knapsack is a softer bolster for his head as he sweetly slumbers between the cornhills, than the downy pillow awaiting his return in his distant home. He has found out the secret that love knows no burdens, feels no hardships, in the service of its object. If the term for which he is drafted should expire to-day, instead of throwing up his cap for joy he would find a recruiting officer and re-enlist for the whole war, bounty or no bounty, for he means to fight till the last rebel lays down his arms, and the land of his fathers is redeemed.

Now, my young friend, do you see the point of this illustration? There are multitudes of conscript Christians pressed into Christ's army by the constraint of the law. They render acceptable service, and will be rewarded for their fidelity, as the grateful country gives pensions alike to the drafted and volunteer soldier, and indiscriminately decorates their graves. But the volunteer enjoyed his service, finding the battle-field a delight because it afforded him an opportunity to suffer for his loved country, while the conscript, just as faithful in the outward act of obedience, never tasted joy in his irksome toils and sacrifices. Which kind of a Christian do you choose to be? You may serve all your life under the constraint of law, or you may serve with gladness in the way of God's commandments under the mighty impulse of love, perfect love, which casteth out all servile, tormenting fear.

These are the two ways of Christian living —the lower and the higher path. Every consideration of greater usefulness, greater happiness, greater security, and, above all, greater glory to the blessed Lord Jesus, should constrain you to seek the higher path.

> " If our love were more simple,
>   We would take him at his word ;
> And our lives would be all sunshine,
>   In the sweetness of the Lord."

CHAPTER XXI.

ADDRESS TO SEEKERS OF FULL SALVATION.

WE would now address those who are sincerely and earnestly seeking perfect love, but who fail to understand the exhortation to a full surrender to Christ, and to have no will of their own. We are so created that we must regard our own welfare. Self-love is implanted in our natures. If it could be destroyed, there would be nothing to which God or man could appeal. Neither threatening nor promise would move such a soul. Moreover, self-love has the approval of Christ in his epitome of the moral law. He makes it the measure of our love to our neighbor. " Love thy neighbor as thyself." But selfishness differs from self-love in this, that self is exalted into the supreme law of action. The well-being of others and the will of God are not regarded. This is the self that is to be crucified. Says St. Paul, " I am crucified with Christ; it is no longer *I* that live, but

Christ that liveth in me," (Gal. ii, 20, as punctuated by Alford.) The former *ego* of selfishness has met with a violent death, having been nailed to the cross, and Christ has taken the supreme place in the soul. The very fact that the death was violent implies that it was instantaneous—a very sharply defined transition in St. Paul's consciousness. There is some one last rallying point of selfishness, a last ditch, in which the evil *ego* trenches itself. It may be some very trifling thing that is to be exempted from the dominion of Christ —some preference, some indulgence, some humiliating duty, some association to be broken, some adornment to be discarded. "Reign, Jesus, over all but this," is the real language of that unyielding heart. This trifle, held fast, has been the bar which has kept thousands out of that harmony with the Divine will which precedes the fullness of the Spirit.

But when this last intrenchment of self-will has been surrendered to Christ, he is not long in taking possession. The fullness, as well as the immediateness, depends on the faith of the soul in the Divine promise. For there is a difference between the subjugation of the rebel and his reconstruction in loyal citizenship between the death of sin and the fullness of Christian life. But the great distinctive and godlike feature of man is his free will. The memorable event, the pivotal point on which destiny, heaven or hell, hinges, is the hour of intense spiritual illumination, when sin is deliberately chosen—the soul saying, " Evil, be thou my good "—or voluntarily rejected. Submission to Christ is an act of faith. It could not be possible without confidence in his veracity and goodness. Hence justification and emergence into the " higher life " frequently take place when the only preceding act which impressed itself on the memory was not an act of faith but of surrender, which is grounded on trust as its indispensable condition.

Some writers on advanced Christian experience magnify the will, and say to inquirers, " Yield, bow, submit to the law of Christ;" while the evangelist of the Wesleyan type says, " Believe, believe Christ's every word." Both are right. Perfect trust cannot exist without perfect consecration. Nor can we make over all our interests into Christ's hands without the utmost confidence in his word. Hence crucifixion with Christ implies perfect faith in him, not only when he is riding in triumph into Jerusalem amid the huzzas of enthusiastic men and the hosannas of willing children, but when the fickle multitude are crying, " Crucify him." From the beginning Jesus intimated that discipleship must be grounded on an acceptance of himself, stripped of all the attractions of riches or honor. To know him after the flesh, is to know him from some selfish and worldly motive; it is to fail to know him in that way which insures eternal life. To an enthusiastic scribe who has just seen the glorious display of power in the healing of Peter's wife's mother and the casting out of demons, and who was taking only a romantic, rose-colored view of discipleship, prompting the thoughtless promise, " I will follow thee whithersoever thou goest," Jesus replied, " The foxes have holes, and the birds of the air have nests, but the Son of man hath not where to lay his head." Let him who follows me know that he is following a pauper fed at the tables of friends, and soon to be buried as a beggar at their expense. " If any man will be my disciple let him deny himself, take up his cross daily, and follow me." Here, over the very gateway of the kingdom of Christ, stands chiseled the stony words, " Crucifixion of self." The requirement looks toward the highest spiritual life. The higher the degree of life the higher the required consecration.

Hence, love made perfect requires as its antecedent that perfect surrender which, in the strong language of St. Paul, is crucifixion with Christ. The difficulty with average Christians is that they faint beneath the cross on the *via dolorosa*, the way of grief, and never reach their Calvary. They do not by faith gird .on strength for the hour when they must be stretched upon the cross. They shrink from the torturing spike and from the spear aimed at the heart of their self-life. This betokens weakness of faith. But when the promise is grasped with the grip of a giant, no terrors, no agonies, can daunt the soul. In confidence that there will be, after the crucifixion, a glorious resurrection to spiritual life and blessedness, the believer yields his hand to the nail, and his head to the thorn crown. That flinty center of the personality, the will, which has up to this hour stood forth in resist-

ance to the complete will of God, suddenly
flows down, a molten stream under the furnace blast of Divine love, melted into oneness
with the "sweet will of God." After such a
death there is always a resurrection unto life.
An interval of hours, or even of days, may
take place before the angel shall descend and
roll away the stone from the sepulcher of the
crucified soul, and the pulsations of a new and
blissful life be felt through every fiber and
atom of the being. It is not the old life that
rises, but a new life is breathed forth by the
Holy Ghost. The believer can then truly say
that he is "dead indeed unto sin, but alive
unto God through Jesus Christ."

> " He walks in glorious liberty,
>   To sin entirely dead :
> The Truth, the Son, hath made him free,
>   And he is free indeed.
>
> " Throughout his soul thy glories shine,
>   His soul is all renewed,
> And deck'd in righteousness divine,
>   And clothed and filled with God."

He who enjoys this repose is brought so intimately into sympathy with Jesus Christ that
he is all aflame with zeal, and aroused to the
24

utmost activity to save lost men. As a venerable preacher, widely known, quaintly expressed it, " I enjoy that *rest* of faith that
keeps me in perpetual *motion.*"

We come now to the practical question,
"How may I enter into this rest, this resurrection with Christ, this Divine freedom?" If
you ask this question in sincerity, it evinces
that you have the first condition requisite for
its attainment—a sense of spiritual bondage.
Till you realize the indwelling of sin—the great
spiritual despot—you will make no efforts to
secure the intervention of the great Emancipator. The second requisite is, that you believe that he is "mighty to save;" that "he
is able to save to the uttermost all that come
unto God by him." So long as you doubt
that Jesus is a complete Saviour, you will be
reluctant to yield yourself to him. You must
believe that "the blood of Christ cleanseth
from all unrighteousness," before the Holy
Spirit will apply the blood of sprinkling to
your heart. We are not bound to explain the
necessity of this faith. It seems to be the
only doorway through which God enters into
the soul to set up his kingdom. Every spirit-

ual blessing enters the soul by the same avenue. It cannot enter through the senses,
which apprehend only the material world. It
cannot be grasped by the reasoning faculty,
which apprehends only relations. It is not an
object of the natural intuitions; it is the object of the spiritual intuitions, or the faith faculty. The grounds of this faith are the Divine
promises; its object the Lord Jesus Christ.

But this faith itself has its subjective conditions. The chief of these is the complete
surrender of self, the entire submission of the
will to the law of Christ—the law of love—
and the entire consecration of all to him.
The sinner's submission at his conversion
is different from the believer's surrender before entire sanctification. The one seeks
only pardon, the other the glory of his king
—King Jesus. Hence the great transformation called entire sanctification, or the shed-
ding abroad of perfect love, is possible only
to one who completely identifies himself with
Christ, discarding all separate purposes and
selfish ends. The coming of the abiding Comforter into the consciousness of the believer is
promised only to those who ask in the name

of Jesus. This signifies not only by the authority and through the merit of Jesus, but *for
the promotion of his glory*. Many seekers after
this great treasure of " rest in Jesus," or " the
higher life," or " perfect love," or "complete
holiness," fail at this point. Selfishness or
the desire for happiness, instead of a desire to
add luster to Jesus' crown of glory, is the
vitiating element which renders their faith of
no avail. Self-love, the measure of our required love to our neighbor, is lawful and
right. But selfishness, which has interests distinct from the honor of Christ and the advancement of his kingdom, never elevates but
always degrades the soul. As genuine heroism
always regards some object beyond self—for
which to sacrifice and devote itself to destruction, if need be, so true faith goes beyond self,
and apprehends Jesus Christ's glory as its
object of desire. It is at this point that the
seeker of purity of heart finds his severest
tests. It has been said that it is a long road
to the end of self. But the illumination of the
Holy Spirit will, in a very short time, show to
the sincere and importunate soul the end of
that long road. He can carry a lighted candle

through our souls, and in a few moments uncover the idols of which we ourselves may
have been unconscious. He will make demand after demand, till he has exhausted self.
A friend of the writer became sick in Paris.
He sent for the most eminent physician in the
city, who, after a careful diagnosis, informed
his patient that he was attacked with a fatal
fever then prevailing in the French capital.
Said he to him, "You will soon lose your reason, and then sink into a state of insensi-
bility, from which it is not certain that you
will rally. But I will do my best to carry
you safely through the deadly disease. Make
your will, and deposit it with me. Put into
my hands your trunk and its key, your watch,
your purse, your clothes, your passport, and
every thing else which you prize." The sick
man was thunderstruck at such demands by
an entire stranger, who might administer a
dose of poison, and send the patient's body to
the potter's field, and appropriate the surrendered treasures to his own use. A moment's
reflection taught him that the demand was
made out of pure benevolence, and that it
was more safe to trust himself and his posses-

sions to the hands of a man of high professional repute than to run the risk of being plundered by a hungry horde of hotel servants. He surrendered all his goods and himself into the charge of the physician. He sat by his bedside, saw his prophecy fulfilled, reason go out in delirium, and intelligence sink into stupor. He watched the ebbing tide of life with all the solicitude of a brother. At length he saw the tide turn, and detected the first faint refluent wave which was to bring the sick man back to the shores of life. He recovered, and found his purse and all his treasures restored to him. Thus must you do if you would avail yourself of the skill of the all-healing Physician, Jesus Christ. Make your will, and give it to him. Commit your purse to his keeping. A consecrated pocket-book always attends a sanctified heart. Without this attendant, the heart-work is not real and genuine. Put yourself, your possessions, your reputation, your future, into Christ's hands by an act of consecration, and then BELIEVE that he will do his work without any assistance from you. You cannot improve your own condition. You cannot expel the dire disease of sin from its hold upon your very vitals. Jesus only can free you.

> " His precious Blood both wounds and heals,
>   When faith the balm applies,
> My peace restores, my pardon seals,
>   My nature sanctifies.
> His precious Blood the life inspires
>   Which angels live above,
> And fills my infinite desires,
>   And turns me all to love."

My first word of advice to you who are indifferent to the subject, yet are willing to be convinced and incited to seek perfect love, is to gain a clear intellectual view of your spiritual need, and of your wealth of privilege in Christ Jesus, whom you have already claimed as your pardoning Saviour. Understand that he came, not only that you might have spiritual life, but that you might have it more abundantly. When you sought forgiveness you looked away to Calvary, and saw by faith Jesus crucified; now that you are seeking the fullness of the Spirit, lift your eyes above the summit of Calvary, even to Jesus glorified on the mediatorial throne. The glorification of the Son of God opens a new dispensation in the unfolding of the Gospel. Previous to that great event in the heavenly world, Jesus had power on earth to forgive sins; but since he has mounted to his Father's throne, and by his hand has been crowned with the royal diadem, it has pleased him to give proof of his continued interest in all believers by sending down the fullness of the Holy Ghost. To this Jesus distinctly referred when he stood among the jubilant priests sounding their trumpets in the last great day of the feast of tabernacles, and made this wonderful promise: "He that believeth on me, as the Scripture hath said, out of his inmost self shall flow rivers"—not brooklets, vanishing in the drought—" of living water." That Jesus was speaking of some future dispensation of blessings to believers, St. John, guided by Divine inspiration, distinctly declares: "But this spake he of the Spirit, which they that believe on him should receive: for the Holy Ghost was not yet given, because that Jesus was not yet glorified." In the gift of the Holy Ghost the Gospel dispensation culminated. John the Baptist, when Jesus came to be baptized, saw this privilege of believers towering above all other blessings, an event in the future history of the Son of man eclipsing all other events, the end and aim of his incarnation, atoning death, glorious resurrection, and triumphant ascension, that he might mend the -severed link between God and man by the fusing, unifying power of the Holy Spirit. " After me comes one who shall baptize you with the Holy Ghost and with fire." The Comforter came on the day of pentecost—came to stay. His work is not an indefinite and general operation, but an individual transformation.

2. Though you live in the dispensation of the Spirit, the benefits of his presence are to be appropriated to you by faith. You say that you have always been told to believe, and that you find it difficult. I will not blame you. Sometimes faith preached to young Christians with no exemplification or simplifying of the act, is as inappropriate as to set a bushel of wheat before a half-starved sucking babe with the invitation to eat. You cannot believe without an object of faith. He stands forth before you in the Gospels, Jesus the Son of God. You cannot believe without grounds or evidences. They are found in the Gospels, in the miracles and sinless character of Jesus Christ, and in the effects of his Gospel in human hearts and

lives, and in its beneficent influence on the nations which have received its blessed light.

The evidences of Christianity are the gift of God to you. In this sense, faith is the gift of God. But to receive their convincing effect you must study them with a candid mind, willing to follow wherever the truth leads. If you would have faith in Christ, become familiar with his character and his teachings. It may be that we have four gospels in order that the Son of God, in the perfection of his manhood and the splendor of his Godhead, may pass four times before your eyes. As he who would be a perfect orator or poet is exhorted by Horace "to handle the Grecian models with a daily and a nightly hand," so must the believer who aspires to be a perfect Christian sit before the great Exemplar by day and by night. An enduring faith is largely grounded in the intellectual grasp of the truth. There is a sense in which we must know in order to believe. A man's character must be favorably known to the banker before he will intrust him with his money. The more we know of Jesus by the study of his fourfold biography, the deeper and broader the foundation for our

faith in his promises. It also greatly assists
our faith to know what marvelous effects have
followed it in the history of the Church, especially in the opening chapter—the Acts of the
Apostles. Trace again and again the triumphant march of our holy faith from Jerusalem,
conquering the inveterate prejudices of Jew
and Gentile, as narrated by St. Luke in the
Acts. You will find that faith is contagious.
Association with some capacious soul who em-
braces the amplitude of the promises, and holds
fast to them with an unrelaxing grasp, helps
the feeble sinews of spiritual infancy to grow
strong. St. Paul is such a soul. He is a spiritual giant. He is accessible to you all. His
enthusiastic ardor, his invincible faith, which
neither stripes nor prisons, plotting Jews nor
riotous Gentiles, could shake, will be a tonic to
your spiritual weakness. Lock arms with him
and walk through his epistles till you catch
his gait and measure up to his Titanic strides,
as he boldly approaches the throne of grace in
the name of the ever living High Priest. "What
part of the Bible do you read the most?" said
a Scotch minister to an old woman of remarkable faith in God. "The glorious epistles,"

was the quick reply. On this strong meat all the giants of the Church have fed. You will find St. Paul's later epistles especially adapted to enlarge your view of your privilege under the dispensation of the Spirit. It is very evident that the great apostle grew in grace mightily between the day when the scales fell from his eyes·in Damascus and the day when he penned the epistle to the Ephesians. But do not rest satisfied with an intimate acquaintance with the Scriptures.

3. While making this acquaintance with the grounds of faith, endeavor to appropriate to yourself every promise of spiritual grace. St. Paul made the promises and atoning blood of Christ his own private property. Here was the secret of his herculean strength of faith. " The life which I now live in the flesh I live by the faith of (in) the Son of God, who loved *me*, and gave himself for *me*." He did not exclude others, but he was sure to include himself, and to insist, not on a fraction of Christ, but a whole Christ, to be as completely appropriated to himself as if he were the solitary son of Adam for whom atonement had been made. Rutherford, whose name is precious

to all devout Scotchmen as ointment poured
out, and whose letters are indeed a garden of
spices for the walks of believers, had evidently learned this secret of appropriating faith.
He often, with special earnestness, besought
the Father to distribute "the great loaf,
Christ," to himself and to his flock. Let me
advise you to practice writing out the promises of the Lord Jesus, especially the promise
of the abiding Comforter, which Jesus styles
the promise of the Father, and to insert your
own name in the place of the *whosoever*, or
any man, or other general term. This treatment of the promises seems to be the best antidote for that general and indefinite faith
which accredits them as true for the mass but
not for the individual. In this way most of
the promises are thrown away by believers, as
the threatenings are thrown away by unbelievers. But when we write our own name in
them, and bring them to the throne of grace,
we are impressed as never before with the
thought that the promise must be fulfilled to
me personally or it is a failure. You will be
astonished to discover how much your spiritual aspirations will be quickened, and your suit

at the mercy-seat intensified, by so simple a device as this. Thus I have given you advice concerning faith such as the great commentator Bengel gives for searching the Scriptures: " Apply thyself wholly to the text: apply the subject wholly to thyself."

After you have fixed your faith on some promise of full salvation, you are to believe that the fullness is for you. You must believe that God is able to give it to you, and that he is willing to fulfill his word now, for to-day is the day of salvation. " Then," says Mr. Wesley, " God will enable you to believe that he doth it." But you say, "I don't realize any change." Do you not see that you are looking for some token that God is true? You must trust his naked word. The nobleman was told by Jesus, " Go thy way, thy son liveth." He did not ask for some sign that the promise was true; but he believed the word of Christ, and acted on that faith. To wait till you feel the change before you believe, is to walk by feeling and not by faith. It is to put the consequent before the antecedent, the effect before the cause. You are not commanded to feel, but to trust. To feel the change is to know it.

To wait for knowledge is to walk by sight. In an important sense knowledge originates in faith. We cannot know that we are the sons of God till we have trusted the promises up to the moment when the Spirit of adoption cries in our hearts, " Abba, Father." After that hour our sonship is a matter of knowledge.

If I have not attained perfect love, the promise of the Abiding Comforter, who shall be the Sanctifier, and glorify Christ to my consciousness as mine, wholly mine, is a subject of faith. It is our duty to insist on the truth of Christ, and to say that he does now keep his word. When it pleases him to reveal Christ to you as your complete Saviour, your faith on this point will be lost in sight, and your faith will reach up and claim some higher blessing yet unattained. On this Jacob's ladder you will climb up to heaven. This faith, which insists that God doeth the work now, must proceed upon the assumption that you cannot make yourself better by waiting. If perfect love is by faith, it must be now, just as I am. These three must always go together —faith, now, and just as I am. There are also three other things which constitute the creed of the legalist—works, some future time, when I have made myself better.

But you ask the question, Is every believer prepared to believe for entire sanctification and the fullness of God? No. If he has no earnest, insatiable desire for it he cannot believe. Nor can he till he has made an entire surrender of himself deliberately, and forever, to Christ. He must be willing that he should subvert all his life plans, and enter into all his present being and future history. In other words, entire consecration is as necessary to sanctifying, as repentance is to justifying, faith. While you are consecrating yourself, various tests will be presented to your mind. Some of these will be suggested by the Holy Spirit. You must abide them. Others may be suggested by Satan to defeat your purpose. He may thrust some strange or unreasonable and absurd duty forward as a test. How am I to treat these suggestions of the adversary when unable to discriminate them from the suggestions of the Holy Ghost? You should declare your willingness to do all the will of God as it shall be made manifest by the word, the Spirit, providence, and reason conspiring. The suggestions of Satan will disappear when our willingness to obey God fully appears.

The suggested tests of the Holy Spirit will continue to press themselves upon our attention, and demand our compliance after God has given us conscious acceptance. Rev. A. B. Earle was deeply impressed, when seeking the witness of adoption, that he ought to go on a mission to Africa. He struggled against it for some time, and at last said, " I will do God's will in Africa or in any other country on earth." Since that moment the call to Africa has ceased. There was no providential opening, but a wide field for evangelism in America, for which thousands of redeemed souls will thank God through eternity. It is evident that Satan was pressing this deadly mission upon him to drive him from his purpose of full consecration. It is always safe to say in such cases, " O Lord, I will do thy will as interpreted by thy word and thy providence." We have now pointed out a stone against which thousands have stumbled in their approach to the blessing of the fullness of the Spirit, and we have endeavored to show you how you may avoid it.

25

4. In urging your suit, rest wholly on the name of your indorser, Jesus Christ. In his address (John xiv–xvi) in which the pearl of perfect love is again and again promised in the coming of the abiding Comforter, Jesus inserts in every promise the condition, " in my name." This means that we are to identify our plea with the glory of Christ. We cannot fail when we pray for the same blessing for which he intercedes in our behalf. We are sure that selfishness does not underlie our petition when our aim is the glory of Christ only. When we thus use the name of our High Priest, we clothe ourselves with his merit. The name of Jesus is like the signet ring of an absent monarch, purposely left behind to authenticate the acts of his ministers. It transfers his power to them. So has Jesus transferred to our hands the key that unlocks the treasury of heaven, and secures the outpouring of the anointing that teacheth and abideth. " The greatest gift that men can wish or heaven can send."

5. Do not fail, when urging your plea, to remember that you have rights with God the Father in Jesus' name. *You* could not claim his mediatorial work and merit. But since

this work has been done, you may now stand on the high platform of rights with God, and *claim in Jesus' name* all that he has purchased for you. He has invested you not only with a *right* to the tree of life, but to all that prepares you to pluck and eat its fruit. Again, "if we confess our sins, He is faithful and *just* to forgive us our sins, and to cleanse us from all unrighteousness." The word "just" is a jural term, implying rights on the part of the believer and obligation on the part of God ; the obligation not only of veracity, expressed by the word faithful, but also the obligation of justice. He will not wrong us by withholding the greatest blessing purchased by his Son, and sacredly kept by the Father till the hour we come in that influential name and claim our heritage.

> " Bold I approach the eternal throne,
> And *claim* the crown through Christ my own."

6. Faint not. Jesus, in his parables of the unjust judge and of the man awakened by his friend at midnight, and in his interview with the Syrophenician woman, emphasizes intensity of spirit, importunity, and perseverance in

prayer. Especially is the unspeakable gift of the fullness of God to be obtained by persistent and prevailing prayer. Take with you into your closet Charles Wesley's wonderful portrayal of a struggling and victorious soul, "Wrestling Jacob," and make its intense expressions the vehicle of your earnestness—its bold demands, its unshaken purpose, its high resolve, the spirit of your plea—and you must sooner or later prevail. God yields to a thoroughly determined soul! The violent take the kingdom of heaven by force. You will find that this earnestness cannot be aroused except upon the plea which says, "Now, Lord, just as I am, fill me with thy perfect love." If you drop the "*now*," and say at some time, you will find the sinews of your effort paralyzed, and your vehement desire cooled down to indifference.

7. Be patient. "I waited patiently for the Lord, and he inclined unto me, and heard my cry." The Psalmist proved the truth of the adage that the patient waiter is no loser. "For ye have need of patience, that, after ye have done the will of God, ye might receive the promise," that is, the thing promised. From

lack of " the patience of hope," thousands have failed to grasp the prize of " love divine, all love excelling," made perfect in the hearts, as a distinct and glorious work of the Sanctifier. You cannot fail if you persevere. The struggle may be only an hour; it may be a month or a year. Some, after wandering as long as the children of Israel in

> " Sorrows and sins, and doubts and fears,
>   A howling wilderness,"

have emerged at last into this land of promise. Such invariably see that they might long, long before have had their portions assigned to them on the mountain of God by their great Joshua, if they had obediently trusted him.

You will meet with the advice to cease all effort, and to subside into quietude and stillness; to do nothing yourself, but let Christ do all for you. It is true that you can do nothing meritorious to improve your condition. It is also true that you must work the work of God, that is, which he requires. "And this is the work of God, that ye believe on Him whom he hath sent." This may require high and strenuous effort to keep yourself on the divine

altar, to keep down doubt, and to hold un-
waveringly to the word of God. The kind of
stillness which Wesley recommended, you will
be safe in practicing—

> " *Restless*, resigned, for God I wait ;
> For God my *vehement* soul stands still."

The faith that brings us into the "valley of
blessing so sweet," comes out of a furnace of
desire, glowing with sevenfold ardor. It is
not in harmony with the nature of the human
sensibilities that this intensity of desire should
be awakened and sustained in a state of pas-
sivity. Endeavor intensifies desire.

I cannot leave this subject without pointing
out another rock over which many stumble in
seeking both justification and perfect love. I
refer to what, for lack of a better name, I call
tentative faith—believing just by way of experiment. There is unbelief at the bottom of any
such acts of the mind. Christ don't receive
people who surrender to him just by way of
trial, to see what blessings he will bestow,
what rapturous joys he will inspire. There is
no complete surrender possible with this mental reservation, the purpose to take back your

consecration if the results are not satisfactory. As true marriage must consist in a union of hearts for life, in order to the enjoyment of the highest bliss of that sacred institution, so must the marriage of the soul to Christ be an everlasting union, the farthest possible remove from the caprices and criminally reserved rights of free love, coquetting with Christ to-day and the world to-morrow. Ye who fully purpose an eternal wedlock with Christ for better or for worse, approach the glorious Bridegroom in the utmost confidence that he will array you in a robe of clean linen, and present you unto himself as his faultless bride with exceeding joy—joy in his own bosom, joy thrilling your spirit, and gladdening all the angels who witness the nuptials.

> " He comes ! He comes ! The kingly Christ
>   From heaven's eternal shores ;
> His uncreated freshness fills
>   His bride as she adores."

CHAPTER XXII.

ADDRESS TO PROFESSORS.

Stand fast therefore in the liberty wherewith Christ hath made us free.—ST. PAUL.

IT has been said, " Eternal vigilance is the price of liberty." This maxim may not in form be as old as St. Paul's Epistle to the Galatians, but it certainly is in substance. For he says, " Stand fast therefore in the liberty wherewith Christ hath made us free." There is no state of Christian experience in which we may live in ease and carelessness regardless of spiritual foes. It is true that we have the promise that Jesus will keep us. But this promise involves the condition that we keep ourselves on the territory prescribed for our residence, that is, the land of obedience. If we willfully and needlessly go upon the enchanted ground of temptation, presuming that the Lord will deliver us, we shall find ourselves sadly mistaken. We are to keep ourselves in the love of God. This is true of that perfect love which casts out all fear that has torment. But how may I do this? In what direction are my activities to be put forth? An erroneous answer to this question has led many to their spiritual downfall. They have made war directly upon their enemies, and while antagonizing them they have turned their eyes from Jesus, the source of all spiritual power. This was the mistake of Peter on the waters of the sea. As soon as he began to look at the waves he forgot the omnipotent power residing in the arm of Jesus, and dropped down from a faith in the supernatural to a natural view of things. " O, these waves will engulf me!" thought he, and, sure enough, the surface, which had been as marble, at that moment gave way beneath his feet, and he was up to his loins in the sea. It was not till in utter self-despair that he turned to the Master again, and felt his delivering hand laid upon him. We are kept by the power of God through faith. Faith is the human part of our keeping. All power is in our living Saviour above. Faith is the act which links our feebleness to his omnipotence. Scientists talk of the conservation and corre-

lation of forces in physical phenomena. They
mean by these hard words to teach that there
is a fixed amount of physical force in the universe, and that when it disappears in one form
it re-appears in another; heat changing to
electricity, etc.

Whether this theory is true or not, there is
conservation and correlation of spiritual power.
Faith is the point of contact between that
battery and human souls. Whatever be the
form of our religious activity, it is faith that is
at the bottom, whether it be prayer, praise,
watchfulness, resistance to sin, or efforts for
the salvation of others. When St. Paul has
enumerated the weapons which constitute the
Christian's offensive and defensive armor, he
adds, "above" (or over) "all," as a protection
to every other part of the armor itself, "take
the shield of faith"—continually exercise a
strong and lively faith. The ancient shield
covered the whole soldier. Hence the motto
for all Christians, whatever their attainments,
is, "Looking unto Jesus." If your old enemy is
the alcoholic or the narcotic appetite, you are
not to be thinkiug all the time of the decanter
and segar, and bracing yourself against them in

your own strength—the method of occasional
human victory, but more frequently of human
defeat ; but you are to look unto Jesus, to
magnify his power, to dwell upon the promises,
and to supplicate his great gift of the Comforter, to abide within, and to be the keeping
power. The former method of overcoming sin
is, in the words of President Finney, "the religion of resolution ;" the latter is "the religion
of faith." As long as faith in Christ is in exercise, the soul is impregnable ; it dwells in "the
munition of rocks." Then "none shall be able
to pluck them out of my Father's hand."
True vigilance, therefore, the price of spiritual
liberty, is faith in Christ modified by the apprehension of spiritual peril—it is looking
unto Jesus on the battle-field. The beautiful
vignette of a cross grasped by a hand, with the
motto underneath, *Teneo et teneor*—I hold
fast and am held fast—expresses the same
thought. There is no other way of maintain-
ing the higher life. It is rest in Jesus. It is
the rest of faith. They who thus rest are not
exempted from temptation and warfare, but
they are lifted by the power of the Holy Spirit
into such a nearness to Jesus that they find

trust in him a natural and a delightful exercise, and victory over sin easy.

The spiritual life, which was formerly much like a foreigner sojourning in the heart, has at length become a naturalized citizen, and means to stay forever. Formerly faith was a painful effort and spasmodic ; now it is spontaneous, delightful, and continuous, so long as the grounds of faith, the Divine promises, are kept in view by the constant study of the Holy Scriptures.

The higher life has deeper roots than the ordinary Christian life. It is rooted in the soil of the divine word, and, like the century-enduring oak, appropriates therefrom all its elements of strength. " Man shall not live by bread alone, but by every word that proceedeth out of the mouth of God." He who wishes to dwell on this high spiritual plane above the clouds, which intercept the sunlight to the dwellers below, must consent to be a man of one book, and to endure the reproach of being a man of one idea—Christ crucified. He will awake in the morning more hungry for his soul-food than for his breakfast. He will prefer the word of God to the morning

paper, if he has time but for one ; and, if com-
pelled to go forth without his daily spiritual
rations, he will be conscious of faintness and
weakness. Well persons always feel the loss
of their regular meals ; the sick never, because
they have no appetite intensely consuming
their strength.

Let it be understood that the state of full
trust in Christ cannot be maintained by hours
devoted to current literature and minutes
given to hasty glances at the Holy Scriptures.
That is the path to spiritual emaciation,
trodden by multitudes of weak believers,
piteously crying, " O my leanness, my leanness!" There must be time taken to read,
mark, and inwardly digest spiritual truth, that
it may pour its vital elements into the life-
currents of our souls.

Many Christians are in too great a hurry to
live the life of uninterrupted trust. The Comforter came to abide, but the place was too
confused and he withdrew. "As the servant
was busy here and there, he was gone."
Again, the higher life is not a life of solitude.
Society produces great men. They are not
reared in the hermitage. Perfect love to God

does not turn its back upon men, and bury itself in a desert or cloister. It seeks human abodes

" With prayers, entreaties, tears, to save,
To pluck men from the gaping grave,"

The ordinary social means of grace are necessary to the promotion of the life of the most advanced Christian. Beware of undervaluing the gatherings of the Church, where young and old, the mature Christian and the young convert, testify of Jesus' love. Both the faith and the lives of many of them may be imperfect. For this very reason they need your superior light, while you need their society to keep you in the closest sympathy with your fellow-disciples, and to counteract the tendency to segregate into cliques, to the detriment of Christian unity.

It sometimes happens that the repose of the soul in Christ is disturbed by another cause. Ecstatic joy has been erroneously assumed to be the only proof of the presence of the abiding Comforter; and when that rapturous exultation subsides, the individual is apt to say, "I have lost the fullness of the Spirit." The mistake is, the forgetfulness that there are other fruits of the Spirit, which may attest his presence; and, moreover, that the promise of God is still true, though for a brief period we see no evidence of his presence in our feelings. We are to walk by faith and not by feeling. Activity in behalf of the freedom of others is the way to preserve our own. In our recent war it was found that the Republic could not maintain its own freedom without emancipating the slaves within its reach. It is just so with the preservation of that freedom indeed which Jesus, the Great Emancipator, proclaims. The person who sits down to enjoy the delicious sweets of his newly-found liberty, satisfied with the ecstacies of devotion, will soon find his joys expiring. Joy is given as a motive to labor. Great exultation to-day means great toil to-morrow. The gladness of the pentecost was a preparation for the conversion of the three thousand. " The joy of the Lord is your strength." It is designed as a means to an end. "Restore unto me the joys of thy salvation; then will I teach transgressors thy ways, and sinners will be converted unto thee." If we begin to luxuriate in the means as itself an end, forgetful of the divine end, we pervert the blessing bestowed; and the manna, being selfishly hoarded, instead of being distributed to the hungry, "breeds worms."

BEWARE OF FANATICISM.

There are two enemies to the fullness of the Spirit—baptized worldliness, and fanaticism run mad on the subject of holiness. Let us consider the latter. Fanaticism is not limited . to religion. Wild and extravagant views may be indulged on any subject. In our late war we had peace-fanatics, who clamored for peace at any price; and war-fanatics, aching to see every rebel hung and his estate confiscated. In peace, we always have had fanatical agitators on various questions of social interest, such as labor, the sphere of woman, and hostility to immigration. In philosophy, we have fanatics intolerant of opposition, who ridicule as blockheads all who differ from them. Any person whose mind becomes so disproportionately filled with any one idea as to become unsymmetrical and unbalanced, is in danger of those extravagant views and intense feelings which make the fanatic. As religion is an exciting and absorbing theme, so there is especial danger of running into unwarrantable enthusiasm. Religious fanaticism has deluged the world with bloodshed, instituted inquisitions, and invented thumb-screws. Sanctification fanaticism is a milder species of this genus, yet it is none the less mischievous. It brings into reproach the most glorious doctrine of the Gospel—the office of the Sanctifier ; it brings into ridicule the crowning blessing—the most precious experience of our holy Christianity. Here is the portrait of a holiness fanatic, or perfectionist.

1. He abjures and pours contempt upon that scintillation of the eternal Logos, human reason. This lighted torch, placed in man's hand for his guidance in certain matters, he extinguishes in order ostensibly to exalt the candle of the Lord, the Holy Ghost, but really to lift up the lamp of his own flickering fancy. Reason is a gift of God, worthy of our respect. We are to accept it as our surest guide in its appropriate sphere. Beyond this sphere we should seek the light of revelation and the guidance of the Spirit. The fanatic depreciates one perfect gift from the Father of

light, that he may magnify another. Both of these lights—reason and the Holy Ghost— are necessary to our perfect guidance. To reject one is to assume a greater wisdom than God's. Such presumptuous folly he will glaringly expose. He who spurns the Spirit will be left to darkness outside the narrow sphere of reason; and he who scorns reason will be left to follow the hallucinations of his heated imagination, instead of the dictates of common sense.

> " 'Tis reason our great Master holds so dear;
> 'Tis reason's injured rights his wrath resents;
> 'Tis reason's voice t' obey his glorious crown;
> To give lost reason life he poured his own.
> Believe, and show the reason of a man;
> Believe, and taste the pleasures of a God:
> Through reason's wounds alone thy faith can die."

Mr. Wesley was pestered by persons " who imagine that they receive *particular directions* from God, not only in points of importance, but in things of no moment, in the most trifling circumstances of life. Whereas God has given to us our own reason for a guide, though never excluding the secret assistance of his Spirit."

2. The fanatic degrades the word of God by claiming for himself an inspiration equal to its

theopneustic utterances, just as the free-relig-
ionist adroitly belittles the Holy Scriptures by
classifying their inspiration with that of Homer
and Shakspeare. He proclaims new revelations of Christian truth beyond the utterances
of the sacred oracles, forgetting the maxim of
orthodoxy, that any thing essentially new in
Christianity is essentially false. He takes to
his bosom the baneful error that Christianity,
as a system of objective truth, was not handed
down from above a complete whole, but was
left by its Author to be finished by endless
supplements, communicated to individual believers in all ages. John Wesley was called
to preach against this folly of " enthusiasts,
who imagine that God dictates every word
they speak, and that it is impossible they
should speak any thing amiss, either as to the
matter or manner of it." He also styles those
enthusiasts " who *designedly* speak in public
without any premeditation."

3. This fanatic also imagines he has a manifestation of God so immediate that he no
longer needs the ordained means of grace. He
is beyond the sacraments. Prayer is a superfluity. He receives without asking ; or, if he

asks for any thing, he asks but once. To repeat his request would imply imperfect faith.
He omits one petition of the Lord's Prayer,
because he has no trespasses to be forgiven;
although the recording angel is daily noting a
thousand sins of ignorance and infirmity which
need the blood of sprinkling. If he is a
logical fanatic—a very rare bird—he finds all
his time so holy that he has no occasion to
make the commanded distinction between
secular and sacred days. A step further down
this descending stairway brings him to the
Oneida perfectionists—to equal love to all
men and to all women.

4. The fanatical pretender to Christian perfection is characterized by acts professedly
prompted by the Spirit, but which are contrary
to both reason and the word of God.. One
thinks himself called by the Spirit to skip
about or dance in a Christian meeting, and to
make gestures which enforce no truth, because
no words are uttered, though St. Paul insists
that all things be done to edification. Another
whirls on one toe as swift as a top, till she
sinks down exhausted. Another darts like an
arrow across the prayer-room with outstretched

hand, and lays it on the head of a brother to impart the Holy Ghost. Another is impelled to show his humility by leaving his seat in the church, and rolling in the dust in the broad aisle during the sermon. These are specimens of vagaries contrary to common sense and the Bible, which have brought spiritual Christianity under reproach, and have turned away formal professors from seeking the greatest gift that men can wish or Heaven can send— all the fullness of God.

> " Such the credulous dotard's dream,
>   And such his shorter road :
> Thus he makes the world blaspheme,
>   And shames the Church of God ;
> Staggers thus the most sincere,
>   Till from the Gospel hope they move ;
> Holiness as error fear,
>   And start at perfect love."

5. Another feature of the character of such a one is superiority to instruction and reproof. Are they not taught of the Lord ? Shall they, who are receiving the blaze of the Spirit's light, like the full-orbed sun, turn away and follow the pale radiance of some. brother's feebler light, glimmering like a faint star in the skies ? Not they. In vain does the wise and deeply-ex-

perienced Wesley expostulate with Bell and Maxfield, and their band of overheated zealots, who, by their dangerous delusions, were sadly damaging the fair fame of Methodism, and making her a laughing-stock to her many foes. They would not deign to listen to "poor, blind John." After a long forbearance, sixty of these deluded members of the Foundry Society were cut off at once, and left to follow their disordered imaginations, in order to save the whole body from the fatal infection. Many of them "perished in the gainsaying of Korah."

6. We should deserve the reputation of an unskillful limner should we fail to portray the most prominent and most ugly feature of this character,—his uncharitableness. Professing perfect love to God, he grievously lacks tender affection to his fellow-men. All degrees of spirituality and faith below his own are deemed by him worthy, not of sympathy but of censure. If the young convert falls into the hands of such a nursing father or nursing mother, he will have a sorry time indeed, and be more than once tempted to say that there is a mistake in the declaration that "the ways of wisdom are ways of pleasantness." He is

scolded for every unsteady step; at every fall he is berated, and not encouraged to try again. He is judged by an absolute standard, and condemned without mercy if he fails in any particular. It is not our purpose to show the philosophy of so strange a combination of contradictions as this feature of the perfectionist-fanatic presents. Similar phenomena occur in the commercial world. Stock-gamblers, while calling millions their own, are penniless bankrupts. Both characters draw upon their imaginations, and account themselves rich. They do not put gold in their coffers. They are satisfied with the glitter of appearances. Simon Magus fixed his eye upon the worldly glory which the extraordinary gifts of the Holy Ghost would confer, and was baptized, and found that he was still the same poor pagan sorcerer. Christians who seek for ecstatic joys, or showy gifts of the Spirit, or any thing else rather than the pure love of God, make the same mistake. Hence the importance of giving earnest heed to Wesley's admonition, " Let no one be satisfied with the direct witness of the Spirit, without the *fruits* of the Spirit."

APPLICATION :—In the words of Wesley, "Watch and pray lest you fall into so great an evil. It easily besets those who fear or love God. O, beware you do not think of yourself more highly than you ought to think ! Do not imagine you have attained that grace of God which you have not attained. You may have much joy; you may have a measure of love, and yet not have living faith. Cry unto the Lord that he would not suffer you, blind as you are, to go out of the way; that you may never fancy yourself a believer in Christ till Christ be revealed in you, and till his Spirit witness with your spirit that you are a child of God."

" Beware of that daughter of pride, en-thusiasm, (fanaticism.) O keep at the utter-most distance from it ! Give no place to a heated imagination. Do not hastily ascribe things to God. Do not easily suppose dreams, voices, impressions, visions, or revelations to be from God. They may be from him. They may be from nature. They may be from the devil. Therefore 'believe not every spirit, but try the spirits whether they be of God.' Try all things by the written word, and let all bow down before it. You are in danger of enthusiasm every hour if you depart ever so little from Scripture; yea, or from the plain, literal meaning of any text, taken in connection with the context. And so you are, if you despise or lightly esteem reason, knowledge, or human learning; every one of which is an excellent gift of God, and may serve the noblest purposes. I advise you never to use the words 'wisdom,' 'reason, 'knowledge,' by way of reproach. On the contrary, pray that you yourself may abound in them more and more. If you mean worldly wisdom, useless knowledge, false reasoning, say so; and throw away the chaff but not the wheat. One general inlet of enthusiasm is expecting the end without the means; the expecting knowledge, for instance, without searching the Scriptures and consulting the children of God; the expecting spiritual strength without constant prayer and steady watchfulness; the expecting any blessing without hearing the word of God at every opportunity. Some have been ignorant of this device of Satan. They have left off searching the Scriptures. They have said, 'God writes all the Scriptures on my heart.'

O take warning, you who are concerned herein! You have listened to the voice of a stranger."

In conclusion, this question arises. In view of the possibility of such an unlovely character coming into existence under the guise of entire sanctification, would it not be wise to abstain from inculcating this high doctrine, lying as it does on the borders of an infatuation so dangerous? Just as wise as it would be to suppress Christianity because its abuse has bred fanatics, bigots, and persecutors. Just as wise as it would be to withdraw all gold and silver coin from our currency because of worthless imitations. Yet this is the way the many are treating entire sanctification. A superior practical wisdom did the great founder of Methodism evince when, notwithstanding the outburst of religious madness and folly which at one time beslimed his London Societies, he insisted on preaching this truth, and enjoined on all his preachers to set forth "perfection to believers constantly, strongly, and explicitly," and exhorted them "to mind this one thing, and continually agonize for it." His brother Charles, constitutionally much conservative, thus expressed his sympathy with this doctrine in this fiery ordeal :—

> " Set the false witnesses aside,
> But hold the truth forever fast."

Many years after the great work of sanctification which was wrought so powerfully in the Wesleyan Societies, beginning in Otley about 1760, and spreading rapidly through the connection, and in some places running into extravagances requiring excision, Wesley calmly reviews that great outpouring of the sanctifying Spirit, and adopts the prayer of a devout Scotchman : " O Lord ! if it please thee work the same work again without the blemishes. But if this cannot be, though it be with all the blemishes, *work the same* work."

Let me exhort you, in the words of Wesley, so full of practical wisdom,

" TO BEWARE OF SCHISM,

of making a rent in the Church of Christ. Beware of a dividing spirit ; shun whatever has the least aspect that way. Suffer no thought of separating from your brethren, whether their opinions agree with yours or not. Do not dream that any man sins in not believ-

ing you, in not taking your word; or that
this or that opinion is essential to the work.
Beware of impatience of contradiction. Do
not condemn or think hardly of those who
cannot see as you see, or judge it their duty
to contradict you whether in a great thing or
a small. O beware of touchiness and testi-
ness! Expect contradiction and opposition,
together with crosses of various kinds. Consider the words of St. Paul, ' For unto you it
is given in the behalf of Christ '—for his sake
as the fruit of his death and intercession for
you—'not only to believe on him, but also
to suffer for his sake.' Phil. i, 29. *It is given!*
God gives you this opposition or reproach; it
is a fresh token of his love.

    " Be particularly careful in speaking of your-
self ; you may not, indeed, deny the work of
God, but speak of it, when you are called
thereto, in the most inoffensive manner possible. Avoid all magnificent, pompous words;
indeed, you need give it no general name ;
neither sanctification, perfection, the second
blessing, nor the having attained. Rather
speak of the particulars which God has
wrought for you. You may say, ' At such a

time I felt a change which I am not able to express; and since that time I have not felt pride, or anger, or unbelief, nor any thing but a fullness of love to God!' And if any of you should at any time fall from what you now are, if you should again feel pride or unbelief, or any temper from which you are now delivered, do not deny, do not hide, do not disguise it at all, at the peril of your soul. At all events go to one in whom you can confide, and speak just what you feel."

Finally, if you must neglect any means of grace, be sure that it is not the ordinary meetings of the Church, the preached word, the class, the prayer-meeting, and the Sunday-school. Separate meetings for the promotion of holiness we cannot but regard as perilous when long continued and attended by the same persons who have experienced full salvation. By exclusive association with one another there is engendered the feeling that they monopolize all the piety of the Church, and they insensibly begin to withdraw sympathy from those of weaker faith, who most of all need the association and aid of those who are stronger. Nevertheless, where there is great opposition to the preaching of full salvation in the ordinary means of grace it may be expedient, as a temporary resort, to appoint a special meeting.

The purpose of this advice is to avoid every divisive tendency, every entering wedge of schism in the body of Christ. We believe there are few evangelical Churches where a modest, guarded declaration of the wonderful work of God in higher Christian experience, with exhortations drawing, not driving, justified souls toward the same sunny heights, would not be received with gladness. There is an intense hunger for the fullness of the Spirit in all the Churches, as is evinced by the widespread popularity of the hymn,

" Nearer, my God, to thee."

Another reason for our advice is, that no truth in the Gospel scheme was designed to be isolated from its connection with the whole system, and magnified out of due proportion by being exclusively dwelt upon. Such treatment of a most vital truth creates error. Justification by faith, preached alone, without the safeguard set up by St. James, runs into the rankest Antinomianism. But justification by works exclusively preached begets Pharisaism. The sovereignty of God may be magnified into the iron scheme of fatalism ; the merit of Christ's suffering and death may be preached to the total neglect of the regenerating and sanctifying offices of the Holy Spirit, and result in Universalism. - So there may be so long and so absorbing a contemplation of the doctrine of Christian perfection as to lose sight of the duty of calling sinners to repentance. We may linger with Jesus so long on the mount as to forget that, at its foot, is a world lying in the " wicked one," greatly needing our added faith to expel the devil from his usurped possession. Hence, while the whole Gospel is preached, the wise workman will be careful rightly to divide the word of truth.

We need not a segregated and select audience, but every class of Christians, the babe in Christ and the father in Israel, as well as the stranger to the covenant of promise, if we would be kept from dwelling too much upon our own subjective states instead of ministering to the varied spiritual wants of our fellowmen. I am not now speaking against an occasional convention for comparing notes, or camp-meeting in which entire sanctification shall be the theme of the preaching and the chief object of desire, but against stated weekly meetings year after year in our churches, attended almost exclusively by those who profess to have attained full salvation through the blood of sprinkling. Such meetings may do much good; in some instances they have done much harm, removed as their members are from all restraints which the presence of a promiscuous gathering would have exercised. Hence it is better to carry this truth from the select few to the concourse of the multitudes, and present it in due proportion with other truths of the Gospel. The course here indicated was followed by the founder of Methodism. He occasionally called together those who had experienced perfect love, and conversed very searchingly with them, and gave them such advice as he thought needful, but he never established a permanent holiness meeting.

THE END.